heart
on my sleeve

ELLEN WITTLINGER

Simon & Schuster Books for Young Readers

NEW YORK   LONDON   TORONTO   SYDNEY

SIMON & SCHUSTER BOOKS FOR YOUNG READERS
An imprint of Simon & Schuster Children's Publishing Division
1230 Avenue of the Americas, New York, New York 10020

Book design by Dan Potash
Manufactured in the United States of America
2 4 6 8 10 9 7 5 3
Library of Congress Cataloging-in-Publication Data
Wittlinger, Ellen.
Heart on my sleeve / Ellen Wittlinger.
p. cm.
Summary: From the end of high school to the beginning of college, Chloe and Julian deal with major changes in their families and friendships and explore their feelings for each other through e-mails, letters, and a visit.
ISBN 0-689-84997-4 (hardcover)
[1. Interpersonal relations—Fiction. 2. Family life—Fiction. 3. Singers—Fiction. 4. E-mail—Fiction. 5. Letters—Fiction.] I. Title.
PZ7.W78436He 2004
[Fic]-dc21
2003002086

For Elizabeth Bluemle, who gave me
the original inspiration;
for Dar Williams, who gives inspiration to so many;
and for Kate and Morgan, who always know the words
to all the songs.

With grateful thanks to my editor, David Gale; his assistants,
Ellia Bisker and Alexandra Cooper; my agent, Ginger Knowlton,
and her assistant, Kelly Going; and Pat Lowery Collins,
Anita Riggio, and Nancy Werlin for their help and advice on
the manuscript. Much gratitude also to Dan Potash, art director,
and Daniel Roode, who brought the book to life.

Special thanks to the Fine Arts Work Center
in Provincetown, Massachusetts.

E-mail Address List

Reply | Reply All | Forward

Chloe Gillespie
smallboyonherbike@boscore.com
chloegillespie@Cartwright.edu

Genevieve Gillespie
ggillespie@Emmett.edu

Julian Casper
jghost@flowire.com

Eli Mather
catch22@boscore.com
elimather@unimich.edu

Martha & Tom Gillespie
mtgillespie@boscore.com

Kate Waverly
KublaKate@boscore.com
katewaverly@uver.edu

Carly Casper
CCinWonderland@hotmail.com

Tyler Robideau
plexiboy@flowire.com

May Forrester
maybee@flowire.com

Nina Greco
justmenina17@flowire.com

Gunnar Tollefson
gunnartollefson@nyuniv.edu

Subj: Are You Out There?
Date: 4/22/02, 9:37 A.M.
From: smallboyonherbike@boscore.com
To: jghost@flowire.com

Hey Julian!

Some weekend, huh? I was so tired last night, but couldn't sleep at
all—got up at 3 A.M., took my guitar into the downstairs bathroom
(most soundproof place in the house), and started writing a new song.
Too soon to tell if it's any good. (Maybe if I could hear *you* sing it,
I'd know.) :)

I was **so** worried beforehand about going to visit Cartwright to meet
hundreds of potential new classmates. You know, it sounded so
perfect in the catalog, but what if I got there and hated the place?
What if all the other pre-frosh were jerks? Or what if they were all
brilliant or something? But I loved it, didn't you? Especially the
open mic night—that sold me. Now I keep thinking, what if I hadn't
applied to Cartwright, or what if I'd chosen a college based on
something totally not important, like the advice of my guidance
counselor (who thinks if you don't go to Harvard you should just
forget about it and go to a state school). I told my parents to send in
the money to Cartwright today!

You're probably too busy for much e-mailing this week since
Godspell opens on Friday. After hearing you sing Saturday night I
know you'll be amazing. Break a leg! (Do people really say that? Or
just dorks like me?)

Chloe

Subj: The Great Unknown
Date: 4/22/02, 9:57 A.M.
From: smallboyonherbike@boscore.com
To: ggillespie@Emmett.edu

Genevieve,

You will NOT believe what happened to me this weekend at Cartwright! Okay, yes, I met a guy. How did you know this would happen? Oh, Omniscient Sister, you are so psychic—you should charge money. I totally wasn't expecting it. I was SO nervous when I got there and we gathered in this huge auditorium and there were all these other kids and we kept looking each other over and I knew I probably had bags under my eyes because I couldn't sleep the night before and I was seriously **STRESSED**. Besides which, I'm still going with Eli, sort of, even though that's been dragging on way too long already, as you keep telling me. But Eli would be so hurt if I broke up with him—he's my biggest fan—he comes to hear me any time I open for anybody or even do an open mic. He's so LOYAL—he's been my friend since kindergarten! Besides which, Meghan and Kate and Joey would be furious with me for screwing up our group. I don't think I even COULD break up with him—it would be like breaking up with your brother. What should I do? I love Eli, but I'm not *in* love with him. He's not my soulmate—when I gaze into his eyes, all I see are brown circles—so I probably shouldn't waste his time anymore.

This guy I met is named Julian Casper—isn't that a great name? And guess what? He's a singer and an actor! He's the Jesus character in *Godspell* at his school, which, as you know, is the LEAD! Yeah, yeah, musicals have never been my favorite thing—okay, I may once have said I hated them, but I'm young, I can change my mind. Anyway, Julian has a *gorgeous* voice, which I know because he sang at this open mic night they had during the weekend. There were a lot of

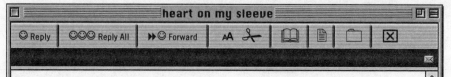

kids who got up to sing or play music (including me, of course), which by itself is SO exciting—I can't WAIT to get to this school. Anyway, he's been auditioning for some national singing contest thing which gives scholarships and he's already at the second level, and if he wins the next two levels, he'll come to Boston in August for the final round! I'll be done working at camp by then, so we can hang out in the city and I can show him around. He told me he *LOVED* my voice and he wants us to work on a duet that we could do at some open mics in Boston! Would that be the coolest thing!?

Do I sound like I've lost it for this guy? I sort of have, but I'm trying to not admit it yet because I'm not sure he feels the same way. He ACTED like he did, but, you know, he might go back to Florida (where he lives) and forget all about me. I mean, maybe it was just a weekend thing. But how fun would it be to go off to college and already have a boyfriend there? God, it would be so great. He says he's definitely going to Cartwright now—he wasn't sure until this weekend, but now he is. I thought I was sure before, but now there's no doubt in my mind!

Veev, I have this feeling you're looking disapprovingly at the screen. You're rolling your eyes, aren't you? You know I wouldn't choose a college based solely on a guy, don't you? Cartwright has a fabulous music program and the campus is gorgeous. I'm *not* picking Cartwright just because I met Julian there. For all I know, he'll change his mind and not even go! Although that would be a shame because I want him to be the father of my firstborn child.

KIDDING! :-}

How's your play going? I wish we were closer so I could come and see you do Blanche DuBois. Have you gotten the usual rave reviews? Has Tennessee arisen from his grave to see your performance? I'm sure his ghost is applauding from the balcony.

Mom just came in and asked me if I'd mind picking up her cleaning and a few groceries—stuff she obviously doesn't need this minute. Dad's morning meeting was cancelled and he doesn't have a class to teach until noon, so they probably want to take advantage of it. Maybe she wouldn't mind if I just took my guitar and went into the downstairs bathroom. You can't hear a *thing* from in there, and I'm not really in the mood to run useless errands.

Do you think I've lost my mind, Veev? What should I do about Eli? What if Julian is my soulmate?

Yours in angst, Chloe

Subj: Of course you've lost your mind
Date: 4/23/02, 2:04 A.M.
From: ggillespie@Emmett.edu
To: smallboyonherbike@boscore.com

Don't :-} me, Chloe! What is all this *soulmate* crap? Soulmate, schmolemate . . . I've tried so hard to inoculate you against the vapid attitudes of our parents, and here you are hoping to see firecrackers in somebody's eyes!

—And furthermore, I did NOT predict the finding of your eternal love-object in Connecticut. All I said was that you'd probably get a big crush on somebody because you're always getting crushes on guys everywhere you go. But you never do anything about it because there's always *Eli,* who would be demolished if you withdrew your slight affection from him. Believe me, it would do the guy good to find somebody who wasn't always thinking about dumping him!

—And *tell* me you aren't still running errands when our parents want a daytime screw? For God's sake, don't they have a lock on their door? Can't they wait until nighttime like normal fifty year olds? What is wrong

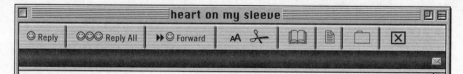

with them? (A question you may remember I have asked for many years.) It was one thing when we were little kids and Grandma lived down the block and they could just send us down there to play so they could sneak in a quickie, but this need for daytime "privacy" at their advanced age is ludicrous. *Nobody* is that much in love after 25 years! Really, these people are starting to make me sick, Chloe. It's a good thing you're going to be hundreds of miles away from them in a few months—they've obviously warped your brain despite my efforts.

—As to this *Julian* person (an ACTOR? Have I taught you NOTHING??), did you sleep with him? Are you thinking he's your *one true love* because you finally gave up the last shred of your virginity to Julian Casper, who is undoubtedly a very friendly ghost? I know it's hard for you to grasp, but some people actually *do* sleep with more than one person in their lives, even though the saintly Martha and Tom Gillespie didn't. (And anyway, how *do* we even know that *for sure*?) Just because this Julian is a singer doesn't make him a higher-level human being. And being an actor probably argues for the opposite.

—Okay, I'm being a bitch. The play's over and you know how I get. Yes, we were wonderful, although the Emmett College audience could not really appreciate it. My Blanche DuBois was inspirationally nuts. And this woman, Alice, who played Stella was fabulous too. We hardly even needed Stanley Kowalski. Anyway, I'm sorry to yell at you long distance, but I can't bear to see you inhaling all that sentimental crap the lovebirds have been handing us over the years.

—Yeah, maybe you'll fall in love with this guy and have a big hot old time with him, and maybe it'll last for 6 months—or maybe 2 weeks— and then cool off. *This happens!* Just because you like somebody doesn't mean you have to get all mystical about it. Or married, for Chrissakes! Yes, you've lost your mind, but only because you were brought up by simpletons. What you should do about Eli is probably

break up with him, but I've been saying that for two years already and I'm not holding my breath. And Julian is NOT your soulmate, because the word is meaningless.

—Veev

Sub: Hey!
Date: 4/23/02, 6:04 P.M.
From: jghost@flowire.com
To: smallboyonherbike@boscore.com

Hey Chloe! Sorry I didn't e-mail you yesterday. We had a late rehearsal and then I had to study for a Psych test. So much goes on at the end of the year, it's like you're racing, racing, racing, and then all of a sudden BOOM: It's all over. It's *really* weird this year since we'll be done with high school for good in 4 more weeks!

Which is fine with me. I'm ready to move on. But it's still weird. I feel kind of bad for my mom being stuck down here in Florida by herself. My older sister is in Texas—I told you about her—and my stepfather left us about six months ago, which is great news as far as I'm concerned, but Mom isn't exactly sure yet. She seems to think the guy had some redeeming qualities. Or maybe she just feels bad that she flunked marriage twice.

It was great to hear from you. I agree, Cartwright seems perfect. I'm definitely going—I'll have to get on my mother to send in the deposit. I *have* to win that damn contest this summer—Cartwright is so expensive. I wish I could hear you sing your new song. What's it about? Springtime in Connecticut?

This week is a killer, but once *Godspell* is over I'll have more time. Thanks for wishing me a broken leg. You, dorky? Not a chance.

Julian

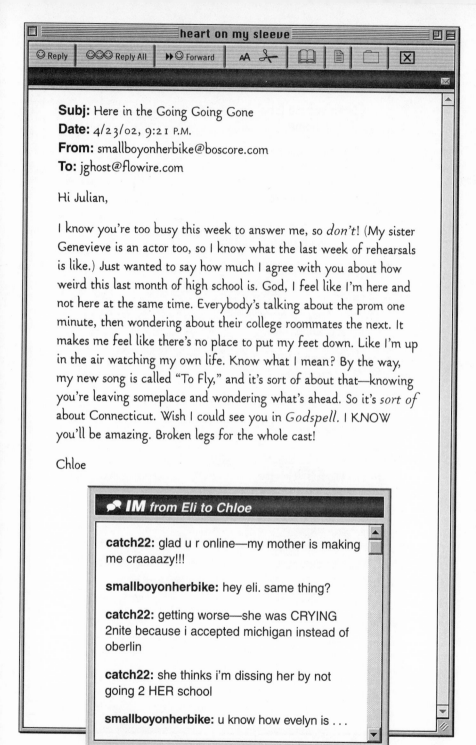

Subj: Here in the Going Going Gone
Date: 4/23/02, 9:21 P.M.
From: smallboyonherbike@boscore.com
To: jghost@flowire.com

Hi Julian,

I know you're too busy this week to answer me, so *don't*! (My sister Genevieve is an actor too, so I know what the last week of rehearsals is like.) Just wanted to say how much I agree with you about how weird this last month of high school is. God, I feel like I'm here and not here at the same time. Everybody's talking about the prom one minute, then wondering about their college roommates the next. It makes me feel like there's no place to put my feet down. Like I'm up in the air watching my own life. Know what I mean? By the way, my new song is called "To Fly," and it's sort of about that—knowing you're leaving someplace and wondering what's ahead. So it's *sort of* about Connecticut. Wish I could see you in *Godspell.* I KNOW you'll be amazing. Broken legs for the whole cast!

Chloe

📢 IM *from Eli to Chloe*

catch22: glad u r online—my mother is making me craaaazy!!!

smallboyonherbike: hey eli. same thing?

catch22: getting worse—she was CRYING 2nite because i accepted michigan instead of oberlin

catch22: she thinks i'm dissing her by not going 2 HER school

smallboyonherbike: u know how evelyn is . . .

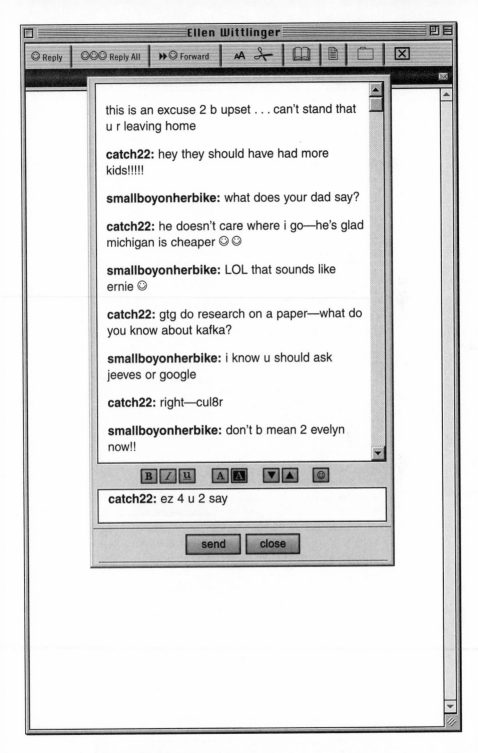

this is an excuse 2 b upset . . . can't stand that u r leaving home

catch22: hey they should have had more kids!!!!!

smallboyonherbike: what does your dad say?

catch22: he doesn't care where i go—he's glad michigan is cheaper ☺ ☺

smallboyonherbike: LOL that sounds like ernie ☺

catch22: gtg do research on a paper—what do you know about kafka?

smallboyonherbike: i know u should ask jeeves or google

catch22: right—cul8r

smallboyonherbike: don't b mean 2 evelyn now!!

catch22: ez 4 u 2 say

send   close

Subj: [no subject]
Date: 4/24/02, 12:37 P.M.
From: mtgillespie@boscore.com
To: ggillespie@Emmett.edu

Dear Genevieve,

Daddy and I were talking at breakfast today and it occured to us that your Tennessee Williams play is opening soon, isn't it? We wanted to be sure to wish you good luck. Daddy asked me if Blanche was the crazy one or the pregnant one, and I said, the crazy one, of course—it's typecasting! (Just kidding.)

Love, Mom and Daddy

🐱 IM *from Kate to Chloe*

KublaKate: ethan finally asked meghan 2 the prom!!! we can all go 2gether ☺☺☺

KublaKate: are we gonna get a limo like last year?

smallboyonherbike: i thought meghan was holding out 4 peter merrick? limo is fine w/me—w/e

KublaKate: peter's back w/elisa ☹ m is ok about it tho

smallboyonherbike: why ethan? didn't think she even liked him (i don't either)

KublaKate: he ASKED her—it's only 3 wks—she has to have a DATE!!!

smallboyonherbike: at least we'll all b 2gether 1 more time

smallboyonherbike: ☺☺☺

KublaKate: DON'T SAY THAT! u will marry eli and i'll marry joey and we'll have 2 daughters each

KublaKate: and live down the st from each other

KublaKate: unless u break up with eli which u CANNOT DO

send   close

Subj: A Ha Me a Riddle I Day
Date: 4/26/02, 2:02 P.M.
To: ggillespie@Emmett.edu
From: smallboyonherbike@boscore.com

Hi Veev,

It's Friday afternoon and I'm e-mailing you from my computer class because there's nothing else to do. We're all sitting here sending IMs to each other. I'm bored silly—why don't they just let the seniors go this last month? So, Julian has e-mailed me once. I can't tell what he's thinking. I'm a little depressed because I realize there's no way in hell I'm going to dump Eli. I mean, he helped me shop for my *prom* dress—I can't not go with him. Anyway, I don't want to **dump** him — this is ELI we're talking about, not some jerky guy or something. He's my best friend.

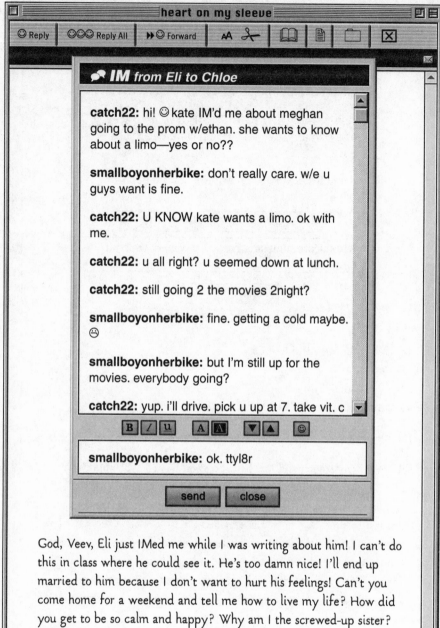

heart on my sleeve

Reply | **Reply All** | **Forward** | AA ✂ | 📖 | 📄 | 📁 | ☒

💬 **IM** *from Eli to Chloe*

catch22: hi! ☺ kate IM'd me about meghan going to the prom w/ethan. she wants to know about a limo—yes or no??

smallboyonherbike: don't really care. w/e u guys want is fine.

catch22: U KNOW kate wants a limo. ok with me.

catch22: u all right? u seemed down at lunch.

catch22: still going 2 the movies 2night?

smallboyonherbike: fine. getting a cold maybe. ☹

smallboyonherbike: but I'm still up for the movies. everybody going?

catch22: yup. i'll drive. pick u up at 7. take vit. c

B *I* u A **A** ▼▲ ☺

smallboyonherbike: ok. ttyl8r

send   close

God, Veev, Eli just IMed me while I was writing about him! I can't do this in class where he could see it. He's too damn nice! I'll end up married to him because I don't want to hurt his feelings! Can't you come home for a weekend and tell me how to live my life? How did you get to be so calm and happy? Why am I the screwed-up sister? HELP!

Chloe

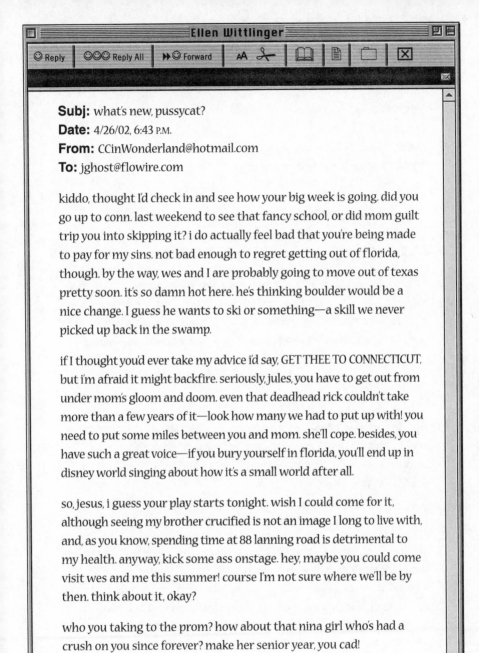

Reply Reply All Forward

Subj: what's new, pussycat?
Date: 4/26/02, 6:43 P.M.
From: CCinWonderland@hotmail.com
To: jghost@flowire.com

kiddo, thought I'd check in and see how your big week is going. did you go up to conn. last weekend to see that fancy school, or did mom guilt trip you into skipping it? i do actually feel bad that you're being made to pay for my sins. not bad enough to regret getting out of florida, though. by the way, wes and I are probably going to move out of texas pretty soon. it's so damn hot here. he's thinking boulder would be a nice change. I guess he wants to ski or something—a skill we never picked up back in the swamp.

if I thought you'd ever take my advice i'd say, GET THEE TO CONNECTICUT, but i'm afraid it might backfire. seriously, jules, you have to get out from under mom's gloom and doom. even that deadhead rick couldn't take more than a few years of it—look how many we had to put up with! you need to put some miles between you and mom. she'll cope. besides, you have such a great voice—if you bury yourself in florida, you'll end up in disney world singing about how it's a small world after all.

so, jesus, i guess your play starts tonight. wish I could come for it, although seeing my brother crucified is not an image I long to live with, and, as you know, spending time at 88 lanning road is detrimental to my health. anyway, kick some ass onstage. hey, maybe you could come visit wes and me this summer! course I'm not sure where we'll be by then. think about it, okay?

who you taking to the prom? how about that nina girl who's had a crush on you since forever? make her senior year, you cad!

gotta go. i'm on 8 to 2 at the bar.

love, carly (the bad seed)

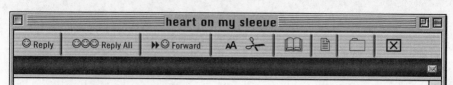

Subj: Putting it behind me
Date: 4/28/02, 3:55 P.M.
From: jghost@flowire.com
To: CCinWonderland@hotmail.com

Godspell's over, thank God. Not that I didn't enjoy it—I did—but it takes so much time and energy to do a musical, and I just feel like I'm currently out of both. I'll be so glad to graduate and be done with high school and all this piddly crap. (I did, however, kick ass.)

I *plan* to get out of Florida, Carly—you know that. I liked Cartwright a lot, but I guess I'm still not sure. Seems like such a big choice and Conn. is so far. And Mom is *not* trying to guilt trip me, but she obviously can't pay for a place like Cartwright unless I win some scholarship money from the contest this summer. She's going to send in a deposit to Cartwright, and also one to University of Florida, just in case—which I happen to think is a good idea.

And, hello? How could I possibly come to Colorado (or wherever you are) to visit you and Wes (whoever he is) when I have three more contest levels to go, and you *know* I have to work as many hours as possible at the Ginger Tree this summer? Duh! Why are you moving again anyway? You've only been in Austin for six months. Aren't you ever going to decide you like someplace?

You are so clueless. I haven't spoken to Nina Greco in about 3 years—she probably doesn't even remember who I am. I'm going to the prom with Tyler's sister Grace, and Ty's taking Inga Matthewson, who's just a good friend. That way we won't have to be all worried about the evening or anything—it'll be easy. You know, no expectations.

Reply | Reply All | Forward | AA ✂ | 📖 | 📄 | 📁 | ☒

I wish you'd stop blaming Mom for everything that goes wrong in the world. I know she can be a drag sometimes, but God, Carly, she's not the devil. Do you even KNOW how much she'd give to have you visit her once in a while? You might just consider it. Yeah, I know, I'm *guilt tripping* you. But you deserve it. All you ever think about is what *you* want. *You* want to get out of Florida. *You* don't want to go to college. *You* need freedom. What does that even mean? Freedom to be a bartender in every college town in America? What for?

Okay, sorry. Now you're pissed at me. I just don't think of going away to college as an escape from Mom, that's all. You don't even see how sad she is about this whole breakup thing. It's not a joke, you know. She loved Rick. Anyway, I have to go—Ty's waiting for me.

Julian (your conscience)

💬 IM *from Tyler to Julian*

plexiboy: figured u were online—phone was busy. when r u coming over?

jghost: now

plexiboy: inga's here 2. u wan2 walk 2 town and get pizza instead of shooting hoops?

jghost: no. i just had lunch. some hoops first?

B | *I* | u | A | A | ▼ | ▲ | ☺

plexiboy: ok—btw nina greco came by w/inga

send | close

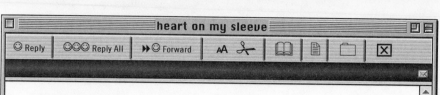

Subj: Small boy?
Date: 4/28/02, 11:57 P.M.
From: jghost@flowire.com
To: smallboyonherbike@boscore.com

Hi Chloe,

I just really noticed your screen name—how did you come up with that? Your subject headings are strange too—am I missing something? Actually I like the image of you as a small boy on your bike. I can imagine you as a little kid in a baseball cap, tooling around the neighborhood at high speed, with baseball cards stuck in the spokes of your bike so you make more noise. Tough, but cute.

Godspell is over, and I'm glad. It was fun, but now I feel like I'm really *done* with high school. Of course there's still a month left, and all those pesky exams to take, and prom and graduation and all that stuff, but Drama Club has *been* my high school life—now that I've had my last performance here, high school seems finished. Do you do any extracurricular stuff? Or does singing/guitar playing take up all your time? Just please don't tell me you're a cheerleader! No, I'm sure you aren't. No small boy on her bike would grow up to yell, "Bobby, Bobby, he's our man! If he can't do it, Jason can!"

I keep thinking about something you said last week at Cartwright—that your biggest hope for college was that you'd find people there you could really *connect* with. You said you had great friends now, nice people, but they weren't that much like you, and you wanted friends who really *got* you. That totally explains me too. My best friend, Tyler, thinks he knows me—we've been friends forever—but sometimes I feel like I'm not really *me* around Ty. You know? I'm who he expects me to be.

I just hope I don't end up like my sister, Carly, who Mom says can't "find herself." Which is probably because she keeps moving every

16

few months—now she's moving from Texas to Colorado, another place I've never been. I think she's lived in most of the western states by now. She's following some new boyfriend to Boulder, but she'll probably dump him when she gets there. Her track record with guys is as bad as with states. I don't get it. She's a really smart person but she never settles down to DO anything, unless you call working in crappy bars a career path. We're so different in that way. I can't imagine wasting my time just drifting around. I like to have goals to work toward.

In two weeks I go to the AMVC regionals (Abraham Menninger Voice Contest) at the University of Alabama. My chorus teacher, Ms. Prescott, has been working with me to get ready. Now that *Godspell*'s over, we work every day after school. Speaking of goals, I am determined to make it to the nationals in Boston! (Not only for the contest, of course.) And speaking of singing, I wish I could hear your new song. As you know, your voice *knocked me out*. Will you at least send me the lyrics when you're finished?

Getting late. More soon.

Julian

Subj: When I Was a Boy
Date: 4/29/02, 12:35 A.M.
From: smallboyonherbike@boscore.com
To: jghost@flowire.com

Hi Julian!

I was up late working on a paper and just checked my e-mail before going to bed and there you were!! (Oops . . . I hate when people use multiple exclamation points, as if everything they say is so dramatic!! And important!!) ☺

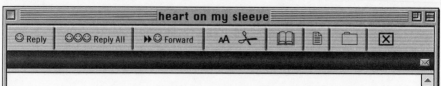

It's very cool that you can see me as a smallboyonherbike. You got it completely, and you obviously don't even know the song. (Restraining myself from exclamation here.) "Small boy on her bike" is a line from a song by Dar Williams (who is one of my very favorite singer/songwriters), and it's from a song called "When I Was a Boy." (See subject line.) I almost always use song titles for my subject lines (unless I'm really lazy or stressed) and they're usually titles from my favorites: Dar, John Prine, Greg Brown, The Nields, Cheryl Wheeler, Patty Larkin . . . and dozens more. You might not have heard of these people, but they're better than lots of the people you *have* heard of. Plus you can see them at small venues or folk festivals instead of those beer-soaked, eardrum-busting screamfests known as rock concerts. (Climbing down off high horse now.)

My sister, Genevieve, and I were both smallboysonourbikes. She was the original, I guess, and I followed her. We're only two years apart in age and Veev usually let me hang around with her—we were sort of a team. As a matter of fact, there was a boy on our street who called us the Sisterbikers, which I loved. (Good name for a band?) We had Magic cards in our spokes, instead of baseball. If there was a newly poured concrete sidewalk, we wrote our names in it. New tar on a road, we walked in it. We left no tree unclimbed. Our parents didn't mind—as long as we lived to tell about it, they didn't much care what adventures we had. But then, as Dar says, there comes the time you have to put on your shirt and start acting like a girl, and it's very depressing for awhile. Anyway, it's one of my favorite songs. I'll make you a mix CD of Dar songs and some other people too. Your education in folk music has begun!

NO, I was NEVER a cheerleader!! (Oops, the exclamation points got out again.) Screaming like that is hell on the vocal chords. Besides which, I can barely do a pushup—they'd never trust me to hold up a whole pyramid of Brimmingham beauties.

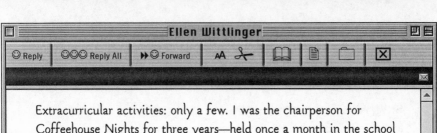

Extracurricular activities: only a few. I was the chairperson for Coffeehouse Nights for three years—held once a month in the school cafeteria. Which meant I had to make sure I had at least three people a night willing to get up and do *something*—sing or play an instrument or read poetry. We sold coffee, soda, and cookies, and charged 2 bucks at the door so we could buy tablecloths for the cruddy cafeteria tables and have candles instead of overhead fluorescent lights. I'm actually going to miss Coffeehouse Nights . . . although I guess there will be stuff like that at Cartwright too. YEAH!

That's the only activity I'm in charge of. I'm on the literary magazine staff too, and sometimes I write an article for the newspaper. I guess I spend more time doing things outside of school than inside. The past year, since I've had my license, I make the rounds of the open mics every weekend, and I love doing that.

I know JUST what you mean about being who your friends expect you to be. How does that even happen? I just want to START OVER and be who I am now and hope people will like THAT person. By the way, if you were the real you last weekend, the real me was impressed.

God, it's almost 2 in the morning!!!! I have to get to bed. I'll send you the lyrics for "To Fly" as soon as I finish it.

Yawningly,

Chloe

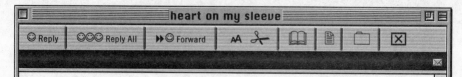

Subj: As Cool As I Am
Date: 4/29/02, 5:21 P.M.
From: smallboyonherbike@boscore.com
To: ggillespie@Emmett.edu

Genevieve,

I just got a LONG letter from Julian. He says my voice *knocked him out*. And he can imagine me as a small boy on my bike, *tough but cute*. His e-mails are turning me into a piddling puddle of goo. I melt for him!

Sorry if I'm making you stick your finger down your throat. When are you out of school, anyway? I need to talk to you in person! You'll be here for my graduation, right? Did you get the letter from Bill about going up to Maple Hill on June 15 to help train the new counselors? It'll be nice to have some time to commune with each other before the brat pack shows up.

I'm feeling bad about not telling Eli or Kate or anybody about Julian. Not that there's much to tell. Of *course* I didn't sleep with him at Cartwright—I just MET him, Genevieve. (And don't give me that *how long are you going to be a virgin* speech again. Until I'm ready.) A little kissing is all that went on. Okay, a lot of kissing, but what's the point of telling everybody? Eli would be hurt and Kate would be furious. But I feel like a creep keeping this secret from them. Which makes ME furious because, God, do I have to MARRY Eli just because I've known him since birth? Answer me!

Chloe

Subj: You don't have to marry anybody!
Date: 4/29/02, 11:18 P.M.
From: ggillespie@Emmett.edu
To: smallboyonherbike@boscore.com

—A piddling puddle of goo is the least of it. You're a peeing poodle of poo. A puzzling pushover of boo-hoo. A pathetic parody of Pooh. A plastic pancake of . . . I don't know, but that was fun, wasn't it? Maybe you *shouldn't* go to Cartwright—I don't know if I can put up with your gloppy gushing over this Julian guy—(am I good at alliteration or what?)—and you haven't even slept with him yet! Have you mentioned this new obsession to Martha and Tom, the loco parenti? Or haven't they come out of the bedroom this week?

—Why are you even TALKING about marrying Eli, for God's sake? You're barely 18. Both Eli and Kate will learn to live with your decision to desert them. The only reason you're getting wiggy over this is because you're leaving for college in a few months and it's making you nervous. Once you're at Cartwright and they're wherever they're going, you'll all start rethinking your lives. Brimmingham, Massachusetts, and its various residents will cease to be of importance to you. Which seems weird now, but it'll be FINE.

—I got Bill's letter, and I've been putting off telling you this. Thing is, I've got a better offer this summer. I went down to NYC a few weeks ago with Alice (Stella, remember?) and auditioned for a small company— they take on summer interns—and we both got in! The pay is lousy, and we'll mostly be understudying and moving furniture, but we'll be in a NYC acting company! It's too good to turn down, Chloe—I'll get to meet people, and I'll be in the city! Pissed off, aren't you? I know—we ALWAYS do Maple Hill. But really, I'm 20 years old—I think I may finally have outgrown summer camp. Don't dissolve—you're too gooey already. I'll be home before the internship starts—for your prom and your graduation—so we can dish dirt about all the locals we love to hate.

—Don't be bummed. Life's too short.

—Genevieve

Subj: Who we really are
Date: 4/30/02, 7:21 P.M.
From: jghost@flowire.com
To: smallboyonherbike@boscore.com

I WAS being the real me last weekend, and if you were being the real you, I think we have a lot in common. Can't wait to get the mix CD. Can't wait to see you again.

Julian

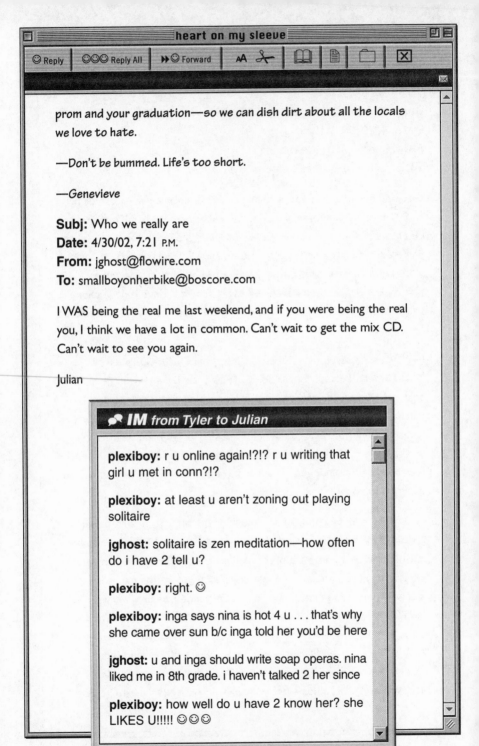

IM *from Tyler to Julian*

plexiboy: r u online again!?!? r u writing that girl u met in conn?!?

plexiboy: at least u aren't zoning out playing solitaire

jghost: solitaire is zen meditation—how often do i have 2 tell u?

plexiboy: right. ☺

plexiboy: inga says nina is hot 4 u . . . that's why she came over sun b/c inga told her you'd be here

jghost: u and inga should write soap operas. nina liked me in 8th grade. i haven't talked 2 her since

plexiboy: how well do u have 2 know her? she LIKES U!!!!! ☺☺☺

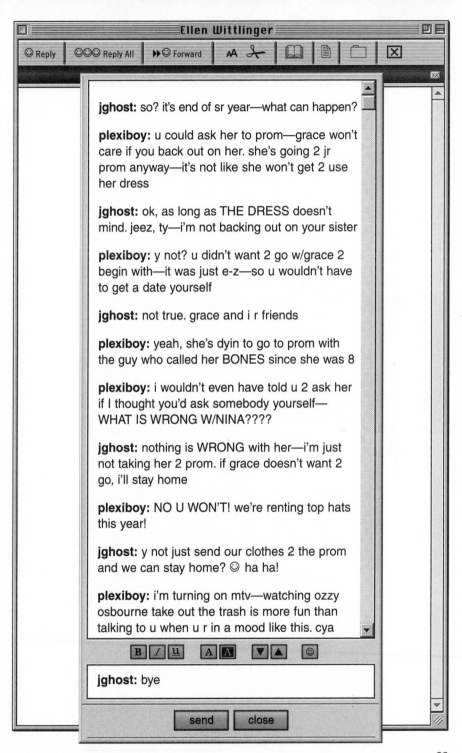

jghost: so? it's end of sr year—what can happen?

plexiboy: u could ask her to prom—grace won't care if you back out on her. she's going 2 jr prom anyway—it's not like she won't get 2 use her dress

jghost: ok, as long as THE DRESS doesn't mind. jeez, ty—i'm not backing out on your sister

plexiboy: y not? u didn't want 2 go w/grace 2 begin with—it was just e-z—so u wouldn't have to get a date yourself

jghost: not true. grace and i r friends

plexiboy: yeah, she's dyin to go to prom with the guy who called her BONES since she was 8

plexiboy: i wouldn't even have told u 2 ask her if I thought you'd ask somebody yourself— WHAT IS WRONG W/NINA????

jghost: nothing is WRONG with her—i'm just not taking her 2 prom. if grace doesn't want 2 go, i'll stay home

plexiboy: NO U WON'T! we're renting top hats this year!

jghost: y not just send our clothes 2 the prom and we can stay home? ☺ ha ha!

plexiboy: i'm turning on mtv—watching ozzy osbourne take out the trash is more fun than talking to u when u r in a mood like this. cya

jghost: bye

send   close

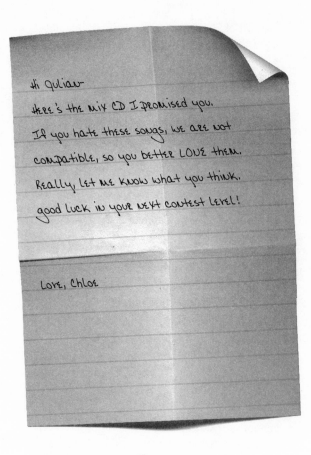

Hi Julian—

Here's the mix CD I promised you.
If you hate these songs, we are not
compatible, so you better LOVE them.
Really, let me know what you think.
Good luck in your next contest level!

Love, Chloe

Subj: Summer Wages
Date: 5/6/02, 5:06 P.M.
From: smallboyonherbike@boscore.com
To: ggillespie@Emmett.edu

Did you even notice that I haven't written to you in a week? You're damn right I'm pissed! I can't *believe* you aren't coming up to Maple Hill this summer! We started as campers there when you were 9 and I was 7, for God's sake—that's 11 years. We've NEVER not gone there for the summer! You always said it was the best thing about having parents who couldn't wait to get rid of you.

How can I go there by myself? It won't feel right. We ARE Maple Hill Arts Camp. Bill will be furious too—who's going to run the theater department? I hope when I go off to college I won't forget all about my old life. But I guess you're too good for MHAC now, huh? Moving props in *New York City* is so much better for your *career*!

Veev, I hardly ever see you anymore. Is this how it's going to be from now on? You'll never even come home for the summer?

I know there's not a damn thing I can do about this. When you make up your mind, it can't be changed. Just don't expect me to like it one little bit.

Chloe

Subj: Frequently Wrong but Never in Doubt
Date: 5/6/02, 5:24 P.M.
From: smallboyonherbike@boscore.com
To: ggillespie@Emmett.edu

Now that I'm speaking to you again (not that you noticed that I wasn't), I have to tell you about being dragged along to a wedding this weekend with Mom and Dad. I didn't even know the people getting married—it was the daughter of that Julia Stevenson woman who's in the garden club with Mom. They tricked me into going by asking if I wanted to join them Sunday afternoon, and I stupidly thought we were actually going to do something as a *family*. Hah!

I don't know why Mom wanted me along—maybe to show that she also has a daughter (or two) and hopes to throw a few shindigs like this herself one day. The reception was outside under a white tent, and there was a band playing schmaltzy waltzes like they always do so the bride and groom can look romantic. But guess who outdid them? Mom and Dad, dipping and sliding around the floor, then *kissing* each other (in public!) every time the music stopped. People were staring at them, then looking over at me and saying stuff like, "Your parents have so much energy!" It was SO embarrassing I wanted to disappear.

Don't they ever notice that other people their age don't act this way? For some reason I keep remembering one time when—I must have been about 14—I asked Mom, "How did you know Dad was *The Right One*?" I was sort of in awe of their *great love* back then, I guess. (Don't snicker.) And Mom got this faraway look and said, "I didn't. It was a lucky accident." What kind of motherly advice is that? *A lucky accident?* What does that even mean?

Chloe

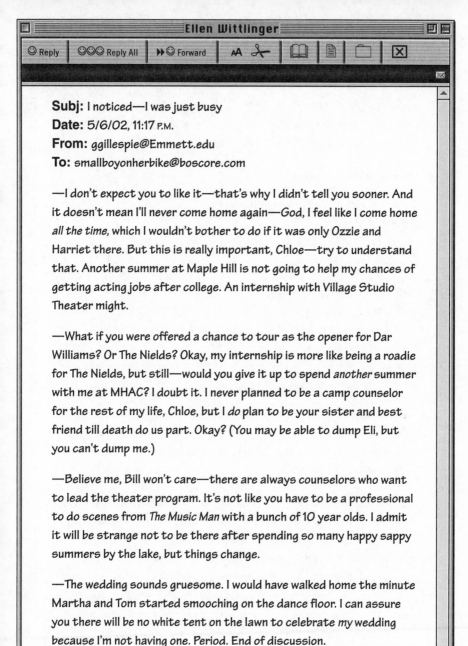

© Reply   ©©© Reply All   ▶▶© Forward   A A ✂   📖 📄 🗀 ☒

Subj: I noticed—I was just busy
Date: 5/6/02, 11:17 P.M.
From: ggillespie@Emmett.edu
To: smallboyonherbike@boscore.com

—I don't expect you to like it—that's why I didn't tell you sooner. And it doesn't mean I'll never come home again—*God*, I feel like I come home *all the time*, which I wouldn't bother to do if it was only Ozzie and Harriet there. But this is really important, Chloe—try to understand that. Another summer at Maple Hill is not going to help my chances of getting acting jobs after college. An internship with Village Studio Theater might.

—What if you were offered a chance to tour as the opener for Dar Williams? Or The Nields? Okay, my internship is more like being a roadie for The Nields, but still—would you give it up to spend *another* summer with me at MHAC? I doubt it. I never planned to be a camp counselor for the rest of my life, Chloe, but I *do* plan to be your sister and best friend till death do us part. Okay? (You may be able to dump Eli, but you can't dump me.)

—Believe me, Bill won't care—there are always counselors who want to lead the theater program. It's not like you have to be a professional to do scenes from *The Music Man* with a bunch of 10 year olds. I admit it will be strange not to be there after spending so many happy sappy summers by the lake, but things change.

—The wedding sounds gruesome. I would have walked home the minute Martha and Tom started smooching on the dance floor. I can assure you there will be no white tent on the lawn to celebrate *my* wedding because I'm not having one. Period. End of discussion.

—I have no idea why they are the way they are. Being less romantic than you, at 14 I assumed it was all about sex. That they were

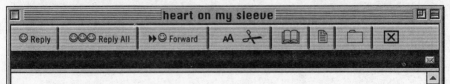
supercharged or something. Or Viagra junkies. Now I think it's more than that, but I don't buy the *greatest love of all* theory either. Lucky and her ducky. I don't have a clue.

—Genevieve

Subj: what's wrong with tending bar?
Date: 5/7/02, 1:02 P.M.
From: CCinWonderland@hotmail.com
To: jghost@flowire.com

jules, are you such a good boy because i was such a bad girl? are you trying to make it up to mom for my miserable behavior? you're better at guilt tripping me than she is, which is quite a feat. why would you even consider staying in florida for college? take out some loans, punk! do anything you have to do! if cartwright is too expensive, go to some other state university, just not in FLORIDA.

i can see now i should have come home more, if only to guide you in this college business. you know, you could just take a year off, like i did, and move someplace new and see how you like it. (okay, my year off has never ended, but still….)

and I don't blame mom for everything, just most things. you were too little to understand how miserable she was to dad. i know, you think he would have left us anyway because he's such a loner, and maybe that's true, but she didn't give him any reason to stick around. and she's been pulling the same stuff on me all my life too—i'm never good enough for her, so why even try? obviously you chose the other route—dedicating your life to pleasing her every whim so she doesn't go ballistic on you. i don't blame you for it—you had to stick around after dad and I were gone and it must have been hell, but now it's time to grow up and get over her. rock out a little bit, bro! (you're not *really* jesus, you know.)

for example, the prom. you're going with *ty's sister*? that skinny thing who thinks she's so brilliant? and you made this choice so there would be 'no expectations' and you wouldn't have to be 'worried about the evening'?? that is pathetic, dear boy. GET worried, GET some expectations, for chrissakes. so what if you're leaving in a few months? what's wrong with dating somebody for the summer? i don't think i ever dated anybody for more than 3 months, did i? in high school, i mean. wes says 6 months is my limit now, and he's worried his time is almost up. (it isn't.)

and i just don't buy all this supposed sadness mom is feeling about rick leaving. couldn't she see the handwriting on the wall? that guy's been packing his suitcase since the first day he moved in. how can you sit around that dingy living room with her sighing and staring off into space all evening? aren't you tired of being a saint?

sincerely,

carly casper, demon spawn

Subj: View from the dingy living room
Date: 5/7/02, 11:53 P.M.
From: jghost@flowire.com
To: CCinWonderland@hotmail.com

Just so you know: As it happens there IS a girl I'm interested in. Very interested, as a matter of fact. And she doesn't live in the hideous state of FLORIDA. I met her at the Cartwright pre-frosh weekend and she's going there next year. She's a musician, a songwriter, and a singer. She looks sort of like Joan Baez in her Bob Dylan days, but softer. I'll see her in August in Boston—she lives near there—if I get that far in the Menninger competition. I liked her the minute I saw her, which NEVER happens to me.

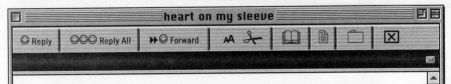

So why does it matter who I go to the prom with? It's one stupid evening. And Grace is all right—it's not like I hate her or anything. And just because YOU never dated anybody for more than 5 minutes doesn't mean that's the standard method. Why even bother going with people—or in your case, living with them—if you aren't interested in a long-term relationship? *Six months?* I don't even buy new *shoes* every six months.

Saint Julian

Subj: Mix CD
Date: 5/8/02, 12:02 A.M.
From: jghost@flowire.com
To: smallboyonherbike@boscore.com

Hey Chloe! I got the CD and it's great. I keep it in the car so I can listen on the way to and from school—even my friend Ty likes it. You're right, I haven't heard of most of these people—are they from around Boston or what? I know the Indigo Girls—I'm not that ignorant—and I've heard of John Prine before, but my favorite of these is Greg Brown, and I really like your favorite, Dar Williams, too. Especially "What Do You Hear in These Sounds?" I could really imagine you singing that one with your gorgeous soprano. Thanks for introducing me to these people. It's funny. Even though I love singing, I don't listen to much modern music. I like classical stuff when I'm studying, and I listen to musicals because I'm always in them, and you can't help but know about the really popular junk because it's on everywhere you go. I thought of this because I wanted to send you a CD in return for yours and I couldn't think what I'd put on it! So I'll just have to give you something else, as soon as I come up with a clever and witty idea that'll surprise the hell out of you!

How are your last days of high school going? In two weeks we have exams, then it'll be the prom, Senior Week, and graduation. I can hardly believe it. *Next* week I go to U. of Alabama for the AMVC regionals. I'm more worried about that than my exams, but Ms. Prescott seems pretty sure that I'll make it to the district level, which is next month in Richmond, Virginia. Wish me luck!

Julian

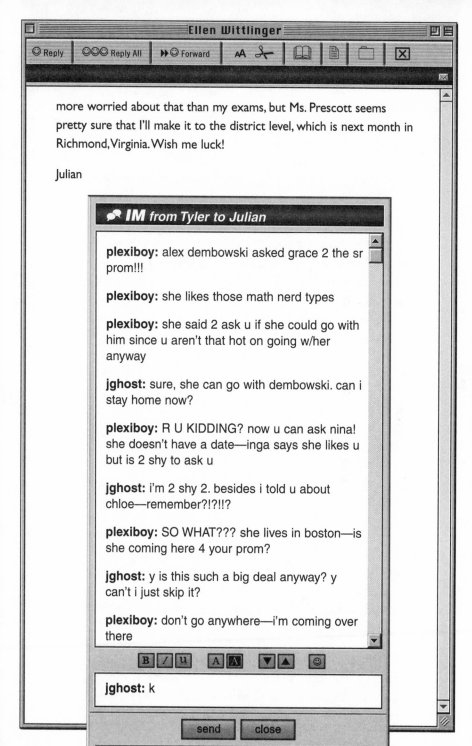

IM *from Tyler to Julian*

plexiboy: alex dembowski asked grace 2 the sr prom!!!

plexiboy: she likes those math nerd types

plexiboy: she said 2 ask u if she could go with him since u aren't that hot on going w/her anyway

jghost: sure, she can go with dembowski. can i stay home now?

plexiboy: R U KIDDING? now u can ask nina! she doesn't have a date—inga says she likes u but is 2 shy to ask u

jghost: i'm 2 shy 2. besides i told u about chloe—remember?!?!!?

plexiboy: SO WHAT??? she lives in boston—is she coming here 4 your prom?

jghost: y is this such a big deal anyway? y can't i just skip it?

plexiboy: don't go anywhere—i'm coming over there

jghost: k

send   close

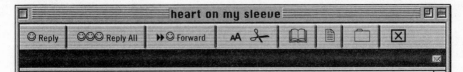

Subj: Financial matters
Date: 5/8/02, 3:12 P.M.
From: mtgillespie@boscore.com
To: ggillespie@Emmett.edu

Genevieve,

Just a heads up. I've decided to go ahead and split my shares of Eli Lilly stock between you and Chloe—you'll remember we talked about this last year. My broker will take care of it and send you some papers—all you have to do is sign and return them. With any luck, the health problems of all us old boomers will make you a comfortable return in future years. Your tax refund check came this week too—I'll send it on. As I recall, you and your sister both got nice little chunks of cash back from your counselor jobs.

Love,

Dad

Subj: What Do You Hear in These Sounds?
Date: 5/8/02, 10:31 P.M.
From: smallboyonherbike@boscore.com
To: jghost@flowire.com

Hey! I'm so glad you like the CD! Isn't Dar great? I love Greg Brown too—I love them all. Some of them started out around Boston—there's a big folk and singer/songwriter scene here, but most of them play nationally now. I like the old folkies too, like Holly Near and Pete Seeger and those guys. I guess I like the whole scene—it's sort of a throwback to the sixties—the era that never dies.

My school is on a later schedule than yours. Our exams are in three weeks :-{ and then all the senior activities start. Meanwhile, we're all

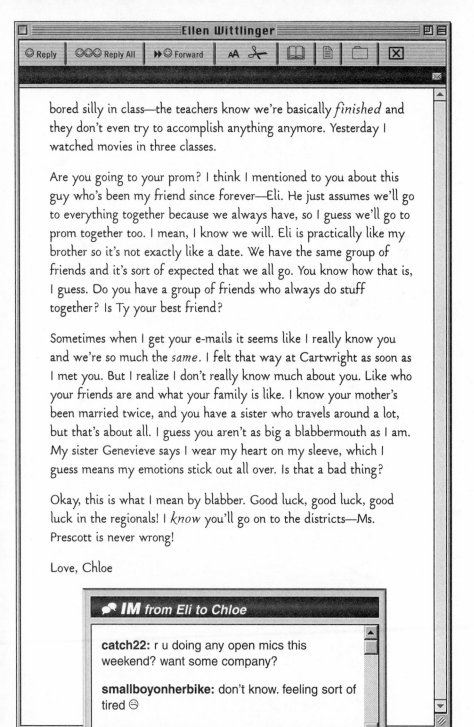

bored silly in class—the teachers know we're basically *finished* and they don't even try to accomplish anything anymore. Yesterday I watched movies in three classes.

Are you going to your prom? I think I mentioned to you about this guy who's been my friend since forever—Eli. He just assumes we'll go to everything together because we always have, so I guess we'll go to prom together too. I mean, I know we will. Eli is practically like my brother so it's not exactly like a date. We have the same group of friends and it's sort of expected that we all go. You know how that is, I guess. Do you have a group of friends who always do stuff together? Is Ty your best friend?

Sometimes when I get your e-mails it seems like I really know you and we're so much the *same*. I felt that way at Cartwright as soon as I met you. But I realize I don't really know much about you. Like who your friends are and what your family is like. I know your mother's been married twice, and you have a sister who travels around a lot, but that's about all. I guess you aren't as big a blabbermouth as I am. My sister Genevieve says I wear my heart on my sleeve, which I guess means my emotions stick out all over. Is that a bad thing?

Okay, this is what I mean by blabber. Good luck, good luck, good luck in the regionals! I *know* you'll go on to the districts—Ms. Prescott is never wrong!

Love, Chloe

💬 **IM** *from Eli to Chloe*

catch22: r u doing any open mics this weekend? want some company?

smallboyonherbike: don't know. feeling sort of tired ☹

catch22: yeah, that school's over—what's next feeling

smallboyonherbike: maybe

catch22: i have it 2—i want it 2 be over already, but also don't want it 2 end

smallboyonherbike: yeah. if i had a new song i'd feel more like going 2 the mics

smallboyonherbike: i'm tired of the same old stuff ☹

catch22: i love your same old stuff ☺☺☺

smallboyonherbike: e, don't u EVER get sick of me?

catch22: noooooope!!!

smallboyonherbike: gtg . . . I'll let you know about the mics

catch22: don't worry so much—all is well!

smallboyonherbike: optimist

catch22: u say that like it's a bad thing!!

send   close

Subj: The Pointless, Yet Poignant Crisis of a Co-ed
Date: 5/9/02, 7:21 A.M.
From: smallboyonherbike@boscore.com
To: ggillespie@Emmett.edu

I've been up all night worrying about this: I sent a mix CD to Julian with a note, and I signed it *Love, Chloe.* When he e-mailed me to thank me for it, he DIDN'T sign it *Love,* just used his name. So last night I e-mailed him again, and I said I had my heart on my sleeve—I don't know WHY I said that—and I signed it *Love, Chloe* again. Do you think he'll get freaked out and never write me again and not go to Cartwright because there's a crazy love-besotted freak after him?

Heart in mouth, Chloe

P.S. And Eli says he never gets sick of me and we're both optimists and everything is going to be fine. I can never break up with him. It would make us both very ill.

Subj: Where your heart is
Date: 5/9/02, 11:53 A.M.
From: ggillespie@Emmett.edu
To: smallgirlonherbike@boscore.com

—It is possible you have forever scared off your one true love, but only if he is a moron. More likely he didn't even notice how you signed the things. He is a *male,* after all. And if he did notice, he's probably flattered no end by your meager declaration which could, as you know, just mean that big-hearted kind of love girls throw around to everyone in sight like beads at Mardi Gras. He's probably wondering how many other guys you're sending your *Love* to. Males almost never use the L-word unless a) they're hoping to get lucky, or b) they actually mean it.

—I can't believe you're letting yourself get so crazed about this person you saw for two days. Or maybe being "love-besotted" is just an excuse to get rid of Eli. Although you don't seem too confident about that possibility either. Even I, your hard-hearted sister, am starting to feel sorry for the guy. He's too nice for his own good. (Or yours, apparently.) My *God*, he helped you pick out your prom dress! What does it look like this year? Are you going in a limo or a pumpkin? Wearing your glass slippers?

—By the way, why are you asking *me* for advice on love? Does it strike you that I've done particularly well with it over the years? Forget about the blind leading the blind—this is more like the *dead* leading the blind.

—*Good* luck getting that heart out of your mouth.

Veev

IM *from Eli to Chloe*

catch22: hey r u there?

catch22: a red bowtie & cummerbund just came in the mail. mom bought them on ebay so we'd match ☺ ☺

smallboyonherbike: gr8!!! now i won't need a red purse

smallboyonherbike: your mom isn't coming with us, is she?

catch22: she WANTS 2 (of course) but i told her she'd have 2 dance w/the limo driver . . . ha ha ha

catch22: our negotiated settlement is she gets to take 200 pictures of us in our outfits

catch22: (in the house, outside the house, by the tree, on the front stairs, in front of the limo, on top the limo, etc, etc.)

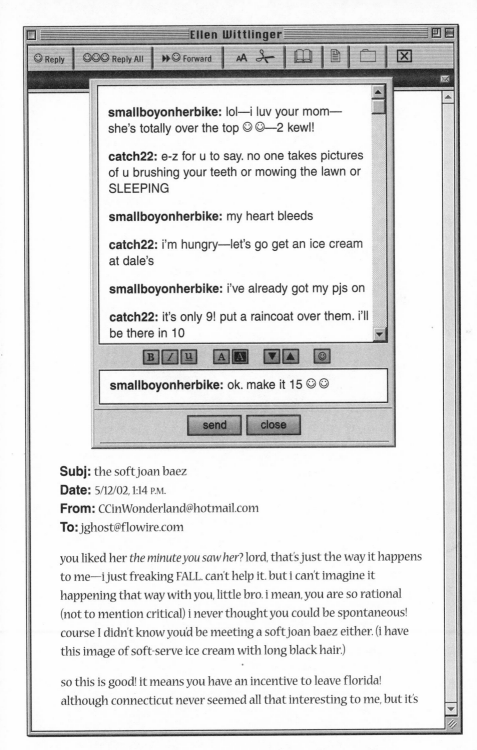

smallboyonherbike: lol—i luv your mom—she's totally over the top ☺ ☺—2 kewl!

catch22: e-z for u to say. no one takes pictures of u brushing your teeth or mowing the lawn or SLEEPING

smallboyonherbike: my heart bleeds

catch22: i'm hungry—let's go get an ice cream at dale's

smallboyonherbike: i've already got my pjs on

catch22: it's only 9! put a raincoat over them. i'll be there in 10

smallboyonherbike: ok. make it 15 ☺ ☺

send　close

Subj: the soft joan baez
Date: 5/12/02, 1:14 P.M.
From: CCinWonderland@hotmail.com
To: jghost@flowire.com

you liked her *the minute you saw her*? lord, that's just the way it happens to me—i just freaking FALL. can't help it. but i can't imagine it happening that way with you, little bro. i mean, you are so rational (not to mention critical) i never thought you could be spontaneous! course I didn't know you'd be meeting a soft joan baez either. (i have this image of soft-serve ice cream with long black hair.)

so this is good! it means you have an incentive to leave florida! although connecticut never seemed all that interesting to me, but it's a first step. the singer thing, though, what's that about? personally i prefer a good banjo picker to yet another girl with a guitar, but that's just me.

guess what? wes and I have passed our six month anniversary and we're still together. i guess i'm moving to colorado with him. and here's your birthday present: i'm coming back to my swampland home for a few days in between texas and colorado, partly to see you graduate and partly so i don't have to do all that packing. you can have the pleasure of informing mom. she'll want to know date and time and all that, so tell her i'll be there when i get there.

Soon,

Carly

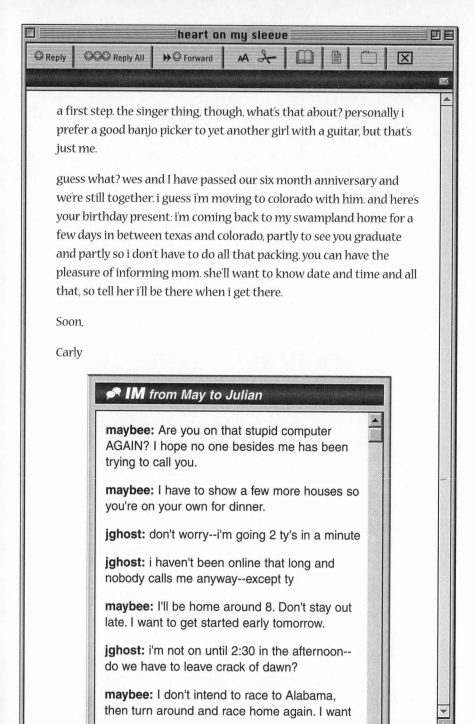

📣 IM from May to Julian

maybee: Are you on that stupid computer AGAIN? I hope no one besides me has been trying to call you.

maybee: I have to show a few more houses so you're on your own for dinner.

jghost: don't worry--i'm going 2 ty's in a minute

jghost: i haven't been online that long and nobody calls me anyway--except ty

maybee: I'll be home around 8. Don't stay out late. I want to get started early tomorrow.

jghost: i'm not on until 2:30 in the afternoon-- do we have to leave crack of dawn?

maybee: I don't intend to race to Alabama, then turn around and race home again. I want

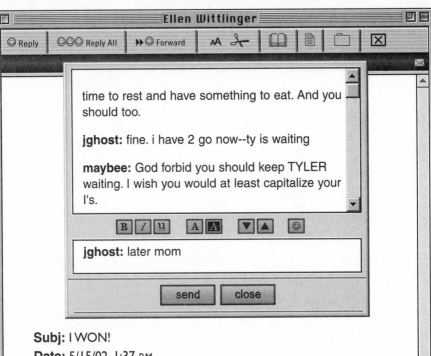

time to rest and have something to eat. And you should too.

jghost: fine. i have 2 go now--ty is waiting

maybee: God forbid you should keep TYLER waiting. I wish you would at least capitalize your I's.

jghost: later mom

send   close

Subj: I WON!
Date: 5/15/02, 1:37 P.M.
From: jghost@flowire.com
To: CCinWonderland@hotmail.com; smallboyonherbike@boscore.com; plexiboy@flowire.com

Hi everybody! Just wanted to let you all know I WON THE REGIONAL CONTEST IN MY CATEGORY (tenor: musical comedy). I got off school yesterday and Mom drove me to U. of Alabama. We got there early so Mom could get lunch and I could get nervous. But it went fine. I sang "My Boy Bill" from *Carousel* which was probably a relief to the judges since most of the other guys were singing stuff from rock operas. I got a plaque and $200. But the NEXT level, the Districts, actually gives $2,000 in scholarship money. And if you win the Nationals—I know I shouldn't even DREAM of it—you get a renewable $25,000-a-year scholarship!

Ty: We got home late last night, so Mom let me stay home from school today, which is why I'm not snoring next to you in calculus right this minute. Call me when you get home.

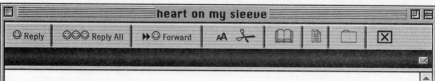

Carly: I told Mom. She said she'd believe it when she saw you.
Chloe: Haven't you finished that song *yet*? I want to sing it!

Julian

Subj: The Poet Game
Date: 5/15/02, 5:31 P.M.
From: smallboyonherbike@boscore.com
To: jghost@flowire.com

Yay for you! I knew you'd win the Regionals! Now all you have to do with that beautiful voice of yours is win the Districts and you can come to Boston in August! I wish it wasn't so far away. August seems like an eternity from now: after graduation, after camp, just before we leave for school.

I guess now you have to start studying for exams. :(Do you have a lot? I opted to do papers instead of exams for English and Psych, so I'm already working on those. I'm not really sweating over them much though—my grades are fine.

So, gulp, I finished the song. I'm currently calling it "To Fly," but that may change. I'm really nervous to send it to you—I haven't shown it to anybody yet. I'll snail mail you a copy with the musical notation so you can see how it sounds, but since I can't wait to get your response, I'll e-mail you the lyrics—see below. If you hate it, don't tell me. No, you can tell me—really. I need to know the truth, even if it's hard. I just hope it doesn't seem too sappy.

By the way, did you ever tell me who you were taking to the prom?

Chloe

To Fly

Everyone's excited to be leaving.
We thought this day would never ever come.
Eighteen years of laughs and make-believing—
At last it's time to run away from home.

But Kate will have to say goodbye to Joey
And Eli's headed west to Michigan.
The next time that we meet it will be noisy
As we tell each other who we have become.

So the only way to go is just to go.
Perhaps you think I oversimplify.
Gotta say goodbye so you can say hello.
Gotta make the leap and trust yourself to fly.

Everyone's excited to be leaving,
As if we can't grow up until we part.
Naively we agree there'll be no grieving—
We embrace as though we know each other's heart.

So the only way to go is just to go.
Up ahead may be a catcher in the rye.
Gotta say goodbye so you can say hello.
Gotta make the leap and trust yourself to fly . . .
Fly! Fly!
Gotta make the leap and trust yourself to fly.

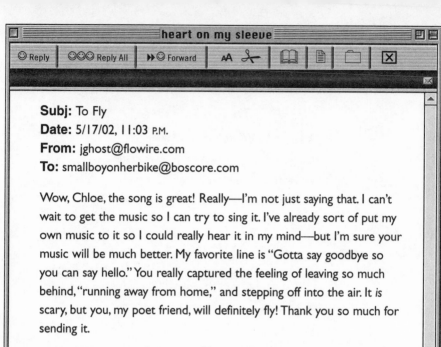

Subj: To Fly
Date: 5/17/02, 11:03 P.M.
From: jghost@flowire.com
To: smallboyonherbike@boscore.com

Wow, Chloe, the song is great! Really—I'm not just saying that. I can't wait to get the music so I can try to sing it. I've already sort of put my own music to it so I could really hear it in my mind—but I'm sure your music will be much better. My favorite line is "Gotta say goodbye so you can say hello." You really captured the feeling of leaving so much behind, "running away from home," and stepping off into the air. It *is* scary, but you, my poet friend, will definitely fly! Thank you so much for sending it.

The prom is a big mess. I don't even want to go but my friend Ty is sort of forcing me to. I was going to go with his younger sister, who I've known forever, but she got a better offer, and then Ty decided I HAD to ask this other girl, Nina, who I hardly even know. So I did and she's going with me, but it's bound to be weird. Why does everybody think they HAVE to go to the prom anyway? I wish you could go with me— *that* would be fun. How come you live so far away? Should I be jealous of this Eli guy? I don't really have a big group of friends like you do. Ty's my best friend and he says I'm a loner, but he has other friends and sometimes I hang out with them if I'm not rehearsing for a play or something. I'm hoping college will be different for me—that I get pulled out of myself a little bit. I felt that way when I was with you at Cartwright.

My prom is May 29 and I graduate June 1. What about you? I want to know when you're doing all that last stuff too. Gotta go study for calc. Just in case you didn't hear me the first time: You are a freaking great songwriter!

Julian

Subj: Eli's Comin'
Date: 5/18/02, 4:21 P.M.
From: smallboyonherbike@boscore.com
To: ggillespie@Emmett.edu

WHEN are you coming home? I need to talk to you in person! You better be here from prom through graduation! I'm writing this fast because Eli is coming over in a few minutes to study environmental science. And then we're going to Kate's house after dinner. Here's the thing: I just got this REALLY nice e-mail from Julian. I sent him a copy of my new song—I'll mail it to you tomorrow (tell me if it's too sappy)—and he seemed to like it a lot. As a matter of fact, he seemed to like ME a lot, like the song reminded him who I was or something. And now I feel *so guilty* about seeing Eli. I haven't told anybody here about meeting Julian because I didn't want Eli to get hurt, but now I feel like I'm hurting him anyway, just because I'm spending so much time thinking about somebody else! Should I tell him? I don't want to lose Eli—he's my best friend (besides you, of course.) Will he hate me? I'm DREADING going to the prom with him, which makes me feel like the most horrible person alive.

Your sister,

Pond scum

Subj: Upstairs by a Chinese Lamp
Date: 5/18/02, 11:13 P.M.
From: smallboyonherbike@boscore.com
To: jghost@flowire.com

Actually I'm upstairs by a gooseneck lamp, but there weren't any titles like that. I'm SO happy you like my song. I've written others in the past, but this is the first one that really seems to work, like I could actually call it a *song*. It's not too sappy, is it? Let me know

when you get the music. Hey, wouldn't it be great to sing it together sometime? Maybe in August!

I wish I could go to your prom with you and you could come here and go with me too! And no, you should NOT be jealous of Eli. I told you, he's an old friend. (We'll just have to pretend we're going together and hope that Eli and Nina won't notice!) ☺

My prom is June 4 and my graduation is June 8. Then a week later I'm off to New Hampshire to Maple Hill Arts Camp. (Did I tell you about MHAC? I've been going there 11 years—this is my second as a counselor.) The last camp session is over August 10 and I'll be home the next day. And your contest is the next week (if you come—which you have to!), so that will be PERFECT. I can show you around Boston.

I just thought of this—do you have a place to stay here? You could sleep in my sister's room—she'll be in NYC all summer. We don't live right in Boston, but I could go in with you on the train or even drive you in for the contest and stuff. What do you think?

I think of you.

Chloe

Subj: YOU WON!
Date: 5/19/02, 2:13 P.M.
From: CCinWonderland@hotmail.com
To: jghost@flowire.com

i'm not the least bit surprised. it's what I expect of you—you're a winner, pal. you liked u. of alabama, huh? maybe you could go there? i'm assuming that smallboyonherbike is the joan baez ice-cream cone you met at cartwright. good screen name. of course you should never have let me know it—it's *so* tempting. so far i have managed to resist sending her a letter of introduction, but how long can i hold out?

okay, i got a plane ticket today. i'll be there on the 30th at noon. can you pick me up at the airport? if you can't i'll have to take a taxi, which i obviously can't afford, because i will NOT ask mom to take one minute off work to come and get me. i'm leaving again on june 2. I would have left on the first, after graduation, but it's a saturday and you have to stay overnight on a sat. to get a cheaper rate. what's that about anyway? i never got that—it's like some kind of republican family values idea where you're forced to sit around with your parents watching bad TV instead of being out partying with normal people.

—CC

Subj: Yes, Your Highness
Date: 5/23/02, 8:32 P.M.
From: jghost@flowire.com
To: CCinWonderland@hotmail.com

Yes, I'll pick you up at noon. Tell me your flight number. Of course the night before is PROM NIGHT, but this will give me a good excuse not to stay out all night with Nina. Not that she'll want to anyway. Yes, I'm going with Nina Greco—shut up. Ty's sister backed out on me, and Ty and Inga set it up with Nina. The whole thing is stupid—I wish I wasn't even going. She hardly even looks at me when I talk to her—how's that going to play out for 5 or 6 hours?

Now, listen to me . . . are you listening? If you DARE to e-mail Chloe your embarrassing, lunatic rantings, you can walk home from the airport. You think you're so funny, but nobody else thinks so. She'll think I put you up to it or something. PLEASE DO NOT WRITE HER! I like this person, Carly. I don't want her to think I come from a family of bizarros. Promise me you won't write to her!

Julian

⊖ Reply   ⊖⊖⊖ Reply All   ▸⊖ Forward   AA ✂   📖   📄   📁   ☒

🗨 IM *from Tyler to Julian*

plexiboy: inga says nina is stoked about going 2 the prom with u

plexiboy: I TOLD U she was in 2 u

jghost: stop telling me this, ty! i don't want her 2 b in2 me! i liked her yrs ago, but i don't want 2 start some big thing NOW!

plexiboy: y??? b-cuz u have a fantasy girl in conn? nina is HERE man—bird in the hand

jghost: BIRD?? hello? welcome 2 the 21st century!

plexiboy: u know what i mean

jghost: i'm trying hard NOT 2 know

B / U   A A   ▼ ▲   ☺

plexiboy: obviously

[send]   [close]

Subj: get a grip
Date: 5/24/02, 1:11 P.M.
From: CCinWonderland@hotmail.com
To: jghost@flowire.com

chloe—a very salinger-esque name, don't you think? by the way, you DO come from a family of bizarros, but god forbid anyone should suspect. i promise i won't write to her ... yet. but you need to take a deep breath, bro. you're wound way too tight. flight # 755—see ya.

—CC

Subj: By next year none of this stuff will matter
Date: 5/24/02, 7:14 P.M.
From: ggillespie@Emmett.edu
To: smallboyonherbike@boscore.com

Dear Pond Scum,

—These hysterical e-mails are getting hard to take. I know this whole prom/Eli/Florida guy thing has you tied like a pretzel, but try to cool out a little, will you? God, you're 18—it's not like you have to choose one of these guys to be with forever! When you finally get around to breaking up with Eli, he'll be hurt. No doubt about it. But it isn't going to KILL HIM! This is just what happens. DON'T break up with him before prom. If you do, you'll both be miserable the whole night, and everybody you know will be miserable too—if you don't, it's only your own guilt you have to deal with. And besides, what do you have to feel so guilty for? I'm telling you, he'll LIVE.

—About the song. I like it—it has your usual melancholy optimism. It is a *trifle* sappy, but that's the kind of song it is, a little heartbreaking, a little uplifting. All in all, it's very good. (It ain't Dar Williams yet, but you'll get there one of these days.)

—Now, 2 cents about MY life: Exams are over and I did exceptionally well, as always. Alice and I are going to NYC tomorrow to try to find a place to live—possibly with a bunch of the other interns at the theater. Then we'll come back here to get our stuff and take it down there. With any luck this will be accomplished by June 4 so we can get to Brimmingham for prom night and graduation. You don't mind if Alice comes with me, do you? If she has nothing else going on? You'll like her—she's much nicer than I am. Warn the 'rents she's coming so they aren't feeling each other up in the kitchen when we arrive. Or going at it in the back seat of the car like that one night I came home with Derek Montoni. Ah, the memories.

—Veev

Subj: Just wanted to say HI
Date: 5/26/02, 6:05 P.M.
From: plexiboy@flowire.com
To: smallboyonherbike@boscore.com

Hi Chloe—you don't know me. My name's Tyler and I'm a friend of Julian's. I noticed your e-mail address when he sent around that letter about winning the district contest, and I just thought I'd send you a short note. Jules and I have been friends since kindergarden, so I know him better than most people, but still, he doesn't like to talk about personal stuff very much. All I know about you, for example, is that you exist. And since I know that much, I assume J. likes you pretty much. He's a great guy, but I guess you know that. Anyway, just wanted to say hi.

—Ty Robideau

Subj: Sensitive New Age Guys
Date: 5/26/02, 6:31 P.M.
From: smallboyonherbike@boscore.com
To: plexiboy@flowire.com

Hi Tyler! I'm glad you wrote to me. Julian has mentioned you a couple of times—I know you're going to the prom together, right? And you set him up with his date, Nina. (Should I be upset about this?) Anyway, it's nice to hear your *voice.* ☺

Julian told me he was kind of a loner—is that true? He didn't seem that way *at all* when I met him at Cartwright. In case he didn't tell you, I like him a lot too—I'm *so* psyched we'll be going to college together! Will he mind that you wrote to me, or that I answered you? I hope not. Maybe I'll actually meet you someday!

Chloe

Subj: A little advice
Date: 5/26/02, 7:23 P.M.
From: plexiboy@flowire.com
To: smallboyonherbike@boscore.com

Chloe: I hope you haven't been using emoticons when you e-mail
Julian. He has a thing about them—he HATES them. If you have—
cease and desist immediately! >:-] Yes, Jules is a loner—he
wouldn't have ANY friends if I didn't force him out of his den from
time to time. Which is why I was so shocked #:-o to hear he'd met
you at Cartwright—without my help! And he would NOT be
pleased to hear we've started up a correspondence, but I just had
to *see* you for myself. He would think we were talking about him
behind his back—which we are. Hugs to you [[[Chloe]]]!

Ty

Subj: Another Mystery
Date: 5/26/02, 8:03 P.M.
From: smallboyonherbike@boscore.com
To: jghost@flowire.com

Hi Julian—I guess your exams are over. How did they go? I've been
writing this damn English paper all weekend and it still sucks. But I
have until Thursday morning to whip it into shape, so I'm not giving
up. Tomorrow is my Physics exam and Tuesday is Trig. Ugh. Who
ever thought up this idea of exams anyway?

Hey, did you know your friend Ty e-mailed me? I guess he got my
address off that e-mail you sent around to several people. I don't quite
know how to take him. Does he have a weird sense of humor? At first I
thought he seemed nice, but in the second e-mail he seemed to be
making fun of me, so I decided not to answer it. Maybe I'm being
paranoid. Does he want you to like Nina? He doesn't even KNOW me.

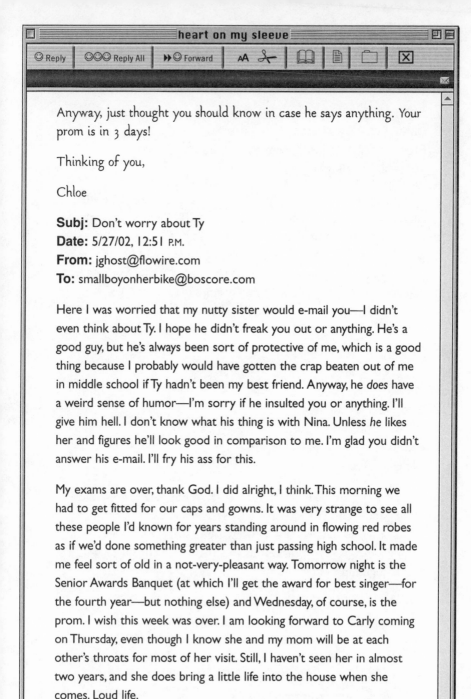

Anyway, just thought you should know in case he says anything. Your prom is in 3 days!

Thinking of you,

Chloe

Subj: Don't worry about Ty
Date: 5/27/02, 12:51 P.M.
From: jghost@flowire.com
To: smallboyonherbike@boscore.com

Here I was worried that my nutty sister would e-mail you—I didn't even think about Ty. I hope he didn't freak you out or anything. He's a good guy, but he's always been sort of protective of me, which is a good thing because I probably would have gotten the crap beaten out of me in middle school if Ty hadn't been my best friend. Anyway, he *does* have a weird sense of humor—I'm sorry if he insulted you or anything. I'll give him hell. I don't know what his thing is with Nina. Unless *he* likes her and figures he'll look good in comparison to me. I'm glad you didn't answer his e-mail. I'll fry his ass for this.

My exams are over, thank God. I did alright, I think. This morning we had to get fitted for our caps and gowns. It was very strange to see all these people I'd known for years standing around in flowing red robes as if we'd done something greater than just passing high school. It made me feel sort of old in a not-very-pleasant way. Tomorrow night is the Senior Awards Banquet (at which I'll get the award for best singer—for the fourth year—but nothing else) and Wednesday, of course, is the prom. I wish this week was over. I am looking forward to Carly coming on Thursday, even though I know she and my mom will be at each other's throats for most of her visit. Still, I haven't seen her in almost two years, and she does bring a little life into the house when she comes. Loud life.

Good luck finishing your English paper. And on your exams too. I gotta admit it's a nice feeling to know I'll never have to take another test at Douglas High School!

Julian

Subj: prom advice
Date: 5/28/02, 11:40 A.M.
From: CCinWonderland@hotmail.com
To: jghost@flowire.com

one last message from your beloved sister before your date with nina greco, who i know you've liked since you were prepubescent, though you won't admit it: talking is not the important part—dancing is, esp. the slow dances. you do dance, don't you? just think of it as an extended hug during which you shuffle your feet around a little. if you can do a soft shoe for *godspell*, you can slow dance at a high school prom. once you have your sweaty hands on each other, it becomes much easier to think of things to say. forget about chloe until september—you've got 3 months to hang out with nina!

by the way, you may not recognize me at the airport: i've lost 25 pounds, cut my hair, and dyed it chinese-restaurant red. don't tell mom—i'd hate to spoil the surprise!

carly

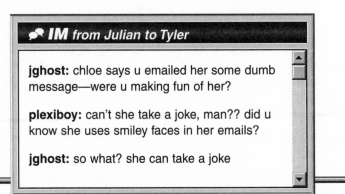

IM from Julian to Tyler

jghost: chloe says u emailed her some dumb message—were u making fun of her?

plexiboy: can't she take a joke, man?? did u know she uses smiley faces in her emails?

jghost: so what? she can take a joke

heart on my sleeve

⌐ Reply | ⌐⌐⌐ Reply All | ▶⌐ Forward | AA ✂ | 📖 | 📄 | 📁 | ☒

jghost: is this about nina???

plexiboy: just lookin out for u jules—nina would b good 4 u

jghost: newflash! picking out my girlfriends is NOT YOUR JOB!!! get over it

plexiboy: fine

plexiboy: r u driving 2 the banquet 2night?

jghost: yeah. r u getting any awards?

plexiboy: maybe latin or spanish. or italian

jghost: no common sense but u r an idiot in 4 languages

B *I* U A A ▼ ▲ ☺

plexiboy: 5—u forgot pig latin—adios, mi amigo eesay ouyay aterlay

send   close

Subj: In Love but Not at Peace
Date: 5/29/02, 2:11 A.M.
From: smallboyonherbike@boscore.com
To: ggillespie@Emmett.edu

I'm so tired. Just moments ago I finished a 15-page paper on Macbeth and Lady, his obsessive/compulsive wife. All my exams are over, and when I hand this baby in tomorrow I will be FINISHED with Brimmingham High School. I can't actually believe it. Also tonight is Julian's prom, so I'm obsessing a bit myself. What if this Nina person turns into a silk purse or something, and he falls for her?

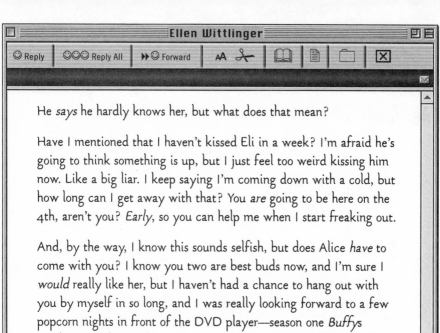

He *says* he hardly knows her, but what does that mean?

Have I mentioned that I haven't kissed Eli in a week? I'm afraid he's going to think something is up, but I just feel too weird kissing him now. Like a big liar. I keep saying I'm coming down with a cold, but how long can I get away with that? You *are* going to be here on the 4th, aren't you? *Early*, so you can help me when I start freaking out.

And, by the way, I know this sounds selfish, but does Alice *have* to come with you? I know you two are best buds now, and I'm sure I *would* really like her, but I haven't had a chance to hang out with you by myself in so long, and I was really looking forward to a few popcorn nights in front of the DVD player—season one *Buffy*s maybe, or early *X-Files*. Just the two of us, getting giddy like old times. If the logistics are too difficult and she has to come with you, I'll bear up. I just hope she likes lots of butter on her popcorn. You'll be here in 6 days! (And so will the prom!@#*%?^$)

Love, Chloe

JUNE

Subj: Hard Times Come Again No More
Date: 6/1/02, 7:31 P.M.
From: smallboyonherbike@boscore.com
To: jghost@flowire.com

You did it! You graduated! Let me be the first (or probably the 57th) to congratulate you! Were you in a big stadium or a gymnasium or an orange grove or what? Was the weather beautiful, the way I always think of it being in Florida? Did your sister show up? How was the prom? (I hate asking this, but I can't seem to stop myself. Feel free to give me a brief answer—I will read things into it anyway.)

God, this graduating stuff is hard, huh? I've got a week full of activities now too, and my sister is coming on the 4th to help me get ready for the prom. NOBODY can make my hair look as good as Genevieve can—I tried to talk her into becoming a hairdresser, but she's got this idea about being an actor. Whatever.

Anyway, write when you come up for air.

Yours, Chloe

Subj: Compromise
Date: 6/2/02, 11:14 P.M.
From: ggillespie@Emmett.edu
To: smallboyonherbike@boscore.com

—Let's just get this out of the way: I LOVE NEW YORK CITY! Alice and I have already found an apartment and moved all our stuff down here— in five days! No phone yet, but you can use my Emmett e-mail address as usual. Things are really working out great—we met the other interns from the program and two of them, Jay and Andrew, had just

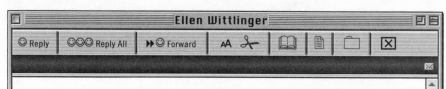

gotten an apartment and were looking for people to share it with, so we took them up on it. The apt. is in the East Village, walking distance to everything important, including Village Studio Theater. Can you believe the luck? Alice says NOBODY finds a decent apt. in NYC this quickly. The bathroom is tiny, but the kitchen is big enough to eat in, and the guys already have dishes and pans and things. Jay and Andrew are really funny—and Jay grew up in Manhattan so he knows the city—he gives us advice so we don't look like bumpkins in Metropolis.

—In spite of the grandiosity of being HERE, I'm still coming to Brimmingham on the 4th. Alice had a great idea—she'll drive me up so she can meet the so-called *family*, then she'll go visit a friend in Cambridge for a few days (so as to allow us our popcorn and cult-TV time), then come back for your graduation. We have to leave right afterward because we start work on Monday, and we want to be well rested to begin our servitude.

—Congrats, by the way, on finishing your sentence at Brimmingham High. You should have told me you had to write a paper on *Macbeth*— didn't you remember that I was the bloody Lady herself in the eighth grade? Mr. MacCandless put it on at the Middle School, which was ridiculous, of course, but he always had such high hopes for us little idiots. I had some wicked insights into character development, if I remember correctly. I told Mr. Mac, "I like playing a character who's pure evil—it's easier than being a good guy." I believe he rolled his eyes. (He didn't think my portrayal of pure evil was *acting*. Similarly, our dear mother told me that my playing the cracked Blanche DuBois was typecasting. I guess I make a good impression on people.)

—Are you telling me Eli has no clue anything is wrong between you two? Even with the no kissing? How can this be true? He's not that stupid, Chloe. Methinks he's hiding from the truth. Poor boy. Could be a stinky prom. Except for how you get to come home and wake your

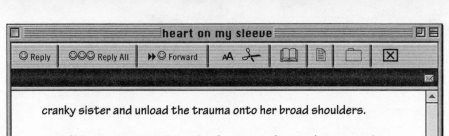

cranky sister and unload the trauma onto her broad shoulders.

—We'll try to get there by early afternoon, after you've stopped your food intake, but before you're feeling nauseous.

—Veev

Subj: Proms and other ceremonies
Date: 6/4/02, 10:45 A.M.
From: jghost@flowire.com
To: smallboyonherbike@boscore.com

Hi Chloe,

I would have written sooner, but I've been working at The Ginger Tree a lot. A couple of the waiters are on vacation so I've been picking up extra shifts—I have to make at least 3,000 bucks this summer. I was also busy for 3 days keeping my mother and sister from eviscerating each other. It was great to see Carly again—it's been almost 2 years— but I forgot what it's like when they're together. They're lunatics. They can't forgive each other for the smallest thing, even if it happened a hundred years ago. One night my mother was going on and on about how Carly had gone for a ride in a car with a boy who didn't have his license yet WHEN SHE WAS FOURTEEN! 8 years ago! Carly couldn't even remember the guy's name. Of course she COULD remember that my mother had once (around the same era) put one of her sweaters in the washing machine—an irreplaceable item that Carly had supposedly saved for months to buy, and which she swears my mother ruined on purpose.

Sorry to bore you with this stuff, but it's hard to take. I like both these people (not all the time, but in general), and I can't understand why they're so terrible to each other. Anyway, Carly had a cab waiting to take her back to the airport the minute I got my diploma. She'd had enough—we all had. But now my mother's acting more depressed than

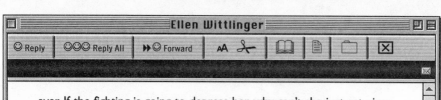

ever. If the fighting is going to depress her, why can't she just act nicer when Carly's here? But I can't blame just one of them—they do it to each other.

My graduation was held in an air-conditioned auditorium. They used to have it outside, but it's usually so hot here a couple of grandparents would have heatstroke before it was over. Florida in June can be miserable, especially if you're not a sun worshipper, which I'm not. Anyway, I've graduated—the ceremony itself was sort of anticlimactic after working up to it for so long. Boring speeches, walk across the stage, throw your hat in the air. Maybe yours will be better.

Okay, the prom, in brief: No limo; I drove. Nina, blue dress. Me, black tux. White corsage and boutonniere. Dinner: prime rib, baked potato, beans. Dessert: chocolate mousse cake (best part of the evening). Some dancing, some talking, both awkward. Ty was amusing, made everyone laugh (second best part of the evening). Inga wore purple dress, red corsage, because Ty likes red and purple together. Not sure she did.

That's about it for the highlights. Ty and Inga went to a party afterward, but Nina had a headache (and so did I), so I took her home. End of evening. So, today is YOUR prom. I wish I could see you in your dress. What color is it? You don't need to send me details—I can imagine how beautiful you look.

Yours, Julian

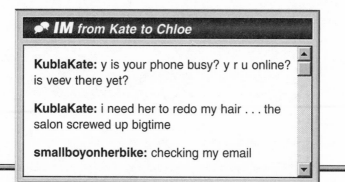

IM from Kate to Chloe

KublaKate: y is your phone busy? y r u online? is veev there yet?

KublaKate: i need her to redo my hair . . . the salon screwed up bigtime

smallboyonherbike: checking my email

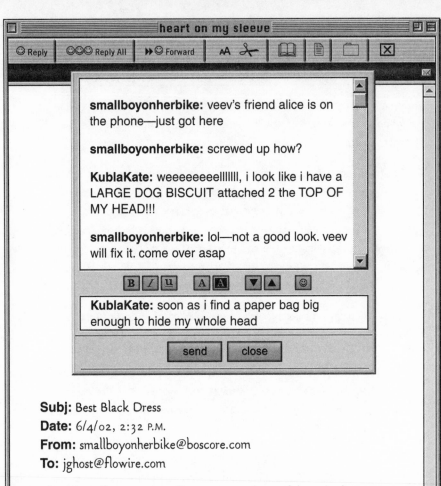

smallboyonherbike: veev's friend alice is on the phone—just got here

smallboyonherbike: screwed up how?

KublaKate: weeeeeeeelllllll, i look like i have a LARGE DOG BISCUIT attached 2 the TOP OF MY HEAD!!!

smallboyonherbike: lol—not a good look. veev will fix it. come over asap

KublaKate: soon as i find a paper bag big enough to hide my whole head

send   close

Subj: Best Black Dress
Date: 6/4/02, 2:32 P.M.
From: smallboyonherbike@boscore.com
To: jghost@flowire.com

Thank you for saying you'll imagine me beautiful in my dress. It's black (as per the title of The Nields's song) and has a long red sash that sort of trails down the back. My sister and her friend just got here so I can't stay online long, but I wanted to say I'm glad you didn't fall in love with Nina at your prom. I mean, I'm glad you didn't have a terrible time or anything—it sounds like it was okay. That's what I'm hoping for too—a decent evening with my friends.

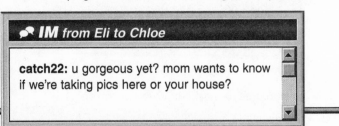

IM *from Eli to Chloe*

catch22: u gorgeous yet? mom wants to know if we're taking pics here or your house?

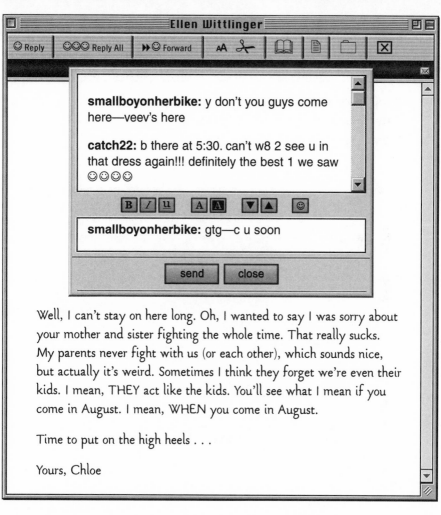

smallboyonherbike: y don't you guys come here—veev's here

catch22: b there at 5:30. can't w8 2 see u in that dress again!!! definitely the best 1 we saw ☺☺☺☺

smallboyonherbike: gtg—c u soon

send   close

Well, I can't stay on here long. Oh, I wanted to say I was sorry about your mother and sister fighting the whole time. That really sucks. My parents never fight with us (or each other), which sounds nice, but actually it's weird. Sometimes I think they forget we're even their kids. I mean, THEY act like the kids. You'll see what I mean if you come in August. I mean, WHEN you come in August.

Time to put on the high heels . . .

Yours, Chloe

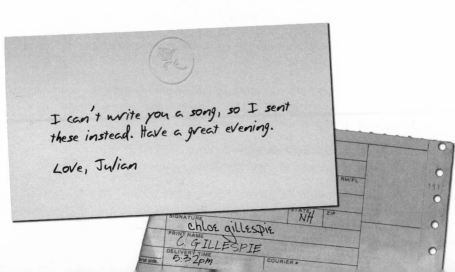

I can't write you a song, so I sent these instead. Have a great evening.

Love, Julian

SIGNATURE   *chloe gillespie*

PRINT NAME   C. GILLESPIE

DELIVERY TIME   5:32pm   COURIER #

STATE/   NH   ZIP

Subj: Might As Well Dance
Date: 6/5/02, 3:44 P.M.
From: smallboyonherbike@boscore.com
To: jghost@flowire.com

Julian! I've never been so surprised in my life! The roses are gorgeous!
God, that was the nicest thing to do—I'm in shock, really. THANK YOU.

So, prom's over. Limo, photographs, eating, dancing, you know how it
goes. Not really worth all the fuss. Every time I thought of those
beautiful roses waiting for me at home, I wished I was back there
with them!

Sorry I don't have time for more than a note today—there's so much
going on this week and I'm still tired from last night. But I'm
thinking of you . . . all the time.

Love, Chloe

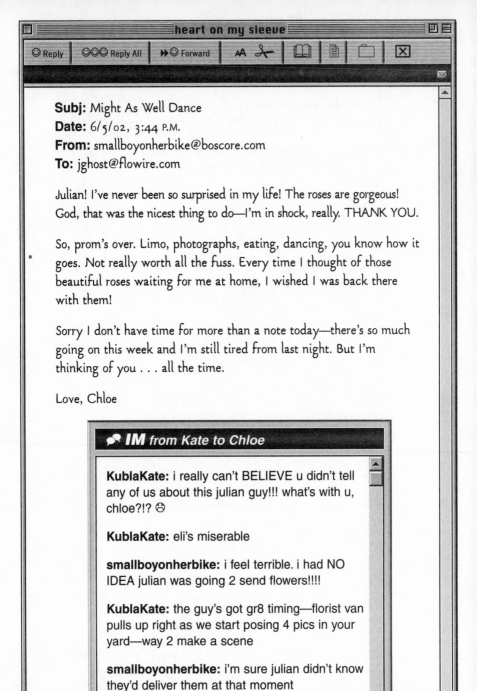

IM *from Kate to Chloe*

KublaKate: i really can't BELIEVE u didn't tell
any of us about this julian guy!!! what's with u,
chloe?!? ☹

KublaKate: eli's miserable

smallboyonherbike: i feel terrible. i had NO
IDEA julian was going 2 send flowers!!!!

KublaKate: the guy's got gr8 timing—florist van
pulls up right as we start posing 4 pics in your
yard—way 2 make a scene

smallboyonherbike: i'm sure julian didn't know
they'd deliver them at that moment

smallboyonherbike: have u talked 2 eli

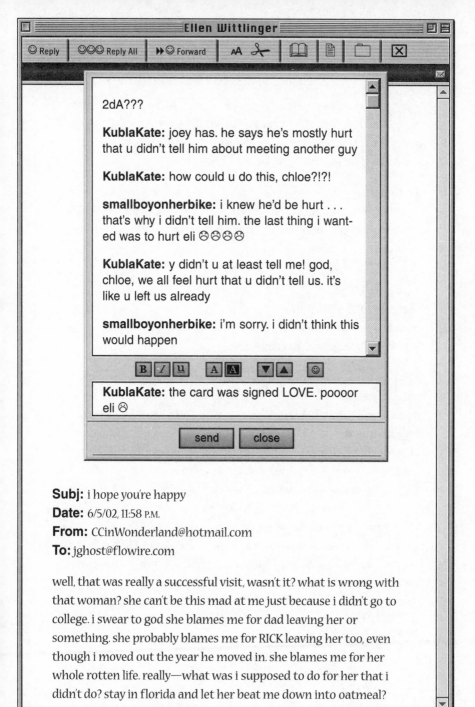

2dA???

KublaKate: joey has. he says he's mostly hurt that u didn't tell him about meeting another guy

KublaKate: how could u do this, chloe?!?!

smallboyonherbike: i knew he'd be hurt . . . that's why i didn't tell him. the last thing i wanted was to hurt eli ☹☹☹☹

KublaKate: y didn't u at least tell me! god, chloe, we all feel hurt that u didn't tell us. it's like u left us already

smallboyonherbike: i'm sorry. i didn't think this would happen

B / u   A A   ▼ ▲   ☺

KublaKate: the card was signed LOVE. poooor eli ☹

send   close

Subj: i hope you're happy
Date: 6/5/02, 11:58 P.M.
From: CCinWonderland@hotmail.com
To: jghost@flowire.com

well, that was really a successful visit, wasn't it? what is wrong with that woman? she can't be this mad at me just because i didn't go to college. i swear to god she blames me for dad leaving her or something. she probably blames me for RICK leaving her too, even though i moved out the year he moved in. she blames me for her whole rotten life. really—what was i supposed to do for her that i didn't do? stay in florida and let her beat me down into oatmeal?

61

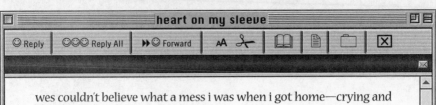

wes couldn't believe what a mess i was when i got home—crying and throwing the stuff out of my suitcase. i think i might actually stay with wes for awhile—he's very *trustworthy*, which probably doesn't sound all that sexy, but it is.

home, by the way, is now boulder, co. it seems okay. i have to get a job, but that's usually easy for me. i'm sorry for dashing out on you, kiddo— i just couldn't take another minute of it. *how can you?*

carly

Subj: Blaming
Date: 6/7/02, 1:03 P.M.
From: jghost@flowire.com
To: CCinWonderland@hotmail.com

For one thing, mom NEVER acts as crazy around me as she does around you. Yeah, she's moody and aggravated sometimes, but she doesn't go ballistic like she does with you. And I know you'll hate me for saying it, but I really think you get nutty around her too. I'm not *blaming* either of you—I'm just saying you provoke each other. I don't get it. Aren't you EVER going to be able to be around her? I think one of you is just going to have to decide not to escalate the war. After you left she was really depressed, and I'm sure she felt lousy about the whole thing too. Maybe she's too old to change. I don't know. But couldn't *you* make an effort? Okay, now you're pissed, I know. Sorry if I made you feel worse, but how do you think I feel that I can never be around my mother and sister at the same time? I need a goddamn fallout shelter.

Julian

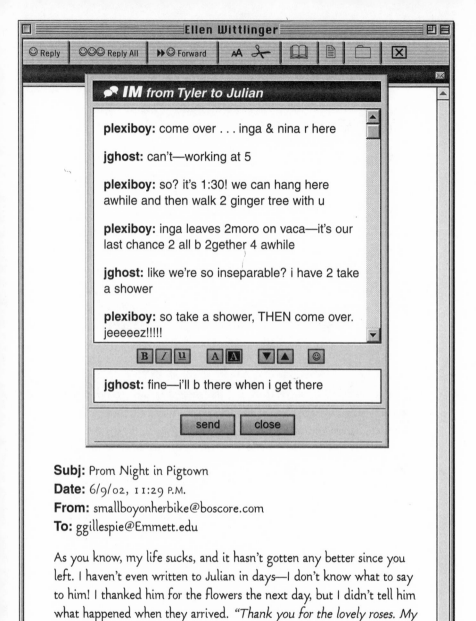

IM *from Tyler to Julian*

plexiboy: come over . . . inga & nina r here

jghost: can't—working at 5

plexiboy: so? it's 1:30! we can hang here awhile and then walk 2 ginger tree with u

plexiboy: inga leaves 2moro on vaca—it's our last chance 2 all b 2gether 4 awhile

jghost: like we're so inseparable? i have 2 take a shower

plexiboy: so take a shower, THEN come over. jeeeeez!!!!!

jghost: fine—i'll b there when i get there

send   close

Subj: Prom Night in Pigtown
Date: 6/9/02, 11:29 P.M.
From: smallboyonherbike@boscore.com
To: ggillespie@Emmett.edu

As you know, my life sucks, and it hasn't gotten any better since you left. I haven't even written to Julian in days—I don't know what to say to him! I thanked him for the flowers the next day, but I didn't tell him what happened when they arrived. *"Thank you for the lovely roses. My boyfriend read the card and had an asthma attack. His mother yelled at him for forgetting his inhaler and then hit a squirrel as she raced back to their house to get it. My friend, Kate, started crying and ruined the makeup job she'd paid 50 bucks for. Nobody spoke to each*

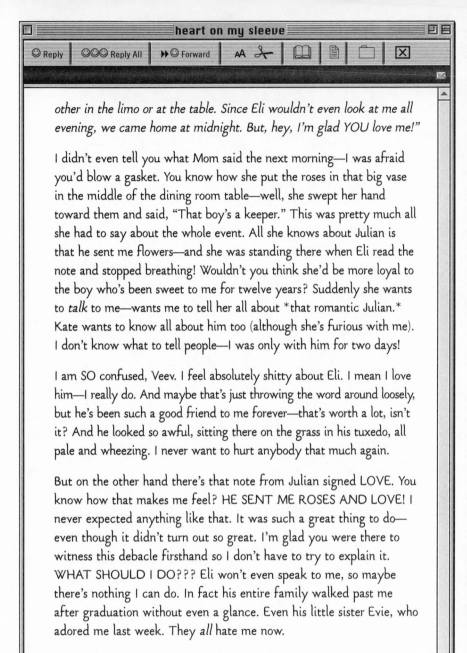

other in the limo or at the table. Since Eli wouldn't even look at me all evening, we came home at midnight. But, hey, I'm glad YOU love me!"

I didn't even tell you what Mom said the next morning—I was afraid you'd blow a gasket. You know how she put the roses in that big vase in the middle of the dining room table—well, she swept her hand toward them and said, "That boy's a keeper." This was pretty much all she had to say about the whole event. All she knows about Julian is that he sent me flowers—and she was standing there when Eli read the note and stopped breathing! Wouldn't you think she'd be more loyal to the boy who's been sweet to me for twelve years? Suddenly she wants to *talk* to me—wants me to tell her all about *that romantic Julian.* Kate wants to know all about him too (although she's furious with me). I don't know what to tell people—I was only with him for two days!

I am SO confused, Veev. I feel absolutely shitty about Eli. I mean I love him—I really do. And maybe that's just throwing the word around loosely, but he's been such a good friend to me forever—that's worth a lot, isn't it? And he looked so awful, sitting there on the grass in his tuxedo, all pale and wheezing. I never want to hurt anybody that much again.

But on the other hand there's that note from Julian signed LOVE. You know how that makes me feel? HE SENT ME ROSES AND LOVE! I never expected anything like that. It was such a great thing to do—even though it didn't turn out so great. I'm glad you were there to witness this debacle firsthand so I don't have to try to explain it. WHAT SHOULD I DO??? Eli won't even speak to me, so maybe there's nothing I can do. In fact his entire family walked past me after graduation without even a glance. Even his little sister Evie, who adored me last week. They *all* hate me now.

Maybe relationships aren't worth the trouble.

Chloe

Subj: If I Wrote You
Date: 6/10/02, 12:21 A.M.
From: smallboyonherbike@boscore.com
To: catch22@boscore.com

Eli—Please read this. I know you're really mad at me, and I don't blame you for not wanting to speak to me anymore, but I thought if I wrote you an e-mail maybe you'd be able to listen to me for just a minute.

The reason I didn't tell you about meeting Julian at Cartwright is that I DIDN'T want to hurt you. It was just one weekend, and I didn't know if I'd ever see him again. I know that doesn't make it right—I should have told you about it—but I didn't really know what to say. Eli, we've been the best of friends since forever—I don't even remember when we started to call it *going together*—we've just always been together. But we're going away to college now, and it seems like things will change anyway. I guess I thought once we were at school we'd naturally see other people and it wouldn't be a big deal.

Not that I would EVER want to stop being your friend, E. I couldn't even imagine that! And I didn't write a song "especially" for Julian—I wrote a song about leaving for college—I showed it to Genevieve too. I don't know why I didn't show it to you. I don't know why, but I'm sorry I didn't. And I'm so, so sorry that I hurt you and you feel like you can't trust me anymore. Maybe it's not worth much now, but I promise I'll never tell you even the littlest lie ever again.

Is there any chance we can be friends again, Eli? You don't have to answer me right now—just think about it. I'm leaving on the 15th for Maple Hill. You can write me there if you want to, same address as every year: Maple Hill Arts Camp, Box 41, Juniper, NH. Please forgive me.

Chloe

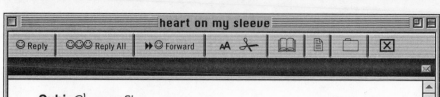

Subj: Closer to Fine
Date: 6/11/02, 1:12 P.M.
From: smallboyonherbike@boscore.com
To: jghost@flowire.com

Hi Julian,

I know I haven't written in awhile—it's been kind of crazy around here. My sister, Genevieve, was here with her hyper friend Alice, which made graduation kind of strange. I don't know how much I told you about my parents, but they don't get excited about much, except each other. They're really not normal at all, but they think they are. Anyway, this Alice is HIGHLY excitable, always jumping into the air and talking very loudly—when she and Genevieve are together, they act like the junior high pep squad. At the graduation I had a straight-on view of the four of them sitting in the bleachers (our ceremony is outside on the football field)—my parents whispering to each other and applauding politely when my name was called, Alice and Veev leaping from their seats and shouting "WHOO-WHOO" complete with pumping arm motions.

The whole week has been weird. First of all, your gorgeous flowers, which are still alive and beautiful because my mother keeps putting aspirins in the water, and which I am still amazed by, did cause a small problem. They were delivered just as my friends had all gathered to take pictures in our prom outfits, and my date, Eli, who's also a good friend, was a little upset. I didn't see the point of telling him about meeting you, so he was surprised by your gift, and now I have to try to patch up our friendship. He's practically like my brother, so I don't want things to be bad between us, especially right before we go off to college. Not that any of it was YOUR fault, of course. I love the roses—nobody has EVER gotten me a bouquet of flowers before!

The other weird thing is that my sister is acting very strangely. Veev and I are really close—we always have been—so maybe I'm just jealous that she and Alice are suddenly such close friends. And it's not that I didn't like Alice either—she was a little over the top, but it was actually nice to see the way that brought Genevieve out of her normally hard shell a little bit. I guess I just felt a little left out. They've moved to NYC together, and they're both interning with an avant-garde theater group this summer and living in an apartment with two gay guys, so they're all about *Manhattan* now and the *theater world*. It was like they had their own language and I couldn't really understand it. Even when Alice left to go stay with her friends in Cambridge, they were on the phone with each other half the time. I needed Genevieve to be thinking about me, but instead she was on her own planet.

I guess I shouldn't complain—it sounds like you had a worse time when your sister was visiting. Families are so complicated—you want to get along with them, but sometimes you just CAN'T.

I leave for camp on Saturday and I'm really looking forward to getting there—seeing my old friends and meeting the new counselors before the hordes of little kiddies arrive. You can write to me at Maple Hill Arts Camp, Box 41, Juniper, NH. Once in a while the counselors get a day off and go into Hanover for a break. If I find an Internet cafe I'll e-mail you—otherwise, I'll do my best with paper and pen. Funny how much harder it seems to write a *real* letter than an e-mail.

When is the District contest? Are you still practicing every day? You HAVE to win—I can't WAIT to see you in Boston!

Love, Chloe

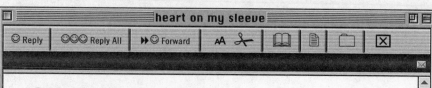

Subj: Punk Junkies from New York
Date: 6/12/02, 10:12 p.m.
From: ggillespie@Emmett.edu
To: smallboyonherbike@boscore.com

Hi Chloe! It was so great to see you last week! I loved meeting your friend Alice! She's so much fun! How was your first day of work at Village Studio Theater?

—You may recall that none of the above was in your last e-mail. Maybe I'm being a tad oversensitive here, but I DID spend four days listening to you whine and moan about your long-distance love life and the emotional mess you're leaving behind you in Brimmingham, not to mention playing hairdo doctor for you and your friends, and applauding like mad at your release from high school. Hello? I have a life too! Sometimes I feel like you don't even see me—you just see some sister/confessor person whose job is to help you get your life together.

—And just because I'm two years older than you doesn't mean I know what you should do about Eli or Florida guy or Kate or Mom and Dad. I'm not trying to be mean here, but, Chloe, you didn't tell anybody the truth (except, I guess, me), and now it's backfiring on you. Maybe you don't even know what the truth is right now. I can understand that, but I think you should start mending things by edging a little closer to it than you have been.

—I do feel bad hitting you when you're down, but, Chloe, I get down too, and you don't even notice.

Veev

Subj: Quit Hollerin' at Me
Date: 6/12/02, 11:05 P.M.
From: smallboyonherbike@boscore.com
To: ggillespie@Emmett.edu

God, I feel like an apology machine these days: I'm sorry, I'm sorry, I'm sorry. Didn't I ever treat anybody right? It's not true, you know, that I don't notice when you're down—it just seems like you never want to discuss your life the way I want to discuss mine. I always thought you were more self-reliant than I am—that you could fix yourself without any help. Okay, AND fix me. I wish you *would* tell me more about your life—not just the good stuff like the plays, but all of it. Yes, I should have told Eli the truth right away—I wish I had now—but do YOU tell everybody the truth? You're not that different from me, Veev—it doesn't *seem* like a lie if you just say nothing.

How was your first (and second) day at the theater? How's life with the hilarious Jay and Andrew? Yes, I did like Alice, although I think I might get tired of the frisky puppy routine if I lived with her. You guys sure got close fast. I guess I'm surprised because you never had many girlfriends before, and now you and Alice are attached at the hip.

Before I go to bed tonight I promise to repeat 100 times: *I will not be so self-centered.*

Love, Chloe

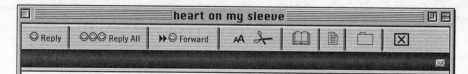

Subj: Angels Running
Date: 6/13/02, 12:14 A.M.
From: ggillespie@Emmett.edu
To: smallboyonherbike@boscore.com

—Okay, you're right. I'm a big fat liar too. I've been thinking about this
all day. No, I've been thinking about this all month. How to tell you,
what you'll think. I was going to tell you while I was in Brimmingham,
but there was never a good time, what with the *crisis* and all. Hell,
there never would have been a good time—as you pointed out, it
doesn't seem like a lie if you just say nothing. So I'm telling you now: I'm
a lesbian, Chloe. Alice isn't just my friend; she's my lover.

—When you think about it, it will answer a lot of questions about me. I
didn't really want you to delve into my life the way I did yours, because
in high school I was so terribly confused about everything. I guess I
knew then that I was gay, but I just couldn't deal with it, which is why I
dated a new guy every month or two. I kept thinking I just hadn't found
the right one yet. And then, after I got to Emmett I just stopped
going out with guys at all—it seemed so hopeless. I'd sort of decided
that I didn't want to be a lesbian, but I obviously wasn't straight, so I
just wouldn't be with anybody. That worked until I met Alice.

—You know how it was growing up in our house with Antony and
Cleopatra. We soaked up all this garbage about romantic love and
finding the one perfect mate. You bought into the idea, but it scared
the hell out of me. Probably because I already knew my perfect mate
was not going to get the *Good Housekeeping* Seal of Approval. Mom and
Dad wouldn't be waltzing and smooching at my wedding. I've been
keeping big secrets, Chloe, from you and from myself. No more.

—Alice has changed my life. Yeah, she's sort of a big puppy, but that's
because she doesn't let anything get her down. I've never been around
somebody who charges into situations like she does, who really enjoys

living. She says she loves me and it makes me dizzy. I don't say it back—not yet—because I'm fairly screwed up when it comes to the L-word. But I hope someday I'll be able to.

—I know this is a big shock for you. I'm sure you had no idea. As far as telling Mom and Dad, I don't care if you want to, but I'm not asking you to either. It's my job and I'll do it soon. God, now that I've written this whole thing, I'm almost afraid to send it. But I will, because I really want you to understand this.

—Don't feel like you have to answer immediately. Think about it a few days. I'm sorry my other letter was so nasty; you're a great sister.

—Love, Genevieve

Subj: how's this for an idea?
Date: 6/13/02, 7:12 A.M.
From: CCinWonderland@hotmail.com
To: jghost@flowire.com

hey bro,

see what time it is? can you believe i'm up this early in the morning? that's because I never went to sleep last night—wes and i have been up all night talking. guess what? *he wants to marry me.* kind of a crazy idea, huh? but when you think about it, maybe not. i mean, i'm 22, people get married at 22. and I really *like* wes. which is more important than you might think. *love*, yeah, i fall in love with everybody, but after a couple of months i usually can't stand them anymore. with wes it's been six months already, and i still like him, so that's kind of unique.

so i said yes. we're gonna do it! not sure when but soon—it'll just be a small thing, justice of the peace, or maybe we'll drive to nevada and do it in one of those funky wedding chapels out there. the only people we

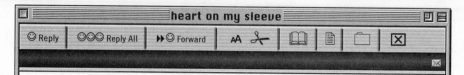

even know here are wes's college roommate and his girlfriend, so i guess they'll be our witnesses. i wish you could come, but i know you can't afford to take any trips this summer. Don't tell mom—i'm gonna wait until it's over to call and tell her. i don't want her here, and she wouldn't come anyway. wes says maybe at christmas we could come east and see his parents in north carolina and then stop in florida too. he has this idea that mom is going to like him—talk about a cockeyed optimist. (although personally I don't see how anybody could NOT like him—he's a very sweet, calm person—an old soul, for sure.)

do you think i should call dad and tell him? california's not that far away, but i know he wouldn't come. last time i talked to him (last year?) he said he didn't go into town for his mail more than once a week—he hates to leave the "peacefulness of my farm." (who else would call a dozen chickens and a little plot of tomatoes and beans a farm?) i know this will sound like i have some kind of weird complex, but wes actually reminds me of dad in some ways—dad before he crawled into a hole.

so, that's the bold news from boulder! your jaw's resting on the floor, jules. write me back and say you're happy that i'm happy.

love, CC

Subj: Happiness
Date: 6/13/02, 11:39 A.M.
From: jghost@flowire.com
To: CCinWonderland@hotmail.com

Dammit, Carly, you've always got to be doing something crazy, don't you? Something nobody would expect of you. Mom always said you'd never get married because you were too fickle to stick to one guy— is that why you're doing this? To show her? I wouldn't tell her about this if you paid me. For one thing, it may not even happen—you're

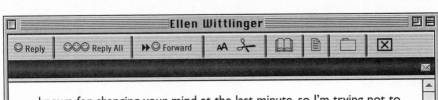

known for changing your mind at the last minute, so I'm trying not to get too upset about this current plan.

Yes, I want you to be happy. Of course I do. But why do you want to get married? And who IS this Wes guy, anyway? You've hardly said two words about him all this time (even when you were here!)—I figured he was just another one of your interchangeable harem of men—and now I find out he's an *old soul* and you're lining up witnesses! And the fact that he reminds you of dad—well, that REALLY freaks me out. I didn't even know you talked to the guy on the phone—I haven't heard from him in years. He raises chickens? Have you been there? Have you seen him?

Don't get mad at me, Carly. I'm just worried for you—I don't think this is a good idea. But since I know you do whatever you want to do whenever you want to do it, it won't surprise me to hear that you didn't take my advice. I wish I could at least see this Wes guy before you marry him. But if you go ahead and do it, well, I wish you good luck. I really mean that—and I'm happy you're happy.

Love, Julian

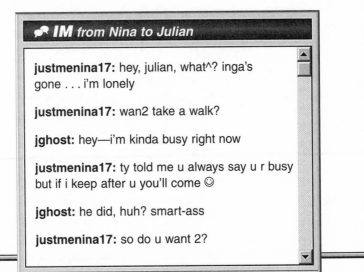

IM from Nina to Julian

justmenina17: hey, julian, what^? inga's gone . . . i'm lonely

justmenina17: wan2 take a walk?

jghost: hey—i'm kinda busy right now

justmenina17: ty told me u always say u r busy but if i keep after u you'll come ☺

jghost: he did, huh? smart-ass

justmenina17: so do u want 2?

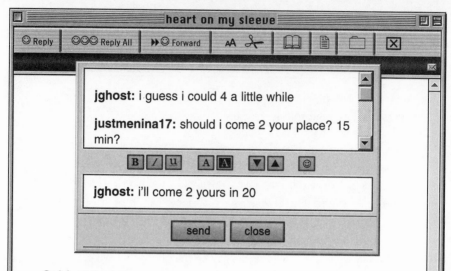

jghost: i guess i could 4 a little while

justmenina17: should i come 2 your place? 15 min?

jghost: i'll come 2 yours in 20

send   close

Subj: Little Lies
Date: 6/14/02, 2:14 P.M.
From: catch22@boscore.com
To: smallboyonherbike@boscore.com

Hi Chloe,

I don't even know what I want to say to you, but I thought I ought to write something before you left for camp tomorrow. I'm not mad at you—I was never really mad. Hurt, yes, I can't deny that. But I guess it's partly my own fault because I never wanted to talk about what would happen when we left for college. Obviously we won't see much of each other with me in Michigan and you in Connecticut, but I guess I wanted to believe that we could make it last anyway.

So it's not just that you met this guy Julian, but the fact that you DIDN'T think we'd make it last. You thought when we went to school we'd see other people and it *wouldn't be a big deal.* I just can't understand that, Chloe. Have you always felt like this? That I was just a high school boyfriend? Or, worse, one of your *best friends*?

I don't know if we can still be friends. It doesn't feel like I can do that. I know I never said it to you, and I never sent you roses with a flowery card, but I did love you. I DO love you. I guess I thought we were so close it didn't need to be said. Or maybe I was afraid to say it in case you didn't say it back.

I'm really confused right now. But I'm not ready to lose touch with you altogether either. So I'll write you again up at MHAC. Have a good summer.

Eli

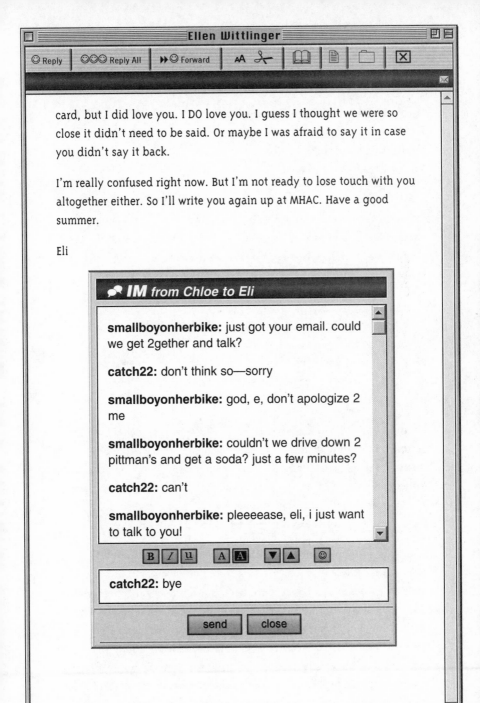

IM *from Chloe to Eli*

smallboyonherbike: just got your email. could we get 2gether and talk?

catch22: don't think so—sorry

smallboyonherbike: god, e, don't apologize 2 me

smallboyonherbike: couldn't we drive down 2 pittman's and get a soda? just a few minutes?

catch22: can't

smallboyonherbike: pleeeease, eli, i just want to talk to you!

catch22: bye

send   close

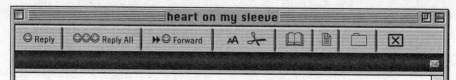

Subj: Speed of the Sound of Loneliness
Date: 6/14/02, 4:57 P.M.
From: smallboyonherbike@boscore.com
To: ggillespie@Emmett.edu

I feel like somebody let all the air out of my balloon. Eli won't speak to me, Kate yells at me, and you've become somebody I hardly know. Somebody who's been keeping a BIG secret from me for a long time. I've spent this whole week trying to decide if what you told me could really be true, and I've decided, of course it is. Like you said, it answers a lot of questions, just not the way I ever thought they'd be answered.

I thought it was odd that the two of you had to talk on the phone twice a day, and when Alice was around she always had her arm hanging around your shoulders. To tell you the truth (there's an idea—let's try it!), it actually crossed my mind that Alice was a lesbian. I wondered if you knew. HA! How's that for denial?

I wish I could say it doesn't bother me at all, Veev, but, you know, I'm getting into truth these days. I've been telling you every detail of my stupid life since I could talk—and you've only been giving me tidbits. It makes me feel like I don't know who you are! And if I don't know who YOU are, or if you're someone completely different than I thought you were, well, it sort of leaves me hanging out on the line, all by myself.

And—truth—the fact that you're a lesbian does freak me out a little bit. I mean I know kids who are gay, but I don't hang out with them— not that I *wouldn't* hang out with them, but it's a very different group than my friends, and I don't feel that comfortable around them. I don't know *how* to know them. I keep thinking about dumb stuff like how you won't have a husband or kids, so my kids (assuming I get married) won't have any cousins. And how we won't all go on vacation together and the husbands go fishing while we eat ice cream and gab. I know I sound stupid, but Veev, you've always been my only *real* family—you know that—and now I feel like you won't be anymore!

I'm sorry if I sound like a total bigot. You know I love you no matter what, but it's taking me a while to digest this whole thing. I'm NOT telling Mom and Dad—you can have that pleasure while I'm safely in New Hampshire (where nobody is angry with me, yet).

I keep thinking of things like when you went out with James Downing for at least 3 months and I was so jealous I wanted to smack you, especially when you broke up with him! I would have killed to date James Downing. I guess you just have to laugh, huh?

Sorry I'm not the perfect sister. Hi to Alice.

Love, Chloe

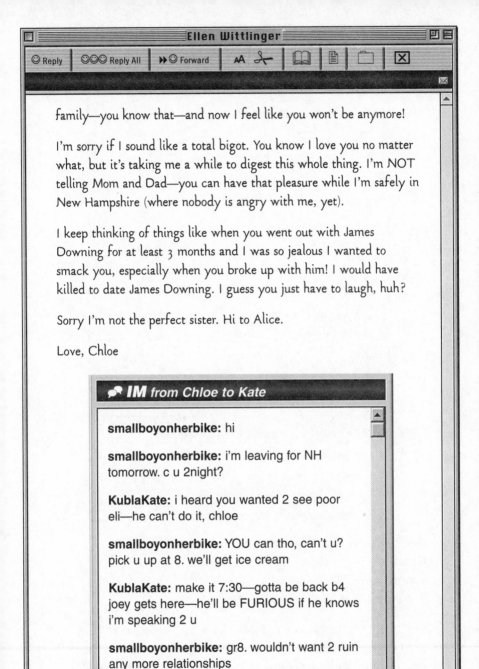

📣 **IM** *from Chloe to Kate*

smallboyonherbike: hi

smallboyonherbike: i'm leaving for NH tomorrow. c u 2night?

KublaKate: i heard you wanted 2 see poor eli—he can't do it, chloe

smallboyonherbike: YOU can tho, can't u? pick u up at 8. we'll get ice cream

KublaKate: make it 7:30—gotta be back b4 joey gets here—he'll be FURIOUS if he knows i'm speaking 2 u

smallboyonherbike: gr8. wouldn't want 2 ruin any more relationships

smallboyonherbike: and could u stop calling eli POOR ELI?

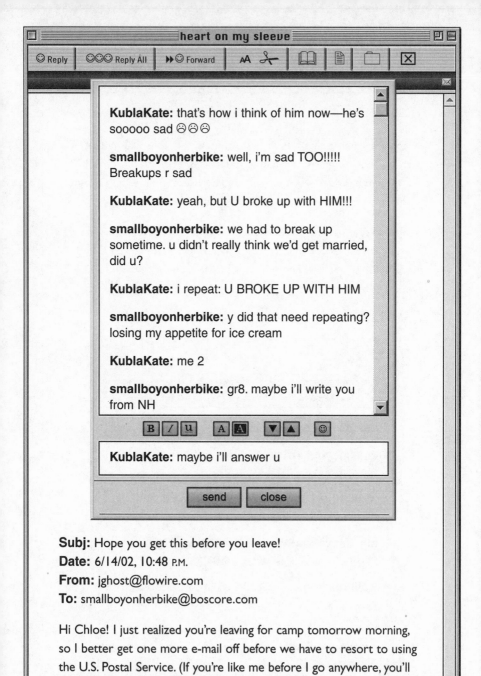

KublaKate: that's how i think of him now—he's sooooo sad ☹☹☹

smallboyonherbike: well, i'm sad TOO!!!!! Breakups r sad

KublaKate: yeah, but U broke up with HIM!!!

smallboyonherbike: we had to break up sometime. u didn't really think we'd get married, did u?

KublaKate: i repeat: U BROKE UP WITH HIM

smallboyonherbike: y did that need repeating? losing my appetite for ice cream

KublaKate: me 2

smallboyonherbike: gr8. maybe i'll write you from NH

B / u A A ▼▲ ☺

KublaKate: maybe i'll answer u

send   close

Subj: Hope you get this before you leave!
Date: 6/14/02, 10:48 P.M.
From: jghost@flowire.com
To: smallboyonherbike@boscore.com

Hi Chloe! I just realized you're leaving for camp tomorrow morning, so I better get one more e-mail off before we have to resort to using the U.S. Postal Service. (If you're like me before I go anywhere, you'll check your messages one more time before you go to bed tonight and probably again in the morning too—preparing for e-mail withdrawal.)

I'm sorry about the flowers arriving just as you and your friends were getting ready to leave for the prom. I wanted them to get there that day, but not that MOMENT. I guess I can understand why Eli is so mad at you, although if he's really just a friend, I wouldn't think he'd care that much. Are you sure he doesn't think you're more than that? Maybe he's just pretending it's only friendship because he knows that's what you want. Sorry . . . I'm not trying to psych the guy out or anything, it's just that relationships with people are usually pretty confusing to me too—I guess I'm just thinking out loud.

It's great that you have such a good relationship with your sister. I'd like to meet her—working for a theater group in Manhattan for the summer sounds amazing! She must be a really good actor. My sister, on the other hand, has completely lost her mind. I won't get into all the details, but she's considering getting married to this guy she hardly knows. Somebody she met in Austin who apparently also likes to move around the country every couple of months like she does. Sometimes I think she just does this stuff to make my mother crazy.

The District contest in Richmond is June 28. I'm really getting nervous. I don't know why I thought I'd actually win this. I mean, this will be all the kids from the Southern District who won their regionals—they'll *all* be good. I don't know if I'll win it or not. I *really* need a scholarship and I really want to see you in Boston! I'll be so mad if I don't win! If I do come to Boston though, I'd love to stay with you. My mom won't be coming with me—the plane fare is expensive and she doesn't like to take much time off from work—so it'll just be me. The contest is August 15 and 16, which is a Thursday and Friday. If I'm not paying for a hotel I could probably stay on for the weekend—we could have so much fun—I just HAVE to win the damn District!

Write me as soon as you get to Camp Gitchy-Goomy. I never went to

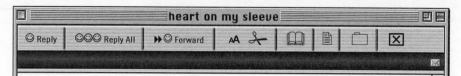

summer camp so I don't really understand what happens at one. Knot tying and 3-legged races? You'll have to fill me in on the specifics. Have fun in the woods while I'm hustling Puu Puu Platters!

Love, Julian

Subj: chapel bells
Date: 6/18/02, 11:18 A.M.
From: CCinWonderland@hotmail.com
To: jghost@flowire.com

so, I guess you heard the news by now. what did mom say when she told you i'd called? she was actually sort of subdued on the phone—she even congratulated me, although not very enthusiastically. then wes got on and tried to talk to her, but apparently they were a little tongue-tied with each other, so they hung up. i wanted to talk to you, but she said you were out with nina greco! (more on this later, chum.)

did she tell you about the ceremony? we decided to go to las vegas because we don't have jobs yet, and wes's friends, jack and nancy, had the weekend off. (jack is a house painter and nancy is a massage therapist.) i'd never been to las vegas—boy, what a trip! since we don't have much money, all we did was play a few slot machines, but it was fun to watch other people lose their money. god, that town is so lit up, it looks like it's daylight all the time.

we stayed in a motel that advertises free weddings if you spend two nights there. jack and nancy only stayed one night, but we stayed two and didn't even have to pay the justice of the peace (who owns the motel and a cafe down the road where newlyweds get a complimentary breakfast). there was a little chapel right in the motel—quite cheesy, with papier-mâché cupids flying around on the ceiling (sort of like pinatas) and strings of red cardboard hearts decorating the little stage where you stand to say your vows. i wore a yellow dress the color of

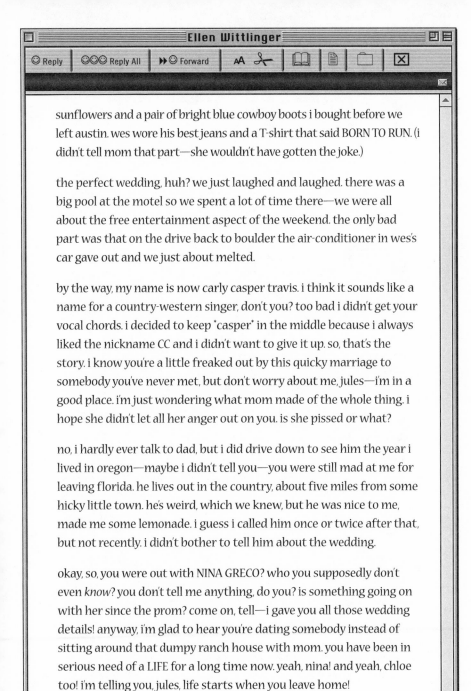

sunflowers and a pair of bright blue cowboy boots i bought before we left austin. wes wore his best jeans and a T-shirt that said BORN TO RUN. (i didn't tell mom that part—she wouldn't have gotten the joke.)

the perfect wedding, huh? we just laughed and laughed. there was a big pool at the motel so we spent a lot of time there—we were all about the free entertainment aspect of the weekend. the only bad part was that on the drive back to boulder the air-conditioner in wes's car gave out and we just about melted.

by the way, my name is now carly casper travis. i think it sounds like a name for a country-western singer, don't you? too bad i didn't get your vocal chords. i decided to keep *casper* in the middle because i always liked the nickname CC and i didn't want to give it up. so, that's the story. i know you're a little freaked out by this quicky marriage to somebody you've never met, but don't worry about me, jules—i'm in a good place. i'm just wondering what mom made of the whole thing. i hope she didn't let all her anger out on you. is she pissed or what?

no, i hardly ever talk to dad, but i did drive down to see him the year i lived in oregon—maybe i didn't tell you—you were still mad at me for leaving florida. he lives out in the country, about five miles from some hicky little town. he's weird, which we knew, but he was nice to me, made me some lemonade. i guess i called him once or twice after that, but not recently. i didn't bother to tell him about the wedding.

okay, so, you were out with NINA GRECO? who you supposedly don't even *know*? you don't tell me anything, do you? is something going on with her since the prom? come on, tell—i gave you all those wedding details! anyway, i'm glad to hear you're dating somebody instead of sitting around that dumpy ranch house with mom. you have been in serious need of a LIFE for a long time now. yeah, nina! and yeah, chloe too! i'm telling you, jules, life starts when you leave home!

love, CC

June 20, 2002

Hi Chloe,

Well, I have to admit that writing the address on the envelope–Maple Hill Arts Camp, Box 41, Juniper, NH–made me feel very strange. I've never written to anybody there because I've always BEEN there. It's MY address, except not anymore. All week I've been thinking about what's going on up there, wondering which counselors are back for another year (Ray? Suzanne? Edie, the nudist?), and what the new counselors are like. Anybody who can do duets with you for Lunch Music? What kids came back? Are Kevin and Kendra there, the Frisbee twins? They are such great kids–tell them I miss them! Is David the Devil back? Or that girl you had in your cabin last year who cried so much she kept barfing? God, I hope not. Who's leading Theater this year? Yeah, I miss it–how could I not? Tell Bill I said hi, and give him noogies from me.

You shouldn't, however, get the idea that I regret coming to NY. The first few days of work were kind of rough since the entire company seemed to think the interns were there to wait on them, and, as with any theater company, there are prima donnas here who are large pains in the ass. But I think, to some extent, they were just testing us to see if we were wienies who couldn't take it. This week most people seem nicer–they're <u>asking</u> us to do things instead of <u>ordering</u> us.

I'll be understudying a couple of parts, though there's no certainty that I'll ever get to perform them, which seems odd–to do all the work to learn the part and then never do it on stage. I keep telling myself it's good experience. So far we've mostly been doing cleaning and maintenance stuff while the actors are blocking the first play. The repertory in July and August: Stoppard's <u>Rosencrantz & Guildenstern Are Dead</u>, <u>The Flies</u> by Sartre, and some one-acts by Christopher Durang. I love Durang, of course, and I'm praying maybe I'll get a small part in one of those, but Jay says not to count on

Ellen Wittlinger

it. I really like Jay-he's a hoot-but Alice and I both think Andrew actually IS a wienie. A whiny wienie who won't do the dishes.

Okay, I'm avoiding again. I'm glad you were honest with me about your feelings, and I don't blame you for being upset that I've been hiding things from you. But try to understand, Chloe, I was afraid to say it out loud-I was afraid to say it to myself. I hadn't been a very good heterosexual; what if I was equally bad at homosexuality? I felt like I was painting myself into a corner. A lonely corner. I probably wouldn't have come out now if not for Alice. Besides, you were always such a hopeless romantic-at last count I believe you've had crushes on 92 boys-and I guess I was afraid you wouldn't accept it. Wouldn't accept me.

I'm sorry I didn't trust you sooner. You don't sound like a bigot at all, and I'm not asking you to be the perfect sister-I'm certainly not perfect, why should you be? I had to laugh though at the part about the "husbands" going fishing. Alice LOVES fishing! So maybe she and your husband can go while we eat ice cream! Seriously, Chloe, these are not things to worry about. For one thing, lesbians DO have children all the time, just not in the usual way. Which is not to say that I want kids-I think about it sometimes and I wonder if my parenting skills would be any better than Mom's or Dad's. They weren't the best role models, you know. Anyway, it's not a decision I have to make now.

I'm sorry it took me so long to tell you the truth. I'm going to try to do better from here on. And by the way, I ran into James Downing last year when his a cappella group from Vassar came to perform at Emmett. Guess what? <u>HE'S GAY!</u> You got it right when you said, "You just have to laugh."

Let's keep laughing.

Love, Veev

P.S. I'm calling Mom and Dad <u>tonight.</u>

June 21 at Maple Hill!

Dear Julian,

I am so glad to be here. The last few weeks at home everything seemed to be turned upside down, but here on the hill it's the same as it always was. I love this place, but when I try to describe it to people I always feel like I'm not doing a good job. Maybe because what it actually looks like isn't what makes it great. There are a couple of big barns that we use for art and theater, an old garage where we play music and dance, a big field for Ultimate Frisbee, long picnic benches in the dining room, cabins which are more like shacks with outhouses, and a buggy path to the lake where mildewed towels and swimming suits hang on a clothesline over a dozen canoes.

But as soon as my car pulled into the parking lot I just felt I was home. The smell of the Arts Barn made me so happy I felt weepy—the smell of the lake pushed me right over the edge, and I embarrassed myself in front of Bill, the camp director. Even the smell of Cookie's carrot-turkey burgers couldn't ruin it for me. (I wonder if every summer camp in America has a cook named Cookie?) Several of the counselors (Ray and Suzanne) were campers here with Peer and me when we were kids, so it's almost like they're my cousins or something. It's weird not having Genevieve here, but I'm getting used to it.

For the most part I like the other counselors this year—there's a girl from Australia and the usual sprinkling of people from across this country. The new theater director (replacing Keer) is kind of annoying, but maybe I'll get used to him. He's <u>very</u> opinionated. Tomorrow the kids arrive! ACK! It's always scary to see who's in your cabin—you don't want a bunch of precocious privileged girls who are only interested in applying makeup, but you don't want homesick scaredy cats either. Since this is an arts camp, we tend to get strong individuals, which is usually fun—the minute their parents' cars pull out of the lot, the kids whip out their pink and blue Manic Panic and start dying each other's hair.

Not to put pressure on you, but you <u>have</u> to win the District contest! I'm so looking forward to seeing you in Boston! We will have a blast!

My fingers are starting to cramp. I'm not used to writing this much in longhand—what did people <u>do</u> before computers? Please write! It makes you look so popular if you get letters at mail call. By the way, do you have any pictures of yourself? I'd like to have something to remember you by during my long, hot summer.

Love,

Chloe

Hiya,

Wish we could have talked before
I left. You and Joey seem madder
at me than Eli does. Did you think
we'd all go away to college and
be nuns and priests? I hate not
being able to talk to you. Please
write me. —Chloe

Maple Hill Arts Camp. Juniper, NH

Kate Waverly
8 Blacksmith Way
Brimmingham, MA
01908

June 22, 2002

Eagle Point, Maine

Dearest Chloe,

Daddy and I came up to the house in Eagle Point yesterday. We had intended to stay in Brimmingham through the weekend so we could help with the Garden Tour—even though our house isn't on the tour this year, I'd promised June to help her staff the luncheon and boutique stands—but after talking to your sister on the telephone Thursday evening and hearing her "revelation," we felt we just needed to get away from everyone and bathe in the solitude of our favorite place on earth.

I have to ask you, darling: Did you know about this? I hate to think that the two of you were in cahoots to keep it from us. Or perhaps you thought you were doing us a favor. You and Genevieve have always been extraordinarily close to each other, so I find it hard to believe this news came as a shock to you too. Yes, we found it shocking, and I am not ashamed to say so. You know Daddy and I have always supported liberal causes, but just because we give money to AIDS groups doesn't mean we appreciate our daughter taking up this offbeat lifestyle. I can't help but think it has something to do with being an actress and the kind of people one associates with in that type of business. Genevieve has always enjoyed calling attention to herself, and I wonder if this isn't just another means to that end.

As you can imagine, Daddy and I are stumped. I appeal to you because you're a young girl too and undoubtedly know more about these things than we do. Is it "cool" for college girls to act like this? (June said she thinks it is.) Is it likely to be a stage Genevieve passes through? And what did you think of Alice when she was here? Of course, I wasn't considering her as my daughter's "significant other" at the time, so I didn't pay that much attention to her. How did she strike you? Loud, of course, but at the time I put that down to youthful exuberance. Now I wonder if she was trying to make some kind of _point_.

If this is what Genevieve intends to do with her life, there's obviously not much we can do to dissuade her. But she can be such a pretty girl, especially when she lets her hair grow out, I hate to see her living some sort of strange, lonely life. You have always had more influence with her than either of us, Chloe, which is why I appeal to you now. Is there anything to be done? Do please give Daddy and me your opinion on this troubling new situation.

We hope you're having a wonderful time at Maple Hill. It was always so surprising to us that you girls loved that dusty, buggy place so much. After the first summer, when we saw how rustic the conditions were, we wanted to switch you to a camp we'd seen in Rhodes Bay up here in Maine—you could have gone sailing and horseback riding there, and the cabins were a good deal less rickety too! But you already loved Maple Hill by then and we couldn't pry you away. Sometimes we've said to each other that that place has had more influence on you girls than either of us ever had.

Have you heard any more from that sweet boy who sent you the roses? What a charmer he must be!

It's so difficult to have a decent conversation with you on that one overused phone they have at camp, so please write and let us know what you're thinking vis-à-vis your sister.

Love,

Mom and Daddy

I'm Coral Tyne in <u>Death Comes to Us All, Mary Agnes!</u> A mean secretary who swings a dead rat! In <u>The Flies</u> A. and I are "townsfolk," and A. understudies Clytemnestra, me Electra. I'm psyched!

-Veev

P.S. Told M&D. Muted response: stoic? don't give a damn?

NEW YORK NY JUN 22 '02

0.20 U.S. POSTAGE PB METER 8397846

Chloe Gillespie
Maple Hill Arts Camp
Box 41
Juniper, NH   03782

Washington Square, Greenwich Village, NYC

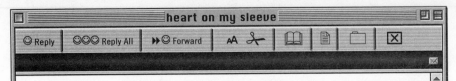

Subj: It's your life
Date: 6/23/02, 12:47 P.M.
From: maybee@flowire.com
To: CCinWonderland@hotmail.com

Carly,

I realize I didn't have much to say to you when you called to announce your marriage. I guess I was kind of in shock. I kept asking myself why did you do something like this? You only knew this Wes a short time and I never even met him. I always think you're doing things to get back at me for something—but then I started thinking about when I ran off with your dad. He was from out of town and he looked so DIFFERENT to me from the boys around here. Well, he turned out to be different all right, that's for sure. But I guess what I mean is that in a funny way I do understand why you got married. It's what you do when you're ready to grow up and to tell everybody you're grown up. I guess you're telling me, huh? Well, I have a lot of work to do this afternoon so I can't spend all of it goofing off like this. I just wanted to say to you that it's your life, after all. I made my mistakes and you have to make yours. I guess I didn't want you to have to make any, but I guess that's impossible. I hope this Wes guy is not a mistake, but if he is, well, then he is. Good luck to you both. — Mom

June 25, 2002

Dear Peer,

You won't believe the letter I got from Mom and Dad. Well, yes, you probably will. Apparently after you called with your "revelation," they scurried out of town and up to Eagle Point. They even missed the garden Tour, which is Mom's favorite social schmooze of the season. She didn't mention whether their tails were between their legs or not.

It wasn't an awful letter, but I guess I'm mostly amazed at what a narrow life they have. (Does that mean I have a narrow life too?) I think of them as intelligent people, but there are obviously things they don't know dick about. They think they're "liberal" because they give money to AIDS groups. They asked me if college girls thought it was "cool to pass through a stage like this" these days. They think being a lesbian is an "offbeat lifestyle," and I think they think if you let your hair grow out, this will all go away. Maybe the most amazing thing was that Mom managed to write four pages in longhand about "the situation" without once using the words gay, lesbian, or homosexual.

Basically, you have them stumped—Mom even used that word. She wants to know if there's anything that can be done to change you back into the fantasy girl she has in her head. The funny thing is, seeing the weird reaction Mom had made me think my reaction was weird too. Maybe everybody has a weird reaction to news like this if they don't see it coming. But it doesn't mean (I don't think), "Ick-you're gay-I'm disgusted." It just means, "You aren't who I thought you were-you aren't just like me." And in my case that makes me feel more alone than I usually feel. It also makes me feel really young and stupid-I mean, I haven't even slept with a <u>boy</u>, and you're already sleeping with a <u>girl</u>! I guess I had a fantasy sister in my head too, and she wasn't a lesbian.

Thank god for camp! Ray and Suzanne are back, but not Edie. I don't think Bill appreciated her encouraging the 10-year-old girls' cabin to go skinny-dipping last year. Kevin and Kendra are here (yeah!) and the barfer is <u>not</u>. David the Devil, however, has returned, as has that skinny girl, Sally, who just about drowned last year. Never thought I'd see her again, but this year she has boobs, so maybe she'll be able to float. For the most part the new counselors are a great bunch, but the guy who's taken over the theater is a real jerk. His name is Gunnar (believe that?) and he's <u>very</u> annoying. I tried to give him a little advice about how you ran the theater groups the last few years, how the kids could drift back and forth between the impror groups and the actual shows, as long as they committed to a show at least two weeks before the production, and he said, "That sounds very disorganized. I expect the kids to make a commitment to one show the day they sign up. They'll do the musical, the straight play, or the impror, not all three." Who does he think he is—Steven Sondheim? It's <u>camp</u>! Kids are supposed to <u>have fun</u> here!

Anyway, everybody asks me where you are—we all miss you. It's <u>great</u> that you got an actual part in a play already! I'm really proud of you.

Thanks for thinking I'm not a bigot. I'm trying.

Love, Chloe

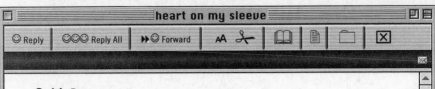
Subj: Born to run
Date: 6/26/02, 3:02 P.M.
From: jghost@flowire.com
To: CCinWonderland@hotmail.com

I guess nothing you do should surprise me anymore, but getting married in a Las Vegas motel—so you can have a complimentary breakfast—to a guy wearing a Born to Run T-shirt, tops most of your earlier performances. God, Carly, when are you going to stop showing off?

You'll be happy to know I think Mom has finally decided to give up on you. She was very matter-of-fact when she told me about the *wedding.* All she said was, "Carly married that man she's been with. They went to Las Vegas over the weekend." No yelling, no anger. When I tried to ask her more about it, she just shrugged and said, "You'll have to ask your sister for the details." (Of course, I KNEW you'd happily supply them before I had to actually ask.) Don't get me wrong, I don't care who you marry, or even when you marry, but I do think you should be out of your adolescence before you make the leap—and I don't see any evidence that you actually plan to grow up. To tell you the truth, I feel sorry for this Wes guy. You've never committed to so much as a yoga class, much less a PERSON.

And don't expect me to discuss Nina Greco with you, or Chloe either. Whatever is going on in my life, it's not going to be the subject for jokes in a bar with your new hubby and his friends. By the way, what does this Wes DO? If you tell me he's in a band, I'll shoot you.

Yeah, I'm really cranky and pissed off tonight—maybe I'm stepping in for Mom or something, I don't know. But I've spent the last month slinging Mu Shu Pork and practicing hitting high C *every damn day* so that on Friday I can go to Richmond and stand there shaking and

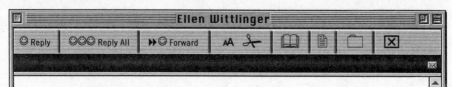

sweating in front of the Menninger jury, so that maybe I can go to a decent college and BE somebody. And it kills me that you're just shrugging your way through life as if nothing counts. For me, everything counts.

Julian

Subj: it's my life
Date: 6/26/02, 9:23 P.M.
From: CCinWonderland@hotmail.com
To: maybee@flowire.com

mom,

i'm surprised to hear you think getting married means i'm grown up. my darling brother just wrote to tell me he thinks i'm still an adolescent and should be spanked for misbehaving. he is so holier-than-thou. (sorry, didn't mean to malign your angel.)

i don't think my marrying wes is anything at all like you marrying daddy. you got married to get out of your parents' house—i was *already* out. also, wes is not a nut job whose goal in life is to have as little to do with other human beings as possible. i'm not being mean—dad's not a bad person—but he's very weird. wes is just a normal guy. he likes to dance and listen to music and go out for drinks and have a good time.

but anyway, i was surprised you took it so well. i'm glad you finally realized not everything i do is about *you*. as you said, it's my life, and if i make mistakes, they're mine too. anyway ... maybe we'll call you sometime. wes says your voice sounds like julia louis-dreyfuss (you know, on "seinfeld.")

carly

June 27, 2002

Dear Chloe,

Well, I guess I can't stay mad at you forever. Besides which, I've been so BORED since you left! My parents aren't even taking us on a vacation this summer (saving it all for tuition), so I'm stuck here until September 2. I got a job at the Gap the day after you left. Don't laugh-at least I've learned how to fold a T-shirt correctly, which I'm sure will come in handy someday. I thought this job would be so good because I'd get a discount on the clothes, but everything is BEIGE this summer- what's that about? I don't want BEIGE clothes-I want RED or ORANGE or GREEN!

So, Joey and Meghan and I have been hanging out with Eli a lot. At first he was in a terrible mood all the time, but I think he's getting over it a little bit. (It probably doesn't hurt that Meghan's always had a crush on him-you knew that didn't you?-and now she can actually flirt with him.) Do you really think we'll all break up when we go away to school? I hate to think that's true-it's too scary. You guys have been my best friends for so long. The idea of having to make new friends gives me a headache. To tell you the truth, I think Joey's sort of looking forward to it, which is depressing. God! I can't imagine starting all over with somebody else! When Joey and I started sleeping together I figured, that was it-we'd always be together from then on. I guess I was an idiot.

Eli says he might write you pretty soon. That's good, huh? Are you having fun at camp? I don't know why you like sleeping in a cabin with ten giggly little girls-I'd rather sort socks. Ugh, I can't write anymore-my fingers are cramping. Write back when you can!

Love (of course),

Kate

Subj: your dad
Date: 6/28/02, 8:37 P.M.
From: maybee@flowire.com
To: CCinWonderland@hotmail.com

Carly,

I just have to ask you, why don't you use any capital letters? It makes your writing seem drab. I suppose it's very "modern" or something. Anyway, I also wanted to tell you that your father liked to dance too, when I first met him. As a matter of fact, we went out dancing at least two or three times a week—he loved disco. He was never a drinker, of course, but he did like to have fun. I'm sorry you don't remember—he was very normal in the early days. How was I supposed to know he'd get so strange? And it's not Julia Louis-Dreyfuss I sound like, it's the mother on "Malcolm in the Middle." That's what everybody says.

Mom

P.S. Your brother just called me from Richmond. He won the District level of the Menninger competition. He gets a $2000 scholarship and a trip to Boston next month. Not enough to pay for that private school he wants to go to though.

Subj: There's a Light Beyond These Woods
Date: 6/29/02, 2:31 P.M.
From: smallboyonherbike@boscore.com
To: jghost@flowire.com

YIPPEE! (For so many reasons!) This is my first day off since I got here 2 weeks ago, so I drove into Hanover to use a computer in the library. I so miss instant communication! Which I realized last night when you called—I'm sorry you had to try for 45 minutes before you could get through to the camp. Friday nights the kids are allowed to call their parents, so it's almost impossible to get through. And then,

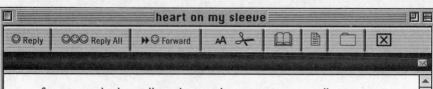

of course, nobody is allowed more than 5 minutes to talk—even counselors. It was so wonderful to hear your voice again and so FRUSTRATING not to be able to talk longer.

But you WON! So we'll be able to talk for 4 long days in August! (And maybe more than talk too . . .) I was so excited last night I couldn't sleep. We HAVE to go to some open mics. Do you think we could duet on "To Fly"? I know we wouldn't have much time to practice it together, but let's try it anyway. It would be SO cool. I want to try to write another song this summer, but right now I'm so busy with the kids I don't know if I'll be able to. Also, I'm wasting far too much effort being furious with the idiot who took over the theater director job. He has to do EVERYTHING his own way. Nobody else can ever have a good idea. Apparently he's going to be a junior at NYU, which means he thinks he knows all there is to know about theater. I just hope he doesn't ruin the fun for the kids. After all, they're the most important thing, not doing a perfect Broadway performance.

Well, I have to write a few other quick notes while I have the computer here. And then go practice up on my Joni Mitchell for campfire tonight—the kids LOVE when I do "The Circle Game."

I'm sending you a big hug and kiss for winning that contest! SMACK!

Love, Chloe

Subj: Wasn't That a Mighty Storm?
Date: 6/29/02, 2:49 P.M.
From: smallboyonherbike@boscore.com
To: Kublakate@boscore.com

Sweet Kate,

Thank you, thank you, for not being mad at me anymore! I feel like a big weight has been lifted off my shoulders—one of the big weights anyway. I'm in Hanover on my day off and I'm trying to write as many people as I can before I have to leave and do my errands. (The other counselors gave me a list of junk food to buy, and I'm not leaving here until I have a Ben and Jerry's too.) So I hope I don't sound crazy—I'm just rushing.

I had NO idea Meghan had a crush on Eli! Since when? Why didn't you ever tell me this? I mean, it's not a big deal, especially now, but I'm surprised I never picked up on it. Did *he* know? I mean, she's been hanging out with us for *years*—did she always like him? I'm actually glad about it. Do you think they'll start dating or something? It's sort of weird, isn't it? Of course you're not an idiot—you're just in love. (Which Veev might say is the same thing, but I wouldn't.)

Which reminds me, I have two big things to tell you. First of all, Julian (the rose sender) is coming to Brimmingham for 4 days in August! So you can meet him, if you want to. He won this singing contest (he has a fabulous voice), and he's competing in Boston for a $25,000 scholarship. I'm so psyched about this, I can't TELL you.

And the second thing is—you better sit down—Genevieve recently told me she's gay. That girl Alice is her girlfriend! Are you freaked out? I don't know how to feel about it—I guess I am sort of freaked out, but I'm trying not to be. Give me advice, Kate. I love Veev, but

I'm sort of dreading seeing her again now. I feel like I won't know what to say. Like she'll be different. She already WAS different when she was here the last time—didn't you think so? On the other hand, Martha and Tom are being creepy about the whole thing, which makes me want to punch them in their overused kissers. (Of course, I won't—I'll just be their usual good girl.) After years of treating us like mildly interesting accessories to their love life, now they're offended that they weren't the first to know about this "troubling new situation." Mom hinted that if Veev grew her hair long again, her heterosexuality might yet be saved. Genevieve's stock has definitely plummeted in their eyes, so I feel like I need to protect her from their jerkiness.

Oh, God, I really ought to write to them while I'm in here too. Write me back a long letter. You don't HAVE to write in longhand, you know. Write it on the computer, run it out, and mail it! I'm so glad we're back!

Love,

Chloe

Subj: Ain't Hurtin' Nobody
Date: 6/29/02, 3:11 P.M.
From: smallboyonherbike@boscore.com
To: mtgillespie@boscore.com

Dear M & D,

Genevieve only told me she was a lesbian a few days before she told you, and I knew she was going to tell you herself, so I left it up to her. I was surprised by it too, but I wouldn't say *shocked.* No, I don't think she's coming out because she thinks it's *cool*—she told me she'd felt this way in high school too, but kept trying to deny it. I

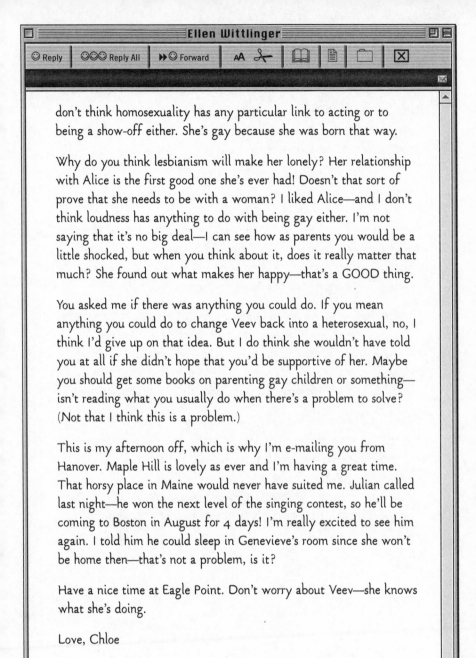

don't think homosexuality has any particular link to acting or to being a show-off either. She's gay because she was born that way.

Why do you think lesbianism will make her lonely? Her relationship with Alice is the first good one she's ever had! Doesn't that sort of prove that she needs to be with a woman? I liked Alice—and I don't think loudness has anything to do with being gay either. I'm not saying that it's no big deal—I can see how as parents you would be a little shocked, but when you think about it, does it really matter that much? She found out what makes her happy—that's a GOOD thing.

You asked me if there was anything you could do. If you mean anything you could do to change Veev back into a heterosexual, no, I think I'd give up on that idea. But I do think she wouldn't have told you at all if she didn't hope that you'd be supportive of her. Maybe you should get some books on parenting gay children or something—isn't reading what you usually do when there's a problem to solve? (Not that I think this is a problem.)

This is my afternoon off, which is why I'm e-mailing you from Hanover. Maple Hill is lovely as ever and I'm having a great time. That horsy place in Maine would never have suited me. Julian called last night—he won the next level of the singing contest, so he'll be coming to Boston in August for 4 days! I'm really excited to see him again. I told him he could sleep in Genevieve's room since she won't be home then—that's not a problem, is it?

Have a nice time at Eagle Point. Don't worry about Veev—she knows what she's doing.

Love, Chloe

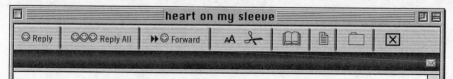

Sub: Killing the Blues
Date: 6/29/02, 3:24 P.M.
From: smallboyonherbike@boscore.com
To: ggillespie@Emmett.edu

Veev—

I'm in Hanover, and I've got 6 minutes of computer time left before the next person's turn, so here's a quickie. Biggest news: Julian won the District contest so he's coming to Boston in August! And Kate is speaking to me again, so I'm no longer bereft of friends.

Big question: When people at camp ask about you, should I tell them about you coming out? Not that it's their business, but people like Bill and Ray and Suzanne (who love you) ask me how you're doing, and I feel a little bit like I'm keeping a secret from them if I DON'T say anything. But, of course, I won't if you don't want me to.

Gunnar, the new theater director, will be very fortunate if he gets through this summer without suffering bodily harm—the kids are ready to mutiny on him, and I'm ready to lead the charge! Guess what musical he's doing: *The Sound of Music!* He says it's appropriate for young children. Maybe so, but not MHAC campers—they did *Cabaret* last year! They want to be strippers, not nuns! WE MISS YOU!

Chloe

June 29, 2002

Dear Chloe,

I hope you can read this—I'm on the bus on the way back to Florida, so my writing is pretty bad. I'm so hyped up I can't read or even watch the stupid Adam Sandler movie they're showing. The only thing I really want to do is write you a letter.

I can't tell you how good it was to hear your voice last night on the telephone. Writing letters and e-mails is great, but hearing your voice really reminded me who you are. I don't know if I'm saying that right. But when you got on the phone I thought, this is really _her_, Chloe! I know her! Does that make any sense? I wish we could have talked longer, but I felt bad about the crying girl who was waiting to call her parents. Hearing all those kids making noise in back of you I felt like I could see you there, being responsible and helping everybody. I could imagine you singing little kids to sleep with guitar lullabies. Do you do that?

I'm sending you a Polaroid that one of the other tenors took of me. (He was photographing everything in sight.) Not great, but at least my ears don't look like Dumbo's. Do you have one to send me?

God, it's impossible to write bumping along the highway. I just wanted to say, I can't wait to get to Boston in August. What contest? I just want to be with you.

Love, Julian

6/30/02

Dear Chloe,

Hey. I talked to Kate a few days ago and we both sort of decided we were being too hard on you. I think Kate was making herself stay mad at you because she felt sorry for me, but I told her to go ahead and write you because I was going to too. So I'm writing. Except I don't exactly know what to say. I guess you're having a great summer at camp as always—I know Maple Hill is like your spiritual home or something.

Things are okay here. I'm working for my uncle again this summer—good money as long as I can take his shit and swallow my tongue. At least doing landscaping gets me outside, and if I'm in a bad mood I can take it out on some rich guy's bushes. In the evenings I hang out with the usual suspects. Since I always miss you in the summer, I keep thinking this year shouldn't be any different, but, of course, it is. Not just because of what happened, but because we'll all be separating so soon. When I start to feel anger knotting up inside me, I remind myself that you were just a few months ahead of schedule—we'll all say good-bye to each other soon.

Growing up sucks sometimes. I mean, I know college will probably be great, but I hate that you always have to give up one good thing to get another. What if these really were the best days of our lives? Anyway, I don't mean to sound depressed. I'm really fine most of the time. The thing I keep wanting to ask you is: Have you wanted to break up with me for a long time or was it just because you met this Julian guy? But I don't really want you to answer me—I just want you to know I'm wondering.

I miss you. I guess I will for awhile.

Eli

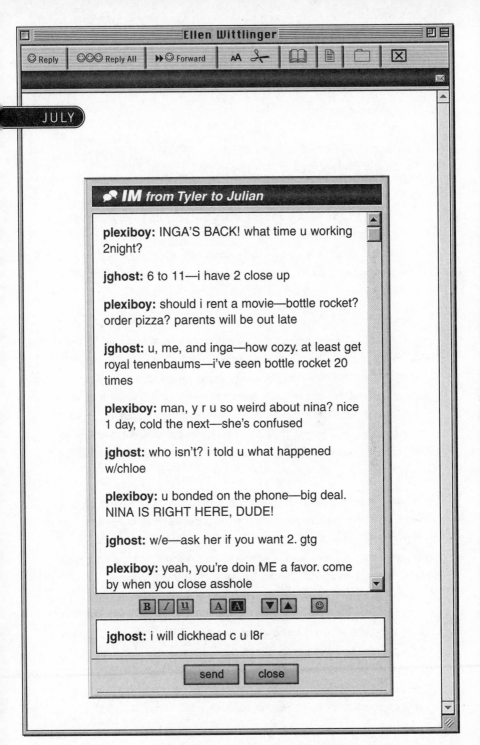

IM from Tyler to Julian

plexiboy: INGA'S BACK! what time u working 2night?

jghost: 6 to 11—i have 2 close up

plexiboy: should i rent a movie—bottle rocket? order pizza? parents will be out late

jghost: u, me, and inga—how cozy. at least get royal tenenbaums—i've seen bottle rocket 20 times

plexiboy: man, y r u so weird about nina? nice 1 day, cold the next—she's confused

jghost: who isn't? i told u what happened w/chloe

plexiboy: u bonded on the phone—big deal. NINA IS RIGHT HERE, DUDE!

jghost: w/e—ask her if you want 2. gtg

plexiboy: yeah, you're doin ME a favor. come by when you close asshole

jghost: i will dickhead c u l8r

send   close

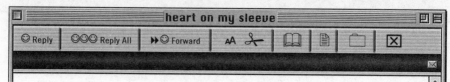

Subj: Who's sorry now?
Date: 7/2/02, 1:31 P.M.
From: jghost@flowire.com
To: CCinWonderland@hotmail.com

Okay, maybe I was a little harsh in that last e-mail. You probably didn't marry Wes just to get the free breakfast. But you took me by surprise, Carly. I never expected you to get *married,* not at 22. Besides which, I was so nervous that week about the competition, I really didn't want to have anything else on my mind, and then you dumped this BIG NEWS on me. Anyway, I'm sorry, mea culpa, sue me.

The weird thing (to me) is that Mom really doesn't seem that bothered by it. I wouldn't say she's HAPPY exactly, more like resigned. But yesterday she said she hopes you can both come here for Christmas because she wants to meet Wes—she thinks *he sounds very nice on the phone!* (Here I thought she was upset because you weren't in college, and it turns out all she wanted was for you to snag a husband! Could that be true?) By the way, she's sold two houses in the past two weeks, so you picked a good time to give her bizarre news; she's very proud of herself for being able to bring home so much bacon.

I know Mom told you I won the Menninger Districts. The other guys were very good—I was amazed to win my division. But that just means that in Boston the competition will be REALLY stiff. I'm trying to convince myself I don't care that much about winning the big prize—it's an honor just to be included, ha, ha. And it's true that one big consolation will be that I get to see Chloe—in fact, I'm even staying with her at her house. I called her at the summer camp where she works to tell her I'd won, and it was so great to talk to her. She's a very cool person. And just to make amends, I'll tell you that I've been seeing Nina once in awhile too. Nothing serious—don't get your hopes up. We're more like chaperones for Tyler and Inga who seem to want to be a couple, but for some reason, don't have the nerve to go for it.

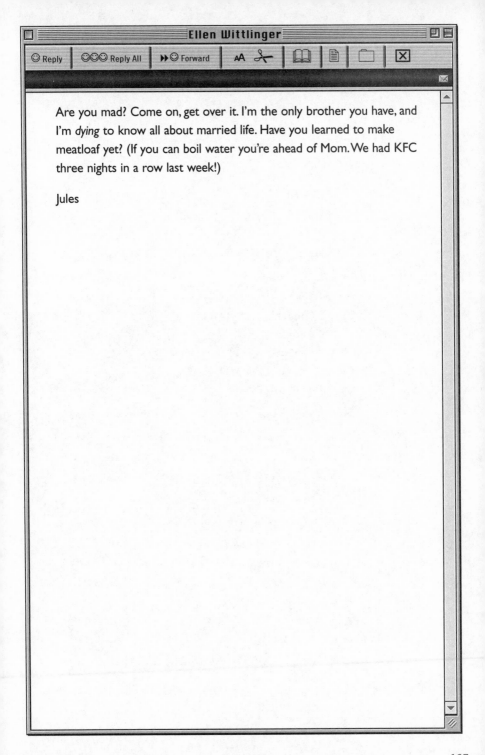

Are you mad? Come on, get over it. I'm the only brother you have, and I'm *dying* to know all about married life. Have you learned to make meatloaf yet? (If you can boil water you're ahead of Mom. We had KFC three nights in a row last week!)

Jules

July 3, 2002

Dear Eli,

Thank you for writing to me. Your letter was wonderful. I can imagine you cursing your Uncle Stan behind his back and reducing somebody's topiary to a pile of sticks. I hope you're not forgetting the sunblock-remember that awful burn you got the beginning of last summer!

It's strange writing to you because I'm not sure what to say. After so many years of yakking about absolutely everything, now I feel like I need to think carefully about every word. I have to tell you one more time that I'm sorry-I really am-the last thing I wanted to do was to hurt you. (I know that sounds like something they'd say on "Dawson's Creek," with tears running down everybody's faces, but I <u>mean</u> it.) I disagree with you about having to give up one good thing to get another-why can't we just add the good things together? Obviously, you can't have more than one boyfriend or girlfriend at a time, but that doesn't mean you have to lose people completely, does it? Please say we can still be friends! I can't imagine losing touch with you, Eli-we're so much a part of each other!

Kate said Meghan is interested in going out with you. Maybe I shouldn't bring it up, but I just wanted to say that (even though it seems a little weird) you should go ahead and date her if you want to. Not that you need my permission, of course—I didn't mean that. I'm just saying, maybe it would make you feel better about this whole thing.

Crap. I hate feeling this way with you, Eli. Like I don't know how to talk to you anymore, or I'm still hurting your feelings or something. You are SO important to me. My entire high school life would have been shit without you there. You know that, don't you? And I feel terrible about the way it came out about Julian, on prom night, for god's sake. I feel like I ruined your senior year or something. Did I?

Anyway, camp is good—I love it here, as you know. It really IS my spiritual home. Just the smell of the place relaxes me. There's a terrific group of counselors here this year, with one exception, and I'm trying to ignore him. I miss having Keer here, of course. By the way, Kate will probably tell you anyway: Keer has come out as a lesbian. It seemed very odd when she first told me, but I'm getting used to it now. I guess nothing stays the same for long, does it? My dad always says, "Roll with the punches." But it's hard when you don't even see them coming.

Eli, I miss you too.

Chloe

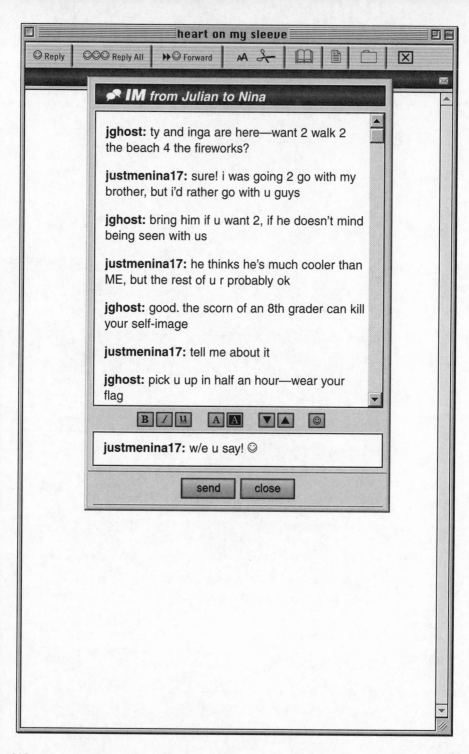

Reply | Reply All | ▶ Forward | AA ✂ | 📖 | 📄 | 🗂 | ✕

💬 **IM** *from Julian to Nina*

jghost: ty and inga are here—want 2 walk 2 the beach 4 the fireworks?

justmenina17: sure! i was going 2 go with my brother, but i'd rather go with u guys

jghost: bring him if u want 2, if he doesn't mind being seen with us

justmenina17: he thinks he's much cooler than ME, but the rest of u r probably ok

jghost: good. the scorn of an 8th grader can kill your self-image

justmenina17: tell me about it

jghost: pick u up in half an hour—wear your flag

B *I* u | A A | ▼ ▲ | ☺

justmenina17: w/e u say! ☺

send   close

July 5, 2002

Dear Chloe,

-Sorry I haven't written you in awhile-there's always something going on around here and I hate to miss any of it. Yesterday Ben Bernstein, one of the directors at Village Studio, threw an enormous Fourth of July party in his loft, which also has a roof garden where we watched fireworks. What an amazing place! Ben has an actual David Hockney painting hanging on his wall which he bought before D.H. was famous, and now it's worth a fortune, I guess. There's fabulous art like that all over the loft. Ben's wife, Adele, used to dance with American Ballet Theater but gave it up when she got pregnant with their kid, Sweeney (which sounds like a name you'd give a dog, doesn't it?). Between them they know a million interesting people and they were <u>all there.</u> Get this: Jennifer Jason Leigh showed up! She's good friends with this guy Craig from V.S.T. She looks even better in person than in the movies-totally electric!

-At first Alice and I felt like party crashers. The only people we knew were from the theater and they weren't interested in spending time with us, as you can imagine. After about 15 minutes of standing around with Jay, we all decided we had nothing to lose; we'd go forth and be brave. I ended up having a long conversation with a guy by the name of Jamison Saperstein whose first novel (called <u>Dust</u>) is due out from Viking next month. He's only 24 and he's already publishing a novel! Made me feel simultaneously hopeful and lazy. It seemed like everybody at the party had some story like that-some brush with fame and/or fortune.

-Oh, New York! It's almost too much for me to take. Is it because I'm such a small-town girl? I love the excitement, but sometimes I feel like I've overdosed on it. Like I want to go inside and rest now, only there is no inside, no place to escape the continual LIFE. We work hard, we play hard, we laugh hard, we argue hard, we get mad at each other hard. It's very intense.

-Andrew and Jay are breaking up. Thank God, Andrew is moving out
and Jay's staying with us. Having the tension of their bickering in the
apartment all the time wasn't helping Alice and me either. I guess she
was a little jealous about me getting the part in the Durang play,
only instead of saying that, she was coming at me sideways. Crabbing
because I changed the radio dial or made too much guacamole-weird
stuff. Finally last night, out on the roof under the fireworks she
started to cry and then came clean about the whole thing. I think
it's straightened out now (or maybe "straight" is the wrong word),
but I realized that my usual response to problems-from my years of
dealing with boyfriends- is that when things begin to go wrong, I cut
and run. Find somebody else and start over. When Alice was getting mad
at me that was my first impulse, but now I'm so glad I didn't give in
to it because going through this hard time-and working things out-has
actually made us closer than ever. (My God, have I ever sounded this
drippy in my whole life? Does happiness make you a sap?)

-On to Maple Hill Arts Camp. Yes, of course, you can tell Bill and Ray
and Suzanne or anybody else you want to, about my coming out. It's a
secret no more. I wonder if any of them suspected? And as for the
new theater guy-cut him some slack, Chloe! Everybody has to find their
own way to do this stuff. I probably wouldn't have dared do something
like <u>cabaret</u> either if I hadn't been at MHAC for years and
understood in my bones the basic tenet of summer camp life: <u>Let's
learn as much as we can about sex while our parents aren't around!</u>
For all you know Gunnar (what were his parents thinking?) never went
to camp himself. And here comes some 18-year-old who thinks he should
do everything just the way her sister did it, and who's rallying the
kids against him! It's hard to come into that place as a new
counselor-he's probably hiding behind all these "rules" he's set up
because he's scared shitless. Couldn't you help the guy out a little
bit? You always helped me with the musical-is anybody helping him? Lord,
I feel sorry for the guy going up against you when you're pissed off!

-Your last letter-the long one-was very perceptive. I understand your reaction to my coming out-that I'm not who you thought I was-I'm not just like you anymore. And it's true, to some extent, except that I was never all that much like you. We liked to THINK we were alike so we'd be a united front against Mom and Dad; we weren't like them. But we weren't twins either, dearie. I'm sorry if you feel you've lost the fantasy me-but the REAL me is still happy to be your sister. Isn't that enough? And the idea that you're alone-come on, Chloe! You have twice as many friends as I ever had! I'm the one who skipped from friend to friend, boyfriend to boyfriend. Do you know I never had anybody over to spend the night, ever? I never had a real friend, except you. So if you think I'm going to give you up now, you're crazy!

-I talked to Mom and Dad again, and they seemed a little less weirded out. They said you'd told them I was indeed a lesbian, and a new hairdo wasn't going to change things. And that you liked Alice and thought she was good for me. I hope that's true and not just something you said to pacify them. I care much more what you think than what they think. Anyway, thank you. I know there are a lot of changes going on in your own life right now-I appreciate how well you're dealing with mine.

-Wow, this is about the longest non-e-mail letter I've ever written. Give everybody a hug for me. And keep the biggest one for yourself.

-Love, Veev

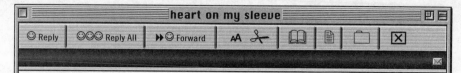

Subj: so shoot me
Date: 7/6/02, 4:15 P.M.
From: CCinWonderland@hotmail.com
To: jghost@flowire.com

wes is in 2 bands: a country western one and a bluegrass one—he
plays upright bass. the first thing he does when he gets to a new place
is find bands to play with—he says music is his life. happy now? other
things about wes I haven't mentioned because I didn't know he was
going to end up being my husband: He has a droopy yellow mustache
that makes him look like general custer. he does finish carpentry to
make money. his drink of choice is dos equis. he's virgo with a moon in
capricorn. he's not a rock 'n roll bum, if that's what you think.

sometimes you can really be a tightass, sweetheart. but i forgive you
because your mother makes you eat too much fast food and your
digestive tract is probably glued together with grease. go buy yourself
some broccoli sometime, or an artichoke. jeez. i do think it's a hopeful
sign that you're interested in TWO (not one but two) females
simultaneously, even if they do live 1,000 miles apart. congrats on the
menninger win, of course. you have as good a chance as anybody else
of winning the whole thing, but I don't think your entire college choice
should be hinging on this one contest! will you honestly not be able to
go to cartwright unless you win? i thought you got some scholarship
money? is u. of florida your only backup plan? you haven't really
thought this through, have you?

mom is being oddly nice about the whole marriage thing. just to
throw me off guard. i guess we will make the parental rounds at
christmastime. wes has this idea that mom is an interesting, kooky
person—i keep telling him she's just a pain in the ass, but he says wait
until i see HIS parents. very white gloves and croquet in the backyard.
are EVERYBODY'S parents bizarre? i always thought having kids made
you boring, but maybe i was wrong—it makes you a raving lunatic!

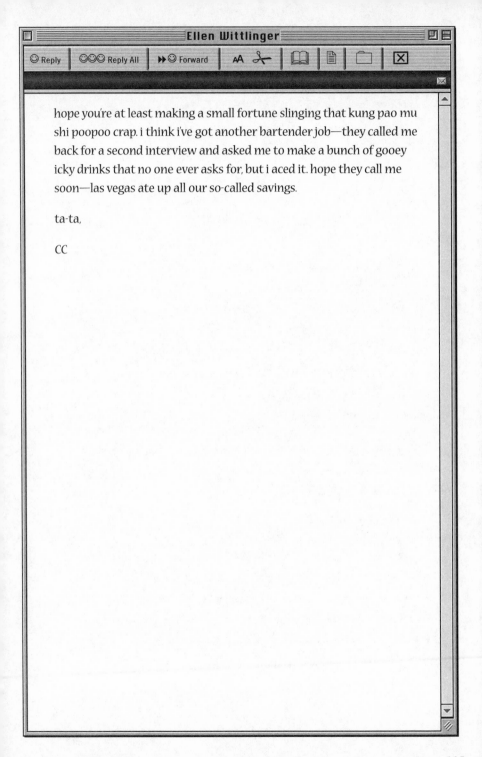

hope you're at least making a small fortune slinging that kung pao mu shi poopoo crap. i think i've got another bartender job—they called me back for a second interview and asked me to make a bunch of gooey icky drinks that no one ever asks for, but i aced it. hope they call me soon—las vegas ate up all our so-called savings.

ta-ta,

CC

July 6, 2002

Dear Julian,

Thank you SO much for the picture! You look so handsome in a suit and tie! Do you have to get all dressed up for these contests? (Where did you ever get the idea you had Dumbo ears?) I thumbtacked the picture above my bunk in the cabin so all my 11-year-old campers could drool. They keep asking me about you, how we met, etc. I can hardly believe I was just like that a few years ago, but I know I was. I remember the year my counselor, Sammie, told us about her boyfriend, who was a college basketball player, and we were all dreamy eyed over the magic of boyfriends!

I have a great cabin of girls this year–very little homesickness and virtually no meanness at all, which is very unusual. We've formed a tight unit, which is an advantage on skit nights because we all work together and there's nobody saying they don't want to do it or they're embarrassed. Everybody puts it out there. This week we wrote a satire called "Survivor-Maple Hill" which was a scream. I won't even try to describe it–I know from past experience that unless you're here, it sounds ridiculous. (EX: We all wore bras on our heads.) Tonight is Spud hunt night which all the kids LOVE. Basically they hide from the counselors and we try to find them, but that doesn't begin to describe the mayhem that goes on.

I guess it sounds a little juvenile, huh? I know some people just don't _get_ this whole camp thing, but those are mostly people who've never done it. The thing about camp is, you don't have to be somebody you aren't. The prissiest girls stop washing their hair and beg to play Ultimate Frisbee. The jockiest guys make themselves a batik T-shirt and try out to be one of the von Trapp children. Somehow they don't have to be who they are at home—nobody judges anybody else—it's so _comfortable_ here.

Have you heard from your sister again? When you get used to it, it probably won't seem so weird that she's married. My sister has just come out of the closet—that still seems weird too, but I'm hoping it will start to seem like a normal thing for me very soon.

I'm enclosing a photograph that one of the campers took of me and developed in our photography lab. Black and white, of course, but I sort of like it. Makes me look serious, don't you think? Which is just what I'm NOT, especially at camp.

Write when you can. I'm thinking of you. And I've started writing another song!

Love, Chloe

Eagle Point

July 9, 2002

Dear Genevieve,

Daddy and I had such a lovely day today. We went sailing with the Eberhardts on their new boat, which is quite luxurious. I took a Dramamine, just in case, and felt fine all afternoon. Mr. Eberhardt (Henry) has just taken early retirement and they're in the process of selling their home in Newton and moving up here permanently. I must say the idea made Daddy and me think twice! Wouldn't we love to do the same one day soon?

Anyway, I don't know if it was being out on the water, no land to be seen and the sort of intimacy that affords, or the fact that we've always felt more at ease with Henry and Stell than with most of our Brimmingham friends, but suddenly I found myself telling them about you, dear, and your friend Alice. I suppose there is a way in which Daddy and I feel responsible for what has happened, and perhaps I just needed a friendly shoulder to cry on. (Not that I <u>cried</u>, of course.) Well, it turns out that Stell and Henry have a niece who is a lesbian. (I do wish there was another word for it—that one sounds so harsh.) So Stell and I spent quite some time discussing it. She says her niece is a beautiful girl—as are you, of course—and her parents had a terrible time believing she could be homosexual, but after a few years they all seem to have come to terms with it. The niece and her girlfriend even come to family holidays together and no one minds.

I suppose it helped me just to know that this does happen in other families too—that Daddy and I didn't do something awful to you during your childhood to cause it. You don't think we did, do you? We've spent a few sleepless nights pondering where we'd gone wrong, but we honestly couldn't see where! It seemed to us we had always role-modeled a loving heterosexual lifestyle. And then we realized that if it was something <u>we</u> had done, your sister would probably be homosexual too, wouldn't she? Please don't tell me she is! I know she dates boys, but so did you, so that's not a reliable indicator. I feel confident that Daddy and I will be able to get past this issue with you, and that we'll all be one big happy family again, but if we were to find out that Chloe is a lesbian too, well, it would be very hard for both of us.

We do hope you're enjoying your time in New York City. We've always found it to be such an exciting place to visit! And, of course, we're proud that you've been given a part in one of the short plays. Just be careful, Genevieve. The city is such an exuberant place it can make you lose your head a little bit.

I didn't want to send this by e-mail because I hate the idea that one's words fly around out there in space for years and anybody can get at them. A letter in an envelope seems so much more private. Of course, if you'd rather e-mail your reply, that's fine—I know putting pen to paper is a lot to ask of a busy young person.

Wish you were here in Maine with us!

Love, Mom and Daddy

Eagle Point

July 9, 2002

Dear Chloe,

Daddy and I had such a lovely day today. We went sailing with the Eberhardts on their new boat, which is quite luxurious. I took a Dramamine, just in case, and felt fine all afternoon. Mr. Eberhardt (Henry) has just taken early retirement, and they're in the process of selling their home in Newton and moving up here permanently. I must say the idea made Daddy and me think twice! Wouldn't we love to do the same one day soon?

We know you must be enjoying camp because you always do. And you'll be glad to know that Daddy and I are using our vacation time to try to come to terms with your sister's new lifestyle. Along those lines, may I ask you one question, dear? Do you feel that there was anything Daddy and I did that might have led Genevieve down this path? We have thought long and hard about this, but we don't see what it could have been. Certainly we have modeled normal heterosexual behavior as much as possible. Perhaps you remember it differently—could this be our fault?

We wanted to let you know that we'd love to meet your Florida boyfriend (if that's what you call him), and we'd be delighted to have him stay with us while he's in the area. He must have a beautiful voice to have come so far in such a prestigious contest. (I hadn't heard of it before, but Stell Eberhardt had.) You must be so happy that you'll have a boyfriend immediately when you get to college!

Well, I really need to get this knot out of my neck and the only way to do that is to hop into the Jacuzzi.

Wish you were here in Maine with us!

Love, Mom and Daddy

Thought you'd like to see what _my_ lake looks like. Imagine me paddling a canoe full of 11-year-olds all singing "Row, row, row your boat" at the top of their lungs! One more month until we're together!

- Love, Chloe

Lake Wachunee, New Hampshire

JUNIPER
JUL 12'02
NH

= 0.20
PB METER
8397840
U.S. POSTAGE

Julian Casper
88 Lanning Rd.
Douglas, FL 32043

Dear E, I guess you must have
a few dozen postcards of this
lake, huh? Camp is half over
already. As usual I feel two
ways: 1) can't wait to sleep in
my own bed and take a hot
shower, and 2) never want to
leave this place, ever. Why
can't I do both?

    - Chloe

Lake Wachunee, New Hampshire

Eli Mather
2 Jasper Court
Brimmingham, MA
01908

JUNIPER
NH
JUL 12'02

0.20
U.S. POSTAGE
PB METER
8397840

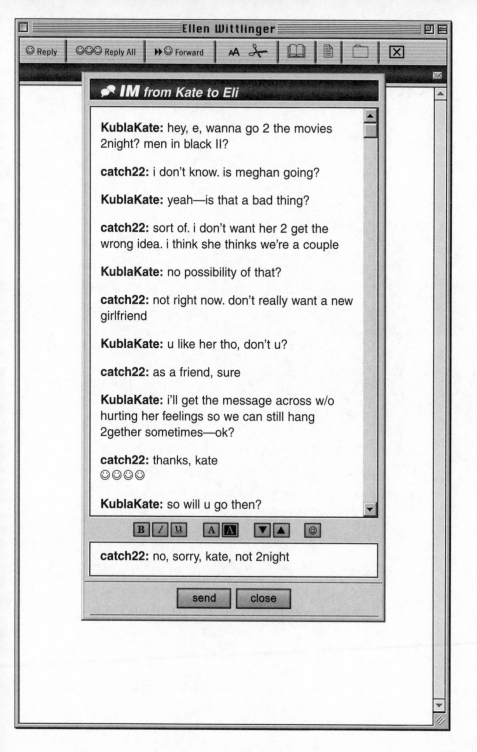

Reply   Reply All   Forward   AA   ✂   ☐ ☐ ☐   ☒

IM *from Kate to Eli*

KublaKate: hey, e, wanna go 2 the movies 2night? men in black II?

catch22: i don't know. is meghan going?

KublaKate: yeah—is that a bad thing?

catch22: sort of. i don't want her 2 get the wrong idea. i think she thinks we're a couple

KublaKate: no possibility of that?

catch22: not right now. don't really want a new girlfriend

KublaKate: u like her tho, don't u?

catch22: as a friend, sure

KublaKate: i'll get the message across w/o hurting her feelings so we can still hang 2gether sometimes—ok?

catch22: thanks, kate
☺☺☺☺

KublaKate: so will u go then?

B / u   A A   ▼ ▲   ☺

catch22: no, sorry, kate, not 2night

send   close

July 12, 2002

Dear Veer,

I just got another annoying letter from Mom (or "Mom and Daddy" as she always signs her letters, as if they were one inseparable entity). She wanted to know if I thought they'd done anything wrong to make you gay. Please tell me I can say YES. Mom says she thought for sure she and Dad had "modeled normal heterosexual behavior as much as possible." Yeah, Mom, more than most, I'd say! Please, can I tell them it was the time you caught them rolling around behind the hydrangea bushes that did it? I'll say it was the hypocrisy of that lie about spraying for aphids.

And now Mom's all excited about meeting Julian when he comes in August because her snooty friend Stell Eberhardt has heard of the Menninger Competition, which gives it a layer of importance it could never have otherwise. I don't even WANT him to meet them now. His family is normal compared to these two.

So, okay, I'm taking your advice about the gunnar problem. I guess I was being a little crazy because somebody other than YOU was running the program. Even before you pointed it out, I could tell that some of the kids really did like him, but they didn't want to get on my bad side by admitting it. So I'm being cool now. I told him if he needed help with the music, I could help him, and he was obviously relieved. I'm rehearsing the kids who have solos so they'll be up to speed in 3 weeks. I still think it's nuts to be so rigid about things, but I have to say, the plays are coming along really well, especially the musical, so I guess it's just the way he has to do it. The nun chorus sounds so great, I tear up when I hear them.

We had the BEST Spud hunt last week. You would have loved it. The kids were very creative in trying to fool us. You know how you have to leave one part of your body sticking out when you hide? Well, they all traded clothes around and painted their nails with other people's polish and wore wigs and it was great! We laughed until I thought we'd all wet our pants. (Actually, Ashley Corrigan did.)

gotta go get ready for Music Night. Our cabin is serenading with "goodnight Irene" and "The Water Is Wide." We sound awesome!

Love,

Chloe

July 23, 2002

Dear Chloe,

What a great picture of you! A kid took that? You must have a bunch of geniuses up there! I don't have a bunk to thumbtack it to so I bought an actual frame to put it in—it looks very nice on my desk. Of course, my mother came into my room, saw it, and wanted to know who you were. I try not to give her too many details of my life because she just nitpicks them to death, but I told her you were somebody I'd met the weekend I went to Cartwright. This look of annoyed enlightenment came over her face. "Oh, so <u>that's</u> why you want to go to that expensive school!" Now, I've been talking about going to Cartwright for at least a year you know what a great music program they have! Sometimes you wonder if they even listen to what you're saying. Not that it doesn't make me want to go there even more knowing that you'll be there—of course it does—but I wouldn't base my decision on something that shallow.

It's interesting to hear you talk about your camp. I guess I always thought camp would be very competitive, like gym class all day long or something. "Let's hike: First one to the top wins! Let's swim: First one across the lake wins!" That sort of thing. Maybe an arts camp is different. Skit night and Spud Hunt both sound like fun. I think it's great if your camp is a place kids can be themselves without being judged—I wish I'd found a place like that when I was a kid. I have a feeling you're the counselor all the kids want to have in their cabin. Am I right? (Hey, I'd want you in my cabin.)

When you say your sister just came out of the closet, you mean she's gay? You said it so matter-of-factly, like it wasn't a big deal, so I wasn't sure. I told you, "My sister got married," and you said, "Oh yeah, my sister's gay," like they were sort of equal. I have to admit it would blow me away to find out my sister was gay. It would be like I never even knew her. Maybe people are more casual about stuff like this in the Northeast—do I sound like a backwoods dope? I don't think I'm prejudiced against gay people, but I don't actually know any either. It weirds me out a little bit.

Anyway, my life continues to be boring as I wait to go to Boston next month. I work as many hours as possible, then hang out with Tyler (you remember him) and his sort-of girlfriend, Inga. We watch way too many old movies and eat way too much pizza. Your summer sounds much better.

Thinking of you,

Love, Julian

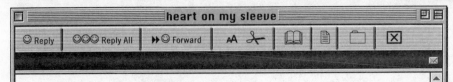

Subj: Broccoli and artichokes
Date: 7/13/02, 10:02 P.M.
From: jghost@flowire.com
To: CCinWonderland@hotmail.com

Just wanted you to know that I'm sitting here at the computer eating a huge bowl of broccoli with artichoke sauce over the top of it. Yum, yum. Later I plan to cook up a batch of eggplant and turnips, lightly sautéed with brussels sprout juice. My digestive tract is purring.

So, Colonel Mustard is in TWO bands. Two is fine; I was only going to shoot you if he was in one band. And only if it had a name like Uncle Toejam's Acid Crematorium or something. But bluegrass is good, and hey, music is MY life too. Maybe I'll actually like the guy (assuming he's around long enough). Just don't write and tell me you're in the process of stirring up some baby Custard-Mustards.

No, my entire college choice does not hinge on getting the Menninger scholarship, but if I DID get it, I could certainly go to Cartwright. Otherwise, I don't know. Mom would have to take out a million loans, and I don't think it's fair to ask her to do that right now when she's just sort of getting back on her feet again. Cartwright gave me a little scholarship money, but mostly loans. I could always go to U. of Florida for a semester or two and then transfer. Or even defer college for a year and just work. I'd feel better if I could pay some of it myself up front. And it's pretty funny to hear you talk about me not thinking things through— I'm the great thinker in the family, hon. You're the spontaneous one.

I'm not seeing as much of Nina anymore. I felt like she was getting the wrong idea. I'm VERY into Chloe, and it's too confusing to be seeing Nina at the same time. I know seeing two people simultaneously was never a problem for you, but for a sane person, it is.

Hope you got that bartender job   — Julian

July 16, 2002

Dear Chloe,

—I can't wait until we can e-mail again—this letter thing is too slow and deliberate. I feel like my words are traveling by donkey up to the wilds of New Hampshire. Okay, you <u>got</u> my letter about the July 4th party, didn't you? And about meeting all those people? And about arguing with Alice and Andrew moving out? Do you not respond to stories about my life because it makes you uncomfortable? You're the one who's afraid that you don't know me well enough, or you won't now that I'm out, but when I tell you stuff, you ignore me! This was all big deal stuff, but all you write back about is Spud Hunt! (Which I want to hear about too, but not <u>only</u>!)

—Yes, I got a nutty letter from "Mom and Daddy" too. She also asked me if they'd made any big bloopers that resulted in my gayness. I'm thinking of telling her the truth: I probably would have confessed my lesbianism even sooner if not for the passionate display of heterosexuality that was constantly thrown in my face. It made me think my own feelings were terribly wrong. I knew I could never live up to their example and I was ashamed of it. So Mom should be happy she was such a saucy wench—she kept me in the closet a few extra years anyway.

—Also, I have a feel Mums wasn't asking about Julian just because of his musical accomplishments. Seems she's worried that if I'm gay, you might be too. This is not a genetic theory but an environmental one—if they did something to ruin me, perhaps they've ruined you too. She's happy that you have a boyfriend, but, as she learned from me, that's not a reliable indicator! So you might want to put her mind at ease. Or you might not. I leave it up to you.

—I'm glad you decided to get along with Gunnar and help him with the musical. It's hell to do all that stuff alone with a bunch of little kids.

Which is why I never worried about perfection, but if he _does_, it'll be twice as much work. Is Ray helping with the scenery again? See if you can pull some people together to help this poor schmuck.

-I don't mean to keep yelling at you. It's just that my life here is so full and emotional and BIG, and when you didn't comment on anything I'd told you, I felt sort of hurt. But I know you have lots going on too. I'm not mad-I just want you to see me too. Alice and I had a great weekend. Jay was visiting some friends, so we had the apartment to ourselves. We went up to the Whitney Museum Saturday morning, then dug through a bunch of used bookstores in the afternoon. We had to work at the theater that evening-_Rosencrantz_ is up and running-but afterward we got Chinese food and a movie and snuggled in bed while we ate. Sunday we didn't get up until almost one o'clock, which was such a luxury. I think I'm finally beginning to feel like I live in New York. I'm a New Yorker!

-Go hunt some spuds for me.

-Love, Veev

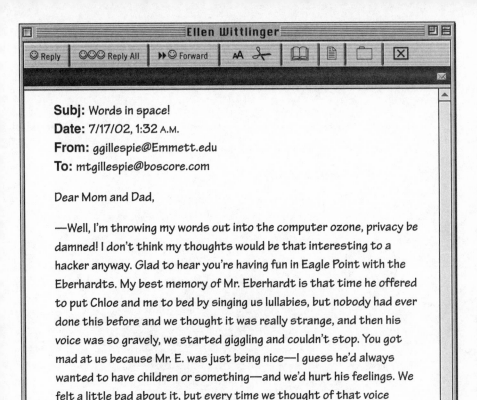

Subj: Words in space!
Date: 7/17/02, 1:32 A.M.
From: ggillespie@Emmett.edu
To: mtgillespie@boscore.com

Dear Mom and Dad,

—Well, I'm throwing my words out into the computer ozone, privacy be damned! I don't think my thoughts would be that interesting to a hacker anyway. Glad to hear you're having fun in Eagle Point with the Eberhardts. My best memory of Mr. Eberhardt is that time he offered to put Chloe and me to bed by singing us lullabies, but nobody had ever done this before and we thought it was really strange, and then his voice was so gravely, we started giggling and couldn't stop. You got mad at us because Mr. E. was just being nice—I guess he'd always wanted to have children or something—and we'd hurt his feelings. We felt a little bad about it, but every time we thought of that voice again, hysterics! Anyway, you can tell them hello from me.

—I'm not that surprised the Eberhardts have a lesbian niece. One-tenth of the population is gay, you know. I'm sure a lot of your Brimmingham friends have relatives hidden in their closets too. And no, I don't think you did anything to make me this way. People are born homosexual (or heterosexual), not made. As for Chloe, I doubt she's gay, but you'll have to talk that over with her.

—It just occured to me that the two of you might want to come down to New York to see the play I'm in. The run is from August 2 to the 25—I can get you comp tickets if you tell me ahead of time when you might be able to come. Maybe Chloe can come too. You haven't seen me in a play since high school—two years already!

—Love, Genevieve

July 19, 2002

Dear Mom and Dad,

Glad to hear you're having such a good time in Maine with Mr. and Mrs. Eberhardt. Tell them I said hello. Have you been stalking great blue herons again?

Camp is great. The new theater director is having the kids do <u>The Sound of Music</u>, which I thought they'd hate, but it turns out they love the whole schmaltzy thing. And it also looks like I'm going to have to be Mother Superior because the girl who was cast in the part slipped on the tennis court yesterday and broke her foot, so she's going home. Everybody else who wanted to be in the musical already has a part and nobody was interested in being an old nun, so I've been elected, whether I like it or not. Acting is not exactly a strength of mine, but I don't suppose it matters much in this production. At least I can hit the high notes.

You asked me whether you had anything to do with her being gay. You need to read some books. It's nobody's <u>fault</u>. She's just gay, that's all. And, in case you were wondering, I'm not. Ever since I saw Tom Cruise in <u>Jerry Maguire</u> I was quite sure of that.

Gotta go. It's time for lunch and I'm doing Lunch Music again—there are only three singer/guitarists here this year, so I'm getting a workout, but I never mind performing (unless I have to wear a habit).

Love, Chloe

I was going to get you something practical, like some towels or dishes, but then I didn't know what you might already have. And it doesn't seem like you're ready to settle into one spot yet anyway. So I thought a check would be the best way to go. Use it for something you need—not another trip to Las Vegas.

Love, Mom (May)

P.S. Welcome to our little family, Wes.

July 20, 2002

Dear Chloe,

It seems like you've been gone forever. I'm sorry I haven't written more often. I'm so tired when I get home from work I just want to collapse. Standing up all day sucks. And I HATE when people ask me how something looks on them. After awhile nothing looks good on anybody!

Well, the Meghan and Eli thing isn't working out. He's not interested in her. I guess he's not really over you yet. It's too bad because Meghan was REALLY starting to like him. She always thought he was cute—I figured you knew that. Now she's sort of pissed off at you that you could have him and don't want him when she wants him and can't have him. I'm not getting in the middle of that argument.

I DO want to meet Julian when he comes in August—I even like his name. When you told me about Genevieve I thought, well, things could be worse. At least you'll probably get married to SOMEBODY, and we can still have babies at the same time and be friends forever, right? I didn't know what to think about the whole lesbian thing at first. I talked to Eli about it—he said you'd told him too. It was strange because I always thought I knew exactly who Veev was—I sort of idolized her when we were younger—but finding this out made me think I didn't at all. It made me wonder who ELSE is gay and I don't know it yet. I guess I was sort of freaked out for awhile, but Eli calmed me down about it. He says Genevieve is the same person she always was, only now she's not keeping any secrets from us. That made me feel better.

And I DID think Veev and Alice were awfully touchy-feely for two girls. Duh! Now that I think about it I'm surprised none of us picked up on it. I guess we were just too excited about the prom, and then too upset when the flowers came from Julian. We weren't thinking about anybody else much. Are you still freaked out? I bet once you see Veev and start talking to her, it won't feel like things have changed that much. God, you two have the best sister relationship of anybody I know.

So Joey and I have been having some big talks lately too. We'll be so far apart once school starts, he thinks it makes sense for us to see other people while we're at school. Just the idea makes me sick to my stomach, but maybe I'll feel different when I get to Vermont. He says we shouldn't talk about it as "breaking up" because that's too sad and final, so we're just going to agree that we can date other people, but still consider ourselves a couple. A couple who sees other people? What does _that_ mean? Sometimes I feel like a big idiot for thinking we'd be together forever. As if sleeping with somebody is the step right before engagement. Obviously, Joey doesn't see it that way. Some days I wish I was 12 years old again.

Not TOO much longer until you're home. Thank God! I need to talk to you FACE TO FACE!

Love, Kate

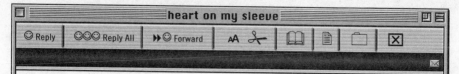

Subj: Butthead
Date: 7/20/02, 2:14 P.M.
From: smallboyonherbike@boscore.com
To: ggillespie@Emmett.edu

Hi Veev,

Your letter arrived yesterday, and I've been feeling shitty ever since. I'm so glad I get a day in town today so I can answer you right away. I am the biggest butthead. It *isn't* that I'm not interested in hearing about your life—that letter about the 4th of July party with Jennifer Jason Leigh and the David Hockney painting and American Ballet Theater—I didn't know what to say about it. It made me feel very dumb. I don't know the first thing about New York City. I couldn't find Central Park with a map and a guide dog. And here you are doing all these amazing things and meeting famous people and being in a play and watching fireworks from the director's roof and going to the Whitney and eating Chinese food in bed with your girlfriend (those last two were in the later letter, but anyway). . . . It's like you suddenly have this big grown-up life, and here I am spending another summer playing Duck Duck Goose.

But you're right, I should have said something. I was *massively* impressed by everything you said and in awe of you living in New York and being so comfortable around all those incredible people. I think of you and Alice living *Sex and the City* (without the men). And I'm sorry I haven't said it before now. Am I forgiven?

I'll assume I am since I'm your favorite (and only) sister. And now, back to Maple Hill Arts Camp, because it's the only thing I know about since I'm miles from civilization (or at least 1/2 hour from Hanover). I got Ray to say he'd get a group of his painting kids to help make the scenery for the musical, and Suzanne and Bess (counselor from Australia) are helping the kids figure out costumes.

(They got a bunch of discount bedsheets and dyed them black for the nuns.) One of the older campers has worked with theater lighting at his high school, so he'll be able to deal with our primitive system here. And during the production I'll be playing the guitar (when I'm not Mother Superior) with Suzanne on piano. At first Gunnar acted like he wasn't sure he wanted to give up his tight-assed control of the whole thing, but as soon as he saw what people were willing to do for him, he softened up like a wet sponge. I think he was actually terrified of having to do the whole thing himself, but didn't know how to ask for help. He's so much more easy-going now that he's relaxed a little bit. Maple Hill makes another convert!

Okay, I have one more thing to tell you, and I've been going back and forth all morning about whether I should or not. But I think I should because it's making me crazy. You know how I asked you about telling your friends here about you coming out, and you said I could go ahead and tell them? Well, I told Ray and Suzanne and they were very cool about it. Ray's college roommate is gay, and he said when he first met him he was a little weirded out about it, but now they're good friends, and he has to laugh at the silly ideas he had before he knew him. Suzanne knows some lesbian couples at her school too, and although she was a little surprised, it wasn't a big deal to her. I guess when you start knowing people who are gay, you stop caring so much about the differences.

So then I told Bill. I'd just finished with my singing group, and it was rest time for the kids. Bill was sitting on the picnic bench under the big maple in front of the dining hall, finishing up some kid's lanyard for him—I guess he must have made about a thousand of those things by now. So I sat down next to him and we were talking and I told him. He just stared at me for a minute, like I was making it up, and then he looked away and made sort of a *hmpf* sound. I didn't know what to say. . . . I didn't know what he was thinking, so I

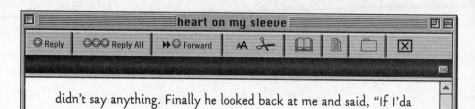

didn't say anything. Finally he looked back at me and said, "If I'da known that, she wouldn't have been a counselor for these little girls the past 3 years."

Can you believe that? I almost started to cry it hurt me so much. Then I said, "You mean you wouldn't have hired Genevieve, even though she was one of the best counselors you ever had, if you'd known she was gay?" He had the nerve to pat me on the knee, like I was such an innocent, I wouldn't understand. "I can't be too careful, Chloe," he said. "This is a sensitive business I'm running. I've got nothing against Genevieve, but these children's lives are too important to take a chance."

I jumped off that bench so fast I almost fell face first. I screamed at him, "*What* chance? If you think hiring Genevieve was taking a *chance*, you're crazy!" He just sat there shaking his head. I couldn't believe it—I ran off into the woods so I wouldn't have to talk to anybody for awhile. I was so shocked! I've always loved Bill. I always thought Bill loved *us*! How could he say something like that? I don't know what to do about it. I mean, he might not bring it up again, but I feel like I should. Like I should make him understand that you aren't a different person just because you're gay. But I don't know how to do it. I feel so betrayed, and then I think, it's not even me he said it about. Have other people acted this way when you told them, Veev? It makes me want to cry just thinking about it. Maybe I shouldn't have told you, but I don't know what to do. Just the idea that you wouldn't have been here the last 3 years if he'd known—I don't want to hate Bill, but I'm starting to.

Now I really miss you. Can I come down to NY before you leave? Maybe to see your play? I have to talk to you before I leave for school!

Love, Chloe

Subj: The Babysitter's Here
Date: 7/20/02, 3:07 P.M.
From: smallboyonherbike@boscore.com
To: jghost@flowire.com

Hi Julian,

As you can see, I'm in town again using the library computer. I really needed the break this week—about this time of the summer I start to feel overwhelmed by everything. It always happens halfway through; some of the kids are starting to have arguments—the best friends and boyfriend/girlfriend situations are starting to crack and they all want *my* advice about what to do. They start hanging on me and it makes me nuts. At the same time we're heavy into rehearsals for my choral group and the plays ("Sound of Music" is the musical—I'm helping out on it.) There's just so much going on all the time, and you can't escape it as long as you're at camp. So a day in town is a big relief.

I'm glad you liked the photograph I sent. The girl who took it is an amazing photographer already and she's only 13. It's funny that your mother thinks you want to go to Cartwright just because I'll be there. My mother is thrilled about "the boy who sent the roses," because she thinks it proves I'm not gay like my sister. Parents are always looking for ways to figure you out. Why don't they just sit down and *talk* to us for a change? Maybe we'd tell them what we're thinking. (Although, maybe not.)

No, you don't sound like a backwoods dope—there are people here who don't know what to think about my sister being gay either. For some people it's no big deal, others were freaked out at first but are getting over it (this includes me), and some people are downright hostile about it, like the camp director here who told me he never would have hired Genevieve as a counselor if he'd known she was gay because he *couldn't take a chance with the lives of the kids!* I'm so blown away by

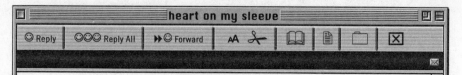

this, I don't know what to do. Veev and I have been going to this camp since she was 9 and I was 7. I would have said I knew Bill as well as I knew my own parents—and respected him more! How could he be such a bigot? This conversation is the worst thing that's ever happened to me at Maple Hill, and I'm having a hard time getting over it.

Part of it is that I'm really tired. I'd love to spend a few nights in my own bed without the midnight giggling and groaning of a bunch of little girls. But I know this is just midsummer exhaustion, and in another few weeks I'll be upset to think I'm leaving them. Happens every year. Wish I could take the weekend off though, and watch old movies and eat pizza with you and Tyler and Inga. That sounds great!

Three more weeks of camp—3 1/2 until I see you again! YES!

Love, Chloe

Subj: real life
Date: 7/21/02, 1:12 P.M.
From: CCinWonderland@hotmail.com
To: jghost@flowire.com

hey kiddo,

is there something strange going on with mom? like does she have a new boyfriend or something? did you know she sent wes and me $300 as a wedding present? i just about fell over! this is the same woman who 6 weeks ago (when i asked to *borrow* $50) told me i'd made my bed, now i had to lie in it. it's like marriage has washed away my sins. we didn't even have a ceremony or anything—i didn't even *invite* her—i didn't expect her to give us *anything*!

do you think this is another guilt trip? i know that's low. but i actually do feel guilty now, which i HATE. does she even have an extra $300? i know you said she sold a couple of houses this month—maybe that's

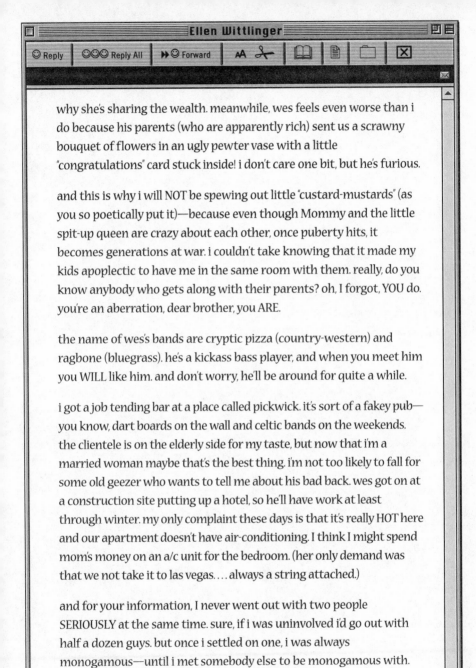

why she's sharing the wealth. meanwhile, wes feels even worse than i do because his parents (who are apparently rich) sent us a scrawny bouquet of flowers in an ugly pewter vase with a little "congratulations" card stuck inside! i don't care one bit, but he's furious.

and this is why i will NOT be spewing out little "custard-mustards" (as you so poetically put it)—because even though Mommy and the little spit-up queen are crazy about each other, once puberty hits, it becomes generations at war. i couldn't take knowing that it made my kids apoplectic to have me in the same room with them. really, do you know anybody who gets along with their parents? oh, I forgot, YOU do. you're an aberration, dear brother, you ARE.

the name of wes's bands are cryptic pizza (country-western) and ragbone (bluegrass). he's a kickass bass player, and when you meet him you WILL like him. and don't worry, he'll be around for quite a while.

i got a job tending bar at a place called pickwick. it's sort of a fakey pub—you know, dart boards on the wall and celtic bands on the weekends. the clientele is on the elderly side for my taste, but now that i'm a married woman maybe that's the best thing. i'm not too likely to fall for some old geezer who wants to tell me about his bad back. wes got on at a construction site putting up a hotel, so he'll have work at least through winter. my only complaint these days is that it's really HOT here and our apartment doesn't have air-conditioning. I think I might spend mom's money on an a/c unit for the bedroom. (her only demand was that we not take it to las vegas. . . . always a string attached.)

and for your information, I never went out with two people SERIOUSLY at the same time. sure, if i was uninvolved i'd go out with half a dozen guys. but once i settled on one, i was always monogamous—until i met somebody else to be monogamous with. but those days are over now, pal. i found my MAN.

carly

July 23, 2002

Dear Chloe,

It's taken me awhile to write back to you because I don't know what to say either. You don't need to keep apologizing to me though—I know you didn't mean to hurt me—that's just what happens when couples break up. I hope we can be friends someday too, I really do, although right now I don't think it would be very comfortable. I mean, I can hardly write you a letter—how would I sit next to you at a movie or in a restaurant? What would I talk to you about? It would be awkward and I think I'd feel like crap. I guess you do have to give up something, at least for now.

No, of course you didn't ruin my entire senior year. The prom, yes—but hey, it's just a dance. I'm not going out with Meghan. We hung out a few times, but I felt like I was trying to feel things I didn't really feel. It didn't seem fair to either of us. Besides, it's only a few weeks before we're all off to separate schools—she'll be in Ohio, and I'm ready to make a clean start in Michigan.

Kate and I had a talk about Genevieve being a lesbian. It was odd; I wouldn't have said that I suspected it, but when you told me, I wasn't all that surprised. It seemed to clear up a mystery-she always kept herself a little distant from everybody, except you, of course. Kate was a little weirded out about it, but I think talking about it helped. When people make big decisions like this, you have to respect them for it. You know they've been thinking about it for a long time, and it probably wasn't easy.

Well, I miss you too, but I kind of think there's no sense in writing for awhile. I really don't want to keep rehashing what happened. I'll e-mail you from Michigan and let you know how great the place is. (I hope.)

Love always,

Eli

HELLO, DEAR,

SO GLAD TO HEAR ABOUT YOU AND
TOM CRUISE-HE HAD ME AT "HELLO"
TOO! TOOK YOUR ADVICE AND BOUGHT
A BOOK ABOUT LESBIANS. DADDY'S
HALFWAY THROUGH A BEN FRANKLIN
BIOGRAPHY, SO I'M READING THE
IMPORTANT PARTS OUT LOUD TO HIM.
YES, THERE ARE HERONS
EVERYWHERE!

- LOVE MOM (AND DADDY)

Penobscot Bay, Maine

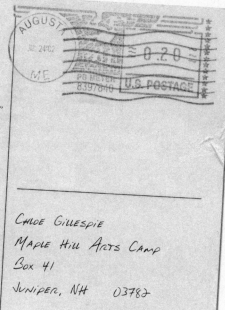

CHLOE GILLESPIE
MAPLE HILL ARTS CAMP
BOX 41
JUNIPER, NH   03782

July 26, 2002

Dear Chloe,

Your last letter sounded kind of down. I would have written sooner, but I've been putting in long hours at work again while other waiters and waitresses are on vacation getting the smell of pork fried rice out of their nostrils. Are you feeling any better by now? I can imagine it's pretty high-stress if all the kids want you to solve their problems for them. I could never stand it. I can't even deal with my OWN problems, much less help anybody else figure out their life. And those kid-relationship things are murder. They're so mean to each other—when do we grow out of that?

I've always kind of liked "The Sound of Music," but please don't ever tell anybody! I know it's mushy and sentimental and ridiculous, but those damn nuns get to me every time. We put it on in 8th grade and I was Captain Von Trapp (of course). How come you're helping out on it—I thought you hated the new theater director?

I can see why Bill's comment upset you, but he probably didn't mean anything personal about Genevieve. If he runs the place and he's responsible for all those kids, I imagine he has to be very careful who he hires. He probably just meant that if people found out he'd hired a lesbian, they might take their kids out of the camp or something. Some people are afraid of homosexuality. When you think about it, it's stupid, but most of us are sort of suspicious of people who seem different from us. How do you change that?

It's so hot here right now you hardly see people outside. It's a little baked town, right out of the oven, without even a gingerbread boy on the street. Anyway, time to shower and go to work. All I do is work. I'm crossing days off the calendar until August 14th. Hey, where's the new song?

Love, Julian

July 27, 2002

Dear Chloe,

-You aren't a butthead. I guess <u>I'm</u> the butthead, dropping names and hoping you'd be impressed. It's not like I <u>talked</u> to Jennifer Jason Leigh. I only talked to that guy nobody ever heard of. So don't apologize-I'm as self-centered as you are. Let us rejoice in our self-centeredness! (I guess it's a family trait, handed down from the you-know-whos.)

-And Duck Duck Goose is not all that different from the chasing-your-own-tail game a lot of New Yorkers play. And you <u>could</u> find Central Park if I was your guide dog, which I intend to be when you come visit us and see my play! Just let me know when you can come. I know it will be after THE BOY leaves, so probably end of August, right? Alice is looking forward to it too. Guess what? I'm getting her into <u>Buffy</u>! We rented the season one DVD-I wanted her to see it from the beginning so she'd really get it-and she did!

-Okay, the Bill thing. Lord, what an asshole. Right off let me say that I never idolized old Bill the way you did, but I can imagine what a shock this was for you. He acts like everybody's favorite uncle as long as you play by his rules, but he's a major control freak. The first year I was a counselor, when you were still a camper, he fired a counselor (remember Ed Christenson?) because the guy kept telling him there was a more efficient way to serve the meals in the dining room! It wasn't a bad idea as I recall, but just the fact that a counselor would overstep his bounds and try to take over something that was Bill's territory made him furious. I never trusted him after that, so his reaction doesn't surprise me that much.

-He said he couldn't take a chance on me, huh? That's Bill to a T. He never rocks the boat, and he doesn't like anybody else to either. I guess I've been lucky that I haven't gotten many lousy reactions when

I come out to people, although I _am_ in New York City, where it seems like half the people I meet are gay. I'm sorry you had to take the brunt of this, Chloe. Prejudice is ugly and hurtful. Thanks for standing up for me, but now you might as well forget it. You're not going to change Bill's mind about gay people-he's one of those guys who knows what he knows-he'll just keep patting you on the knee and ignoring you.

-You don't have to hate him. He's just ignorant, that's all. And the joke's on him anyway, because I _was_ a counselor there for 3 years, one of the best damn counselors he ever had.

-By the way, Mom called to say she'd bought a book, at your suggestion, and she felt she was 'broadening her education about my lifestyle.' Aren't you the smart one? If it's written in a book, Mom believes it.

-Gotta go. Be sure to give Suzanne and Ray big hugs for me. I never doubted their friendship.

-Love, Veev

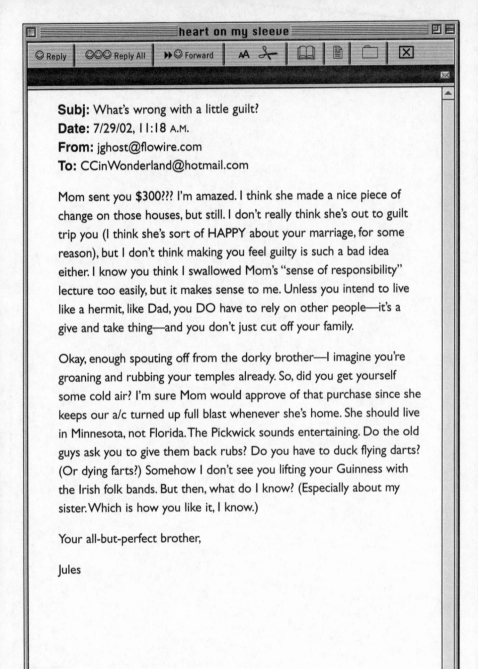

Subj: What's wrong with a little guilt?
Date: 7/29/02, 11:18 A.M.
From: jghost@flowire.com
To: CCinWonderland@hotmail.com

Mom sent you $300??? I'm amazed. I think she made a nice piece of change on those houses, but still. I don't really think she's out to guilt trip you (I think she's sort of HAPPY about your marriage, for some reason), but I don't think making you feel guilty is such a bad idea either. I know you think I swallowed Mom's "sense of responsibility" lecture too easily, but it makes sense to me. Unless you intend to live like a hermit, like Dad, you DO have to rely on other people—it's a give and take thing—and you don't just cut off your family.

Okay, enough spouting off from the dorky brother—I imagine you're groaning and rubbing your temples already. So, did you get yourself some cold air? I'm sure Mom would approve of that purchase since she keeps our a/c turned up full blast whenever she's home. She should live in Minnesota, not Florida. The Pickwick sounds entertaining. Do the old guys ask you to give them back rubs? Do you have to duck flying darts? (Or dying farts?) Somehow I don't see you lifting your Guinness with the Irish folk bands. But then, what do I know? (Especially about my sister. Which is how you like it, I know.)

Your all-but-perfect brother,

Jules

Hi Eli,

I just wanted to thank you for talking to Kate about Genevieve. What you said to her, about Keer being the same person only without secrets, helped me too. In case I never told you before, you're a great person. I won't write you again, but <u>please</u> write me from Michigan.

Love, Chloe

Maple Hill Arts Camp, Juniper, NH

Eli Mather
2 Jasper Court
Brimmingham, MA
01908

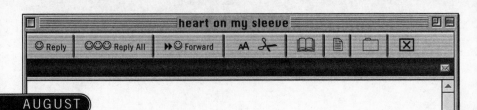

Subj: thanks
Date: 8/1/02, 3:16 P.M.
From: CCinWonderland@hotmail.com
To: maybee@flowire.com

hey mom,

just wanted to say thanks for the wedding present. i didn't expect it, especially since you'll be needing every penny to send jesus to college. we decided to buy an air-conditioner with the money because we were melting in this apartment without one. i guess it's not as hot as florida (or texas for that matter), but it's the first time in my life i've lived without a/c. what a spoiled brat, huh? (i know you'll agree with that.)

jules probably told you i got another bartending job at a pub called pickwick. and wes is working construction at least through the winter, so we're pretty much set for now. that reminds me of something i've been wondering about. when you and dad were first married, before you had kids, did you work? dad was growing weed in the backyard then, wasn't he? did he support the two of you on *that*? i don't remember knowing too much about those years.

anyway, wes says thanks too. getting a wedding present made us feel like we were really married.

Carly

August 1, 2002

Dear Kate,

god, there's only a week and two days of camp left. This year I feel so mixed up about it. Something tells me I might not be coming back here next year, which makes me just about crack up with sadness. Mostly camp is as good as ever, but I had a falling out with Bill, the director, somebody I've always admired. He's not the person I thought he was, which sort of ruins things for me. Or maybe it's just not as good being here without Genevieve.

I wish you hadn't told me that Meghan is pissed off at me. It'll be hard to act normal around her now. Oh, well, as you said, we'll all be going our own ways soon anyway. What is it with you and getting married and having babies? I mean, we have <u>years</u> before we have to think about that stuff. I don't even know if I <u>want</u> babies, although that might be because I've just spent 7 weeks wiping noses and refereeing arguments and finding lost sneakers. Kids are hard work.

I'm glad you talked to Eli about Keer. He is so sensible, isn't he? Okay, I'm just asking you this once and <u>don't tell anyone</u>. Do you think I made a big mistake breaking up with Eli? He really is a great person, and it's killing me that he doesn't even want me to write to him anymore. I feel like I've lost something very important and I don't know if I'll ever find it again. On the other hand, I'm really happy that Julian's coming to Boston, and I wouldn't be able to have Julian stay with me if I was still with Eli, so I guess it just had to happen this way. I really miss him though.

I'm sorry about what's going on with you and Joey. At least you aren't breaking up right now. Remember a few months ago when the acceptance letters were coming in and we were all so excited about getting into our schools? Why didn't it ever occur to us that in order to go to these schools we'd have to leave each other? And that that would be <u>hard</u>?

Anyway, I'll be back soon and we can talk. Oh, and I need some new T-shirts-think I'd look good in beige?

Love, Chloe

August 2, 2002

Dear Julian,

It's August! Eight more days and I'll be able to e-mail you! Twelve days and I'll actually be SEEING YOU! I'm starting to get excited now about all the big stuff coming up. For one thing, the last week of camp is always great—we do lots of special stuff and then, of course, we put on the plays and everything, once just for us and again when the parents get here. That's always SO much fun—the kids are so proud of themselves. It turns out that Gunnar, the theater director, is actually okay. He just wasn't used to a camp like this, which is sort of free-form. Some of us started helping him on the musical a few weeks ago, and now we're all pretty good friends. You know how working on a play can bind people together.

I love "The Sound of Music" now! How did this happen? I guess when you spend a lot of time with something and get past the surface of it, it's hard not to become attached to it emotionally. I even like that stupid "Do, a Deer" song! Speaking of songs, I'm still working on mine. For some reason this one is harder. I keep changing my mind about what I want to say—I've started over four times already. Maybe I'll have something to show you when you come to Boston.

You're right that a lot of people are ignorant and suspicious about anyone who's different from them, but I'm not letting Bill off the hook that easily. Because he knows Genevieve. And nobody would take their kid out of camp because of her—she won "favorite counselor" every single year she was here! Anyway, I've just been staying out of his way as much as possible. I refuse to let him ruin my summer!

So, you're coming to Boston on the 14th, right? How long can you stay? And when exactly is the contest? One day or two? Should I see about us doing an open mic on Friday or Saturday night? God, we are going to have such a great time. Especially after you WIN THE CONTEST!

Love, Chloe

Reply | Reply All | Forward | AA | ✂ | 📖 | 📄 | 📁 | ☒

💬 **IM** *from Tyler to Julian*

plexiboy: hey, thanks, man—since u and nina haven't been hanging with us, inga and i have gotten—close

jghost: what does that mean? you're finally going 2gether?!?!

jghost: btw, i only hung with u because u forced me 2

plexiboy: officially going 2gether—answer 2 my dreams—i've been crazy about inga 4 yrs ☺☺☺☺

jghost: took u long enough 2 admit it

plexiboy: didn't think she'd go 4 more than friends w/me—figured i was lucky 2 get THAT— such a BABE!!!

jghost: hope it survives college

plexiboy: all we need now is 2 get u & nina back 2gether

jghost: would u 4get about nina already!

plexiboy: can't—it would make inga soooooooo happy if u 2 started dating again

jghost: y does she care?

plexiboy: u know how girls r—they don't even go 2 the toilet alone—they wanna do everything w/their friends

B | I | U | A | A | ▼ | ▲ | ☺

jghost: sorry, babe-magnet, not my job 2 keep your gf happy—buh-bye

send | close

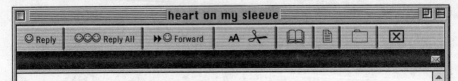

Subj: the early years
Date: 8/4/02, 7:31 P.M.
From: maybee@flowire.com
To: CCinWonderland@hotmail.com

Your father didn't grow enough marijuana in that little plot to get himself
arrested. He liked to brag about it 'cause it made him sound like such a
hippie, but he just grew enough for himself and a few friends. The only
thing he did to earn a dime was pump gas down at Rydell's Mobil a few
days a week. I worked at Eden's Pharmacy until you were born, and then I
got on his back about how he needed to do more work so I could stay
home more. He did. He got that job at the deli at Fishman's, but he hated
it from the beginning. It was downhill after that, and pretty soon I started
as a part-time secretary at the real estate office. That's old news. I'm glad
you put my gift to a good use. I guess you're no more of a spoiled brat
than most kids these days. That's just the way it is.

Mom

August 6, 2002

Dear Verr,

For some reason I'm already feeling blue about camp being over
and I still have four hectic days left. Usually I don't even
THINK about it until the first kid starts packing up, and
sometimes not until the plays are over. Maybe because the whole
thing with Bill makes me sad anyway, and I'm thinking this
might be my last summer here. Just SAYING that makes tears
run down my face. How can I never come back to MHAC again?

There are two girls in my cabin who've gotten very attached to
me-you remember, there are always a few like that-and they've
already been crying at night about leaving. Why does camp do
this to us? How come we don't cry when we leave our friends at
home who we've known for years, but when we have to say good-
bye to people we've been living with for 7 or 8 weeks, we
crumble? I guess camp is more intense because we're with each
other 24/7. But also a lot of barriers come down when you're
away from home-you let people in you wouldn't otherwise.

Speaking of which, I have a confession to make and you can't
tell anyone. It turns out I really like gunnar. I'm not sure how
it happened-I thought he was a jerk at first-but working

together the past few weeks, I've really started to like him.
When he relaxes, he's funny! And the stuff he's done with the kids
is amazing. They <u>love</u> him now—he's gotten incredible
performances from them. Anyway, I'm not going to do anything
about it, obviously, since Julian is coming in a week. Besides
which, I don't think gunnar feels the same way about me. god,
Veer, how many people are you allowed to have a crush on at
the same time? I miss Eli, I'm crazy about Julian. And now I
like gunnar too! At what point am I a nymphomaniac?

I've been trying to write another song, but I can't seem to get
it down. I think the problem is that I want to write it <u>for</u>
someone and there are too many possibilities right now. (Maybe
The Nields already wrote this song and it's called "Cowards.")

I think Julian will be here until Sunday the 18th. How about if I
come down to NYC the next weekend? That still gives me a whole
week to pack up before I leave for school. How are the Durang
plays coming? When do they open? Can't wait to see you swing a
dead rat on a NY stage! It'll be SO good to see you again. We
can both be buttheads!

Love, Chloe

AUGUSTA
AUG 05 '02
ME.
0.20
PB METER
8397840
U.S. POSTAGE

Hello, dear.

Daddy and I are packing up our things to return to Brimmingham on Thursday. The month at Eagle Point always revives me. Sailing, reading, resting, dining out with friends—would that life were always so sweet! We shall see you on Sunday afternoon. Drive safely.

Love, Mom and Daddy

Chloe Gillespie
Maple Hill Arts Camp
Box 41
Juniper, NH 03782

Wild deer in field

Hello, dear.

Daddy and I are packing up our things to return to Brimmingham on Thursday. The month at Eagle Point always revives me. I regret to say I doubt the two of us will be able to make a trip to NYC while you're there this summer, much as we would love to see your play! Break a leg for us!

Love, Mom and Daddy

Chipmunk Family

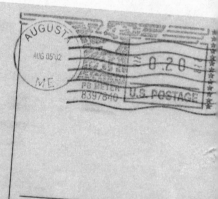

Genevieve Gillespie
401 East 5th St.
Apt. 4E
New York, NY 10003

Hey, Kiddo!

WE'RE HEADED BACK to
REALity SOON, AGAINST MY
BETTER JUDGMENT. I GUESS
YOU ARE TOO. LET US KNOW
WHEN YOU'RE COMING HOME AND
I'll THROW SOME STEAKS ON
THE GRILL.

LOVE, DAD

Black Bear

CHLOE GILLESPIE
MAPIE HILL ARTS CAMP
BOX 41
JUNIPER, NH   03782

Hey, Kiddo!

We're heading for home
this week. Mom's been
force-feeding me books
about homosexuality. Maybe
you *can* teach an old dog
new tricks. Anyway, I'm
trying to learn.

Love, Dad

Moose Bathing in Stream

Genevieve Gillespie
401 East 5th St.
Apt. 4E
New York, NY 10003

August 7, 2002

Dear Chloe,

I hope you get this before you leave on Sunday. I just had to tell you the news on paper so I don't have to say it out loud: I broke up with Joey. I just couldn't stand being around him knowing that once we left for school, he'd be with other girls. It made me crazy thinking he'd sleep with somebody else. I knew I'd be worrying about it all the time, so I just said let's end it now. The worst part is, I don't think he minded that much. I mean, he pretended to because he's a nice person, but I don't think he really did. He's tired of me. It's OVER. I can't believe it and I can't stop crying. I know this isn't the end of my life or anything, but it feels sort of that way. We've been together since freshman year. And now we're finished! I feel so lost, Chloe. I don't know what to do with myself or where to go or anything. Last night I hung out with Meghan, who's also bummed out about Eli, but at least she wasn't ever GOING with him. (I'm not blaming Joey or you-really-but I keep wondering if this is what E. feels like too. How come the two of us were so blind about this whole thing?) Meghan and I went to see <u>Spiderman</u> to take our minds off ourselves. It sort of worked.

Anyway, call me the MINUTE you get home on Sunday. I need to TALK.

Love, Kate

Hi,

I'll be home late afternoon Sunday. Don't expect me for dinner-Kate wants to see me right away-we'll get something to eat out. glad Eagle Point was relaxing. I haven't been there in so long, I barely remember it.

Love, Chloe

Downtown Juniper, New Hampshire

JUNIPER
AUG 07 '02
NH

= 0.20

PB METER
8397840   U.S. POSTAGE

The Gillespies
#2 Seaview Ave.
Brimmingham, MA
01908

August 8, 2002

Dear Chloe,

I hope this arrives before you leave. I'm getting so anxious to get to Boston! I'll arrive on Wednesday at 5:15 P.M. Can you pick me up at the airport? If not, don't worry about it—I can take a taxi. About how far is it from the airport to your house? If it's okay with you (and your parents), I'd stay until Sunday afternoon. If that's not okay, I can get a hotel room or something.

The contest is two afternoons, Thursday and Friday. Then they announce the winners around 7 P.M. Friday night at this big banquet. You can come to that with me if you want—I've got two tickets. So maybe we should do an open mic on Saturday night—that will give us time to rehearse together a little bit. I've got the words memorized, but we'll need to practice the harmonies.

Gotta get to work, but wanted to get this off today. Hope all your plays and end-of-camp stuff go well. I'm anxious to hear your new song, but I'd understand if you're having trouble finishing it. I know I always want to be _perfect_ before I perform. I imagine you're the same with your writing. See you SOON.

Love, Julian

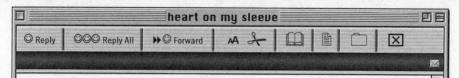

Subj: Car Wheels on a Gravel Road
Date: 8/11/02, 10:07 P.M.
From: smallboyonherbike@boscore.com
To: jghost@flowire.com

Hi Julian,

I'm home! The drive down was sort of grueling—in the summer everybody leaves New Hampshire on Sunday afternoon (which I always forget), and the lines at the toll booths are terrible. I got here about 6 o'clock and went right over to see my friend Kate, who's really upset because she broke up with her boyfriend of 4 years. It's kind of hard for me to believe it too. For so long *Kate and Joey* has been like one word. Just another of these strange changes that seem to keep happening during this weird summer between high school and college. Leaving MHAC was emotional too, so it's been an exhausting day.

But you'll be here on Wednesday, so I'm happy! Yes, of course, I'll pick you up at the airport and you can stay here until Sunday and I'll drive you back to the airport. I am at your service! And, YES, I want to go to the banquet on Friday night when your name is announced as the contest winner! We can do the open mic Saturday night at the Club Morocco in Cambridge—it's a popular club though, so we'll have to get there early to sign up. Maybe we could go to a movie at the Brattle in the afternoon.

I think you're more of a perfectionist than I am, Julian. I almost never think of my songs as "finished," and NEVER as "perfect," but I perform them anyway. I like to hear what people think. This new one just isn't coming together though—I'm not sure why.

Too tired to keep talking. Send me your flight information. I'm excited about seeing you again—hope you feel the same way!

Love, Chloe

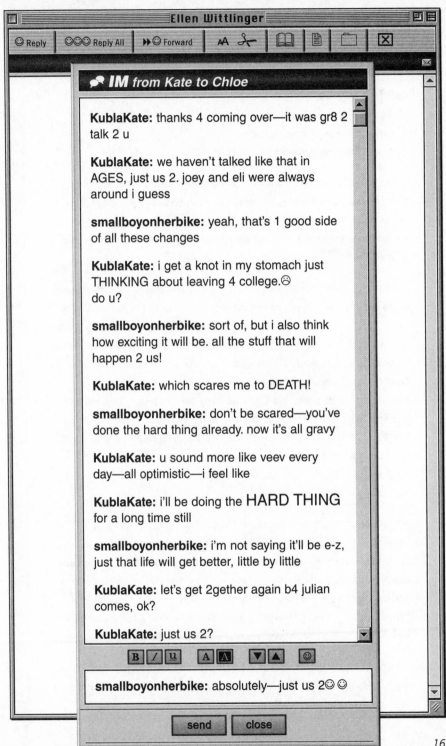

Ellen Wittlinger

💬 *IM from Kate to Chloe*

KublaKate: thanks 4 coming over—it was gr8 2 talk 2 u

KublaKate: we haven't talked like that in AGES, just us 2. joey and eli were always around i guess

smallboyonherbike: yeah, that's 1 good side of all these changes

KublaKate: i get a knot in my stomach just THINKING about leaving 4 college.☹ do u?

smallboyonherbike: sort of, but i also think how exciting it will be. all the stuff that will happen 2 us!

KublaKate: which scares me to DEATH!

smallboyonherbike: don't be scared—you've done the hard thing already. now it's all gravy

KublaKate: u sound more like veev every day—all optimistic—i feel like

KublaKate: i'll be doing the HARD THING for a long time still

smallboyonherbike: i'm not saying it'll be e-z, just that life will get better, little by little

KublaKate: let's get 2gether again b4 julian comes, ok?

KublaKate: just us 2?

B *I* u A A ▼ ▲ ☺

smallboyonherbike: absolutely—just us 2☺ ☺

send   close

167

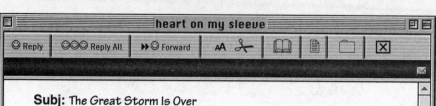
Subj: The Great Storm Is Over
Date: 8/12/02, 11:01 A.M.
From: ggillespie@Emmett.edu
To: smallboyonherbike@boscore.com

—So, what happened? How were the plays? The choral group? Did Gunnar give you a thank-you smooch or a bouquet of poison ivy? Was there the usual sobfest in the parking lot as bewildered parents wrenched their children out of your arms? How did you leave things with Bill?

—I totally remember how exhausting that last day is, so emotionally draining, after which you're expected to clean 8 weeks worth of crap out of your cabin, haul the canoes up to the shed, pack away costumes and art supplies, nail boards over the cabin windows, and lug trash out to the Dumpster. And all the while you keep remembering great things that have happened the past 8 weeks and tearing up: the kid who finally learned to swim, the one who sang her first solo, the one who cried to leave her parents at the beginning of the summer and cried to leave you at the end. Lunch Music, campfire, Skit Nights, Spud Hunt, dance nights on the tennis court with a thousand stars shining overhead. I'll never forget Maple Hill Arts Camp, even if I never lay eyes on it again.

—Here on earth, things are somewhat less lovely, but okay. The Durang plays are still a little bumpy and we open tonight. (Of course, I've mastered my small, bitchy role—more typecasting.) By the time you arrive though, all should be well. I'm so glad you can come down—not just for the show (you've seen me howl at the moon plenty of times), but because I'd like you to get to know Alice a little bit. And New York too. We'll show you everything! (Well, lots.)

—I don't think you're on the nymphomaniac track just yet. An old boyfriend, a new boyfriend, and a crush does not a perversion make.

There would be something wrong with you if you DIDN'T miss Eli—you've been with him forever, even longer than Kate's been with Joey. Although I guess you and Eli were never the out and out lovebirds those two were. Interesting that you fell for a guy who drove you crazy at first. When Alice and I met—for the script reading of *Streetcar*—I thought she was the most arrogant, annoying person on earth. Of course, she thought the same thing about me! (Hard to believe, isn't it?)

—Enjoy Julian when he's there, and don't worry about the other complications. It will all work itself out in time.

Love, Veev

Subj: Leaving on a jet plane
Date: 8/12/02, 7:02 P.M.
From: jghost@flowire.com
To: smallboyonherbike@boscore.com

Hi Chloe,

I'm so nervous today I can barely tie my shoes. It's partly about the contest, and partly about seeing you again. I hope it's as good as it was in April. I hope we have a fabulous time in Boston and I win the contest and we both go to Cartwright next month. I just keep thinking SO MUCH depends on this. Which makes me a little nauseous.

Thanks for picking me up at the airport. My Delta flight gets in at 5:15 p.m. Lots to do before I leave, so this is short.

Love, Julian

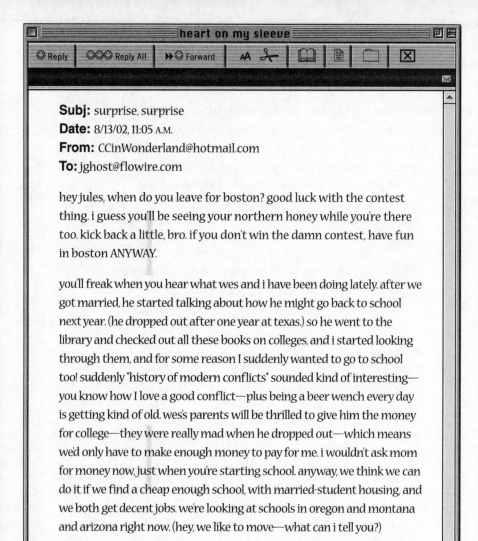

Subj: surprise, surprise
Date: 8/13/02, 11:05 A.M.
From: CCinWonderland@hotmail.com
To: jghost@flowire.com

hey jules, when do you leave for boston? good luck with the contest thing. i guess you'll be seeing your northern honey while you're there too. kick back a little, bro. if you don't win the damn contest, have fun in boston ANYWAY.

you'll freak when you hear what wes and i have been doing lately. after we got married, he started talking about how he might go back to school next year. (he dropped out after one year at texas.) so he went to the library and checked out all these books on colleges, and i started looking through them, and for some reason I suddenly wanted to go to school too! suddenly "history of modern conflicts" sounded kind of interesting— you know how I love a good conflict—plus being a beer wench every day is getting kind of old. wes's parents will be thrilled to give him the money for college—they were really mad when he dropped out—which means we'd only have to make enough money to pay for me. i wouldn't ask mom for money now, just when you're starting school. anyway, we think we can do it if we find a cheap enough school, with married-student housing, and we both get decent jobs. we're looking at schools in oregon and montana and arizona right now. (hey, we like to move—what can i tell you?)

did you know that dad used to work at fishman's deli? or that he pumped gas at rydell's garage? (mom told me.) i didn't know he ever held an actual job. sometimes i think i don't know a damn thing about mom or dad, like, who they were when they were young and happy. or maybe they were never happy. weren't hippies *supposed* to be happy? wasn't that the whole *point*?

let me know how it goes up north.

carly

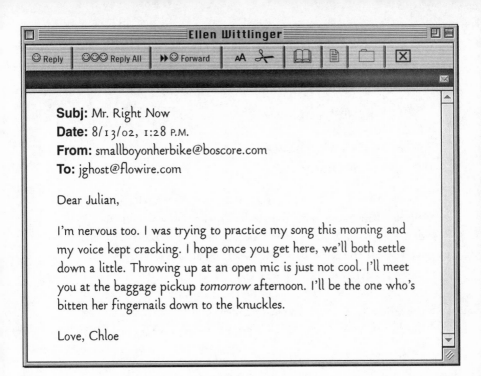

Subj: Mr. Right Now
Date: 8/13/02, 1:28 P.M.
From: smallboyonherbike@boscore.com
To: jghost@flowire.com

Dear Julian,

I'm nervous too. I was trying to practice my song this morning and my voice kept cracking. I hope once you get here, we'll both settle down a little. Throwing up at an open mic is just not cool. I'll meet you at the baggage pickup *tomorrow* afternoon. I'll be the one who's bitten her fingernails down to the knuckles.

Love, Chloe

Hi! We're all having so much fun in D.C., even my brother (who hates everything). I've never been in a big city before and I was a little scared at first, but it's GREAT. Good luck in your contest!

— Nina

Julian Casper
88 Lanning Rd.
Douglas, FL 32043

Subj: This Happens Again and Again
Date: 8/13/02, 2:02 P.M.
From: smallboyonherbike@boscore.com
To: ggillespie@Emmett.edu

Oh, my God, Genevieve, I am so messed up! I keep telling myself it's mostly about camp being over and all that emotional stuff that you described perfectly in your last e-mail, but still, what is WRONG with me? "The Sound of Music" was fabulous—the parents were all sobbing by the end when the von Trapp family carries its children over the mountains and escapes the Nazis. And the kids were euphoric afterward, and so was Gunnar, and so was I, and somehow the "thank-you smooch" turned into something a lot bigger. *Much* bigger.

After our cabins were asleep we sneaked off and met in the woods behind the Arts Barn. God, if Bill had caught us, we'd have been fired right then, even if camp *was* over the next day. Yes, I'm still a virgin, but just barely. All I lost was my mind. Veev, I've never been that excited by a boy before! I didn't even see it coming! Am I a slut or what? Gunnar didn't *make* me go out in the woods with him—I wanted to—boy, did I want to. But I still think I love Julian! Or, at least, I SOMETHING Julian. I like him a whole lot. How many people can you want to make out with at the same time? (Well, not at the same time, but you know what I mean.)

I am so confused. Julian arrives tomorrow afternoon and I can't wait to see him, but now I also feel guilty about this thing with Gunnar. I'm not even done feeling guilty about Eli yet, and already there's more guilt to pile on top of it. I keep imagining what it will be like when I first see Julian at the airport. For awhile I thought we'd run to each other and hug—isn't that what you're supposed to do when you haven't seen your boyfriend for 4 months? But *is* he my boyfriend?

What if we just stand there and stare at each other, like, *who are you*? I don't really KNOW him all that well, although it seems like I should because of the letters. I know Letter Guy, but do I really know Julian Casper?

Kate says I'm becoming more like you (which I think she means as a compliment, but I'm not 100% sure). I hope I am, because you don't get crazy the way I do. I mean, you're dramatic and all, but basically you're sane and rational and you know what you're doing. Do you know what *I'm* doing?

Chloe

Subj: Calm down
Date: 8/14/02, 2:03 A.M.
From: ggillespie@Emmett.edu
To: smallboyonherbike@boscore.com

—I don't get crazy? *Please.* Ask Alice how I was acting the week before we came home together in June. I had intended to *announce* my new status that weekend (at least to you), but I was so nervous that instead I just babbled about stupid crap the whole time we were together. Like when you asked me how big our apartment was and I thought, if I said there were only 2 bedrooms you might ask me questions about sleeping arrangements and then I'd be forced to come clean, and suddenly I wasn't ready. The opening was right there, but I chickened out. Instead I believe I launched into a dramatic monologue about Andrew's hideous taste in furniture so you'd be sidetracked by laughter. Believe me, I've walked the border of cuckooness many a time.

—Try to forget about the guilt stuff for now. I know with Eli it was awful because you'd been friends forever. But the other two you hardly even know. (Although it sounds like you made a few inroads with Gunnar! Go team Chloe!) Anyway, you don't need to beat yourself up

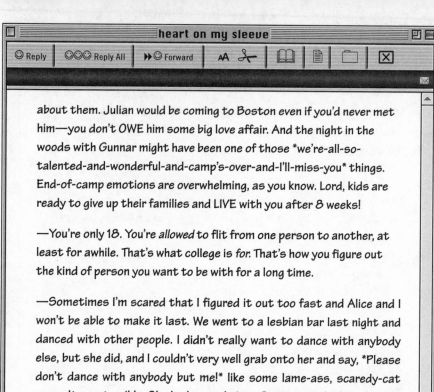

about them. Julian would be coming to Boston even if you'd never met him—you don't OWE him some big love affair. And the night in the woods with Gunnar might have been one of those *we're-all-so-talented-and-wonderful-and-camp's-over-and-I'll-miss-you* things. End-of-camp emotions are overwhelming, as you know. Lord, kids are ready to give up their families and LIVE with you after 8 weeks!

—You're only 18. You're *allowed* to flit from one person to another, at least for awhile. That's what college is *for*. That's how you figure out the kind of person you want to be with for a long time.

—Sometimes I'm scared that I figured it out too fast and Alice and I won't be able to make it last. We went to a lesbian bar last night and danced with other people. I didn't really want to dance with anybody else, but she did, and I couldn't very well grab onto her and say, *Please don't dance with anybody but me!* like some lame-ass, scaredy-cat wuss. It was terrible. She had a good time. So, you see, looking to your *sane and rational* sister for advice is not necessarily a wise move, since she spent an hour this morning hiding in the bathroom, crying. Dramatically stupid. Alice and Jay both slept late so no one even got to see my reddened eyes as I choked down coffee and an entire Entenmann's cheese coffeecake.

—So, Julian arrives. I don't know, kiddo. See how you feel when you see him. Give him a welcome kiss. (If you don't kiss him right away you'll both be way too nervous about when you're *going* to, so get it out of the way first thing.) Forget about Gunnar, for a few days anyway, and have fun. You know what the song says: "Love the one you're with."

—Veev

Subj: Fingers crossed
Date: 8/14/02, 10:24 A.M.
From: plexiboy@flowire.com
To: jghost@flowire.com

I just called your house, but I guess you left for the airport already. Wanted to say good luck—I know how much you need the scholarship money (not to mention the bragging rights). Call me when you get home and give me the final verdict: Cartwright or Florida? Chloe or Nina?

Subj: Thursday in New Jersey
Date: 8/14/02, 1:14 P.M.
From: gunnartollefson@nyuniv.edu
To: smallboyonherbike@boscore.com

Hey Chloe, I'm sitting here eating my lunch and missing the accompaniment of your voice and guitar. It's just not the same to down two hot dogs in silence. It's so weird to be home again. I can't believe we were only up there 8 weeks—it seems like a lifetime. I never went to camp as a kid, so I didn't know this would happen, but I can see why it does. The intensity of living and working with people day in and day out, and taking responsibility for the kids too—it's more intense than any experience you have in your regular life.

When I think of what an asshole I was those first few weeks, I want to shrivel up and blow away. Thank you for not giving up on me. I just didn't get it, the whole camp thing, but you helped me figure out what it was about. I was all into teach-these-kids-a-thing-or-two-about-discipline. But that's not how Maple Hill works. It's funny—I actually feel kind of sorry for my kid-self that he didn't get to go to a great camp like Maple Hill and cool out for a few summers. Maybe I wouldn't be such an aggressive jerk now!

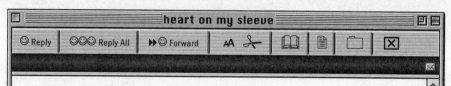
Anyway, I miss you. I'm so glad you gave me a copy of *To Fly*
before you left. It's a knockout song and when I read it, I can
hear you singing it. I hope I'll get to hear you sing it again in
person before too long. Cartwright isn't that far from NYC, you
know. Maybe we can get together after school starts. Don't forget
about me.

Gunnar

Subj: The Bottom of a River
Date: 8/19/02, 11:56 A.M.
From: smallboyonherbike@boscore.com
To: ggillespie@Emmett.edu

Genevieve!

Why aren't you HERE?! How can I possibly explain the entire last 4
days so that you understand just how screwed up I am? I tried to call
you last night, but you were out, and I didn't want to leave a
message because it would have been something like, *Call your sister
before she drowns herself in the bathtub.* Instead I slept about 12
hours and now I feel like death warmed over and I'm ready to spill
the whole sad story out in black and white.

Julian got here Wednesday afternoon, which seems like a month ago
already. I picked him up at Logan and, as you suggested, gave him
mouth-to-mouth in front of three hundred strangers. He kissed back.
So far, so good. We walked to the parking garage with our arms
around each other's waists and I thought everything would be okay.
Big relief. When we got home, Mom and Dad made poached salmon
with some fancy sauce and put fresh flowers on the table and
basically treated Julian like some kind of celebrity, which I thought
was really odd. (I figured they'd go out and we'd order a pizza or
something.) I can't remember them ever paying attention to any of

our other friends, but I think you're right; this is some kind of positive reinforcement for my not being a lesbian. Dinner was awkward, but what did I expect? Mom grilled Julian about whether he liked her cooking (which made him lie) and then about his contest (which made him nervous). As usual, Dad let Mom handle the conversation once he'd made his obligatory remarks about the Red Sox. (Has he ever even gone to a game? Do grown men *have* to pretend to like baseball?)

Once that ordeal was over, they disappeared and Julian and I went for a walk and had a decent talk. It was fine, but I kept thinking, *Who is this guy again?* I mean, writing to him I had this image in my head which maybe got bigger than the actual person. Not an image of what he looked like, but an image of how he acted and talked. How much he *liked* me. Does that make sense? In person he was shorter than I remembered too, as if my memory had totally blown him out of proportion. He was also quieter than he'd been at Cartwright, and we did *not* laugh and smooch and have a fabulous time. When I thanked him again for sending the roses (I was running low on conversation starters) he said he'd gotten the idea from his boss at the Chinese restaurant. I guess that guy always gets them for his wife if she's mad at him. Why did he have to tell me that? I realize a dozen roses isn't exactly an original idea, but still, I thought he'd come up with it himself.

So, okay, Thursday and Friday he was gone most of the day at the contest at the Conservatory in Boston. I drove him to the train and gave him directions, and he called me again to pick him up afterward. Thursday night he was hyper; he regaled M & T with stories of every single other person who was in the contest, where they were from, how good they sounded, what the auditorium looked like, who the judges were, what songs everyone sang. Literally. We sat there through salad, pasta, lamb chops, coffee, and ice cream, and

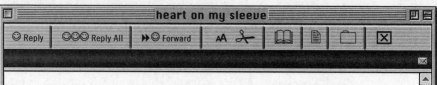

nobody else got a word in edgewise. But he wasn't exactly telling *us* about it; it was more like he was reminding *himself* about the incredible day he'd had. Like we didn't even need to *be* there.

Friday I was supposed to meet him at 6 o'clock for the banquet where the awards would be announced. The dinner was at the Copley Plaza Hotel, very swanky, so I got dolled up as best I could (without your help) and drove into the city. Julian was so nervous by then he couldn't talk *at all*. I kept trying to ask him how the day went, but he just grunted at me. Long story short: Okay, not all that short, but he didn't win the big prize. HOWEVER, he won second prize for the tenors! Which is pretty amazing, don't you think? I mean, there were about 200 kids from all over the country competing in this thing, and he won a second prize! The second prize winners all get $10,000 college scholarships. I was so excited when they called his name, I leaned over and gave him a big hug. He just looked at me with these glazed-over eyes like he didn't know who I was!

All downhill from there. He was in a huge funk! I kept saying, *You won! You won!* but he wasn't buying it. He hadn't won the BIG ONE. He did apologize to me once and said he was sorry for being so upset about it, but it meant he probably couldn't go to Cartwright now. I couldn't believe it! I thought he was *definitely* going to Cartwright—I didn't know he had to win some big impossible contest before he could go!

Saturday we tried to rehearse for the open mic at Club Morocco. He'd been practicing my song *To Fly,* but he had such a different take on it than I do—it sounded like we were singing two entirely different songs. He has a very dramatic voice. It's gorgeous, of course, but my song is more of a folk song—you don't need to throw it at the audience, you just hand it to them. He was singing so loud

and so *wrong* that you couldn't even hear my voice! Finally I got sort of mad and told him, half-jokingly, maybe we should each sing our own stuff at the open mic. Then *he* said, he thought he was doing me a favor by learning my song, but he was tired of singing anyway, after the big contest and all, so I could do it myself!

By that time I just wanted him to leave. We went to the club and I did the open mic, but I could tell he was hardly even listening. I sang *To Fly* and *Romeo* by Jess Klein because that's what I'd practiced. Meanwhile, *my* Romeo kept looking at his watch, obviously bored, and when I was finished, we left. Sunday morning was equally dismal. I took him to the beach at Clayton Head, and he just kept comparing it to some crummy beach in Florida. You *know* there's no place as beautiful as Clayton Head. He stuck one toe in the water and screamed about how freezing cold it was, which made me so mad that I jumped in and swam around for about 15 minutes just to show him. It *was* freezing, of course, and it took me the rest of the day to warm up again.

By the time I drove him back to the airport we were barely speaking. What happened here? We DID have a fabulous time together at Cartwright—I'm not dreaming that! How could he change so completely in a few months' time? I feel like I'm a crazy person or something. Why was I so completely gone on this guy? And now I feel twice as bad about what happened with Eli—he got hurt for nothing. And forget about Gunnar! I'm never writing to a potential boyfriend ever again. No more long-distance loverboys. I'll only get crushes on people who live within 5 miles!

Do I have really terrible judgement or what? I hope he DOESN'T show up at Cartwright now. I don't want to be constantly reminded of what a fool I was. (Meanwhile, M & T didn't pick up on anything; they told me he was *a real winner,* and they hoped I

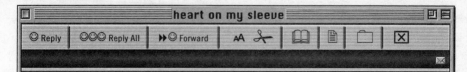
held on to him. I didn't even bother to explain it to them.)

Here I go again, pages and pages about me. I'm sorry that Alice danced with somebody else. I'm sure it didn't mean anything. She came home with *you*! Don't cry and don't eat another coffeecake. Or wait until I get to NYC and we can boo-hoo and load carbs together!

Your desperate and deranged sister,

Chloe

Subj: What do women want?
Date: 8/19/02, 3:31 P.M.
From: jghost@flowire.com
To: CCinWonderland@hotmail.com

Hey, since you asked: I didn't pass Go, I didn't win the contest, and I didn't collect $25,000. I did win second prize for tenors, however, which is a $10,000 scholarship. I'm so confused about the whole weekend, I don't even know if I'm happy about winning or not. Nothing went the way I thought it would from the minute I got to Boston.

First of all, Chloe seemed very different from how I remembered her. Nice, but really aggressive. She planted a big wet one on me the minute she saw me, and I don't know what she told her parents, but they treated me like I was their new son-in-law or something. They're really rich, which I also didn't expect, and it made me feel funny about her. Their house is enormous and she drives her own brand-new little Saab. She didn't seem rich when we met at Cartwright.

I was really nervous about the contest, and I could tell Chloe was not happy that I wasn't jabbering away at her constantly—that's just not me, you know? So, the second day I really tried—at dinner I told them all about what had happened at the contest, but her Dad started yawning and even Chloe kept looking up at the clock! I kept thinking,

What am I doing here? I don't even know these people. C. was with me at the banquet when they announced the winners. They announced them in backward order, so when my name was announced as the second-place tenor, I was sort of happy, but I also realized that now I wasn't going to win the big prize. I felt sort of numb—I didn't know how to feel. Chloe started jumping on me and screaming, *You won! You won!* It was totally embarrassing.

We couldn't even sing together, which was what I think I was most excited about with her. Usually, I just don't know how to act with girls, but Chloe and I hit it off really well, I think, because we're both singers and that made me less nervous. So I practiced this song she wrote so we could do it together at an open mic in Cambridge. It wasn't some terrific song to begin with, but it was okay and I thought I had a really good take on it, but she was all upset that I wasn't doing it *her* way or something. So I just gave up and let her sing it by herself. I was pretty pissed off by that time, so I wasn't going to drip all over her about how great she sounded. The whole idea had been to sing it *together.*

Sunday morning we went to her local beach—pristine white sand surrounded by mansions, with about three people tanning their well-groomed bodies on it (including one of her rich girlfriends who came over to check me out). I'm telling you, the fish probably have to get special permits to swim at this place. I couldn't help thinking how Chloe could afford to go to any college she wanted to, so obviously she had no clue how much getting a scholarship meant to me. We're so *different.*

I'm sort of confused about everything. Women, for one thing. But then I've always been confused about that species. I doubt I'll ever have a girlfriend. And school for another. I COULD still go to Cartwright—the $10,000 is a good start and I have $2,000 from the District win. I could take out loans and work, but now I don't know. Do I really want to be at a school with a bunch of rich kids? Or maybe I mean, do I want to

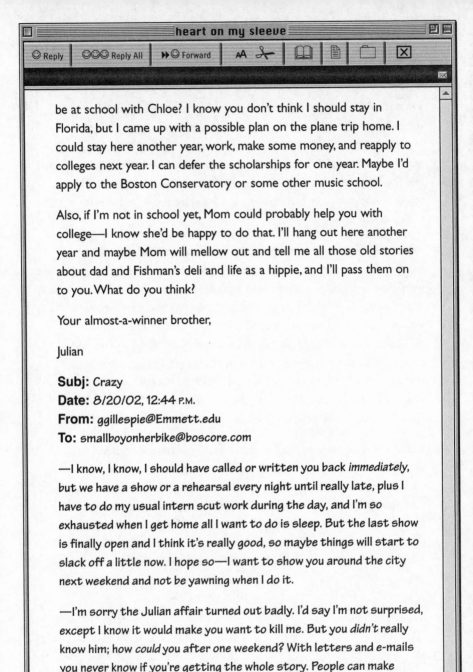

be at school with Chloe? I know you don't think I should stay in Florida, but I came up with a possible plan on the plane trip home. I could stay here another year, work, make some money, and reapply to colleges next year. I can defer the scholarships for one year. Maybe I'd apply to the Boston Conservatory or some other music school.

Also, if I'm not in school yet, Mom could probably help you with college—I know she'd be happy to do that. I'll hang out here another year and maybe Mom will mellow out and tell me all those old stories about dad and Fishman's deli and life as a hippie, and I'll pass them on to you. What do you think?

Your almost-a-winner brother,

Julian

Subj: Crazy
Date: 8/20/02, 12:44 P.M.
From: ggillespie@Emmett.edu
To: smallboyonherbike@boscore.com

—I know, I know, I should have called or written you back *immediately*, but we have a show or a rehearsal every night until really late, plus I have to do my usual intern scut work during the day, and I'm so exhausted when I get home all I want to do is sleep. But the last show is finally open and I think it's really good, so maybe things will start to slack off a little now. I hope so—I want to show you around the city next weekend and not be yawning when I do it.

—I'm sorry the Julian affair turned out badly. I'd say I'm not surprised, except I know it would make you want to kill me. But you *didn't* really know him; how *could* you after one weekend? With letters and e-mails you never know if you're getting the whole story. People can make themselves sound better than they really are, or worse; you have to *know* them before you know how to read the letter!

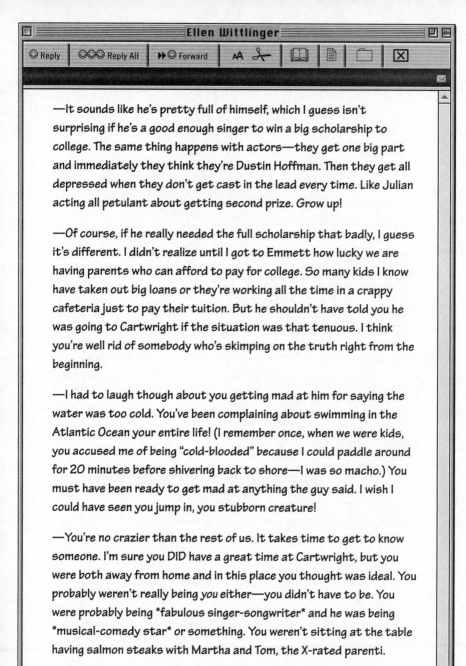

—It sounds like he's pretty full of himself, which I guess isn't surprising if he's a good enough singer to win a big scholarship to college. The same thing happens with actors—they get one big part and immediately they think they're Dustin Hoffman. Then they get all depressed when they don't get cast in the lead every time. Like Julian acting all petulant about getting second prize. Grow up!

—Of course, if he really needed the full scholarship that badly, I guess it's different. I didn't realize until I got to Emmett how lucky we are having parents who can afford to pay for college. So many kids I know have taken out big loans or they're working all the time in a crappy cafeteria just to pay their tuition. But he shouldn't have told you he was going to Cartwright if the situation was that tenuous. I think you're well rid of somebody who's skimping on the truth right from the beginning.

—I had to laugh though about you getting mad at him for saying the water was too cold. You've been complaining about swimming in the Atlantic Ocean your entire life! (I remember once, when we were kids, you accused me of being "cold-blooded" because I could paddle around for 20 minutes before shivering back to shore—I was so macho.) You must have been ready to get mad at anything the guy said. I wish I could have seen you jump in, you stubborn creature!

—You're no crazier than the rest of us. It takes time to get to know someone. I'm sure you DID have a great time at Cartwright, but you were both away from home and in this place you thought was ideal. You probably weren't really being *you* either—you didn't have to be. You were probably being *fabulous singer-songwriter* and he was being *musical-comedy star* or something. You weren't sitting at the table having salmon steaks with Martha and Tom, the X-rated parenti.

—This has nothing to do with your judgment. If you'd met Julian at college and been around him continually, you'd probably have realized in a week or so you weren't that nuts about him and just drifted apart. It was the letters that made you think you were *in love.* However, you were around Gunnar for 8 weeks and you liked him more, not less, during that time, so the situations are not at all the same. Which is not to say you should get into another long-distance thing—not saying that at all—just pointing out that your judgment with Gunnar was probably fine.

—Alice and I are good. We talked about the dancing-at-the-bar thing. She said we wouldn't go back there if it made me uncomfortable, and then I felt bad about it because she'd had so much fun there, so I said of course we'd go back again, but so far we haven't. Relationships are complicated.

—I'll meet you at Penn Station. Come on the train that gets in at 4:30 Friday. I'll buy you a Krispy Kreme donut before we even leave the station. It's going to be so much fun to have you here—we shall wipe out all memory of the dastardly Julian!

—Veev

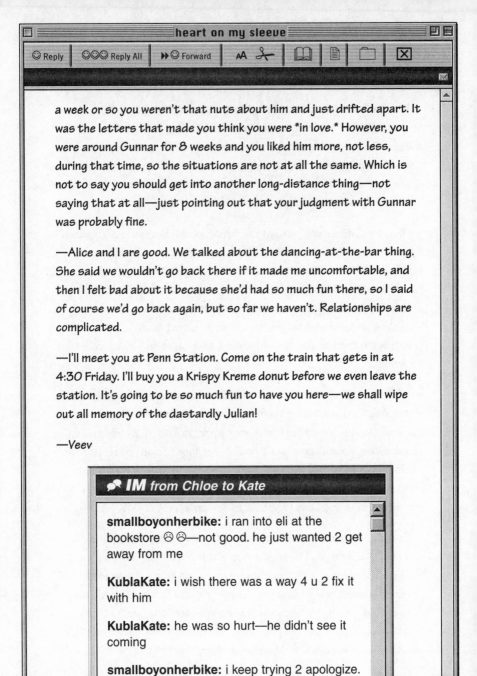

IM *from Chloe to Kate*

smallboyonherbike: i ran into eli at the bookstore ☹ ☹—not good. he just wanted 2 get away from me

KublaKate: i wish there was a way 4 u 2 fix it with him

KublaKate: he was so hurt—he didn't see it coming

smallboyonherbike: i keep trying 2 apologize. it's the only thing i can think of 2 do but he keeps telling me not 2

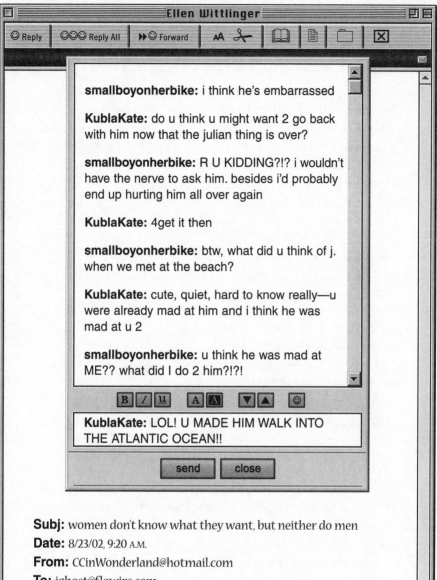

© Reply ©©© Reply All ▶▶© Forward AA ✂ 📖 📄 📁 ☒

smallboyonherbike: i think he's embarrassed

KublaKate: do u think u might want 2 go back with him now that the julian thing is over?

smallboyonherbike: R U KIDDING?!? i wouldn't have the nerve to ask him. besides i'd probably end up hurting him all over again

KublaKate: 4get it then

smallboyonherbike: btw, what did u think of j. when we met at the beach?

KublaKate: cute, quiet, hard to know really—u were already mad at him and i think he was mad at u 2

smallboyonherbike: u think he was mad at ME?? what did I do 2 him?!?!

B I U A A ▼ ▲ ☺

KublaKate: LOL! U MADE HIM WALK INTO THE ATLANTIC OCEAN!!

send   close

Subj: women don't know what they want, but neither do men
Date: 8/23/02, 9:20 A.M.
From: CCinWonderland@hotmail.com
To: jghost@flowire.com

sorry to hear about your lousy visit to boston. but hey, jules, second prize is nothing to sneeze at! you won $10,000! i've never won a damn thing in my whole life (unless you count a pink stuffed frog I won at a fair once). you're like a professional singer now, which is quite awesome!

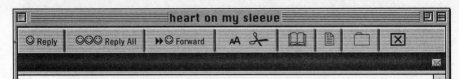

so the chloe thing didn't work out—what were the chances anyway? check her off the list. although you've gotta get over the whole rich/poor hang-up. you didn't KNOW she was rich before you got there, so she must not act snotty about it. maybe you ARE really different from her, but not because she's got money. so she drives a new car— she got lucky. (wes's parents have money too, but they don't give him much of it—you can't blame somebody for their parents.) anyway, you aren't in high school anymore, where it makes such a big difference who has a pool in their backyard and who has a 1982 ford up on blocks. you're not just mom's little boy—you're whatever you say you are. just because she grew up in a bigger house than you doesn't mean chloe is somehow BETTER than you. do i really have to tell you this?

and the never-have-a-girlfriend dirge? enough already. you don't even try. You only made an effort with chloe for 3 days, then worked it into a big deal long distance. you've got nina greco right there in town and you ignore her. why? she's a nice girl (with great knockers) and she likes you! i think you're a big chickenshit, jules. let's hang up the poor-me attitude and get out there and see what happens for a change, huh?

now i DO like your new idea about school, although mom will flip when she finds out you aren't headed straight for college—she'll think you're about to pull a CC trick. but since you're screwed-up about where to go anyway, you might as well hold off a year and rethink your options. unlike your ne'er-do-well sister, you'll probably be able to save a good portion of the money you earn so you can actually pay for college once you get there. of course it does mean another year in florida, but obviously the place doesn't make your hair stand on end like it does mine. and nina greco is going to state, isn't she? convenient.

wes and i have decided to take a couple of courses at the university of colorado as long as we're right here. Then, if school agrees with us, we'll think about transferring someplace else later on. This way we can work full time while we take classes. Can you believe it—me, a multi-tasker?

hey, jules, if you aren't a winner, i don't know who is.

carly

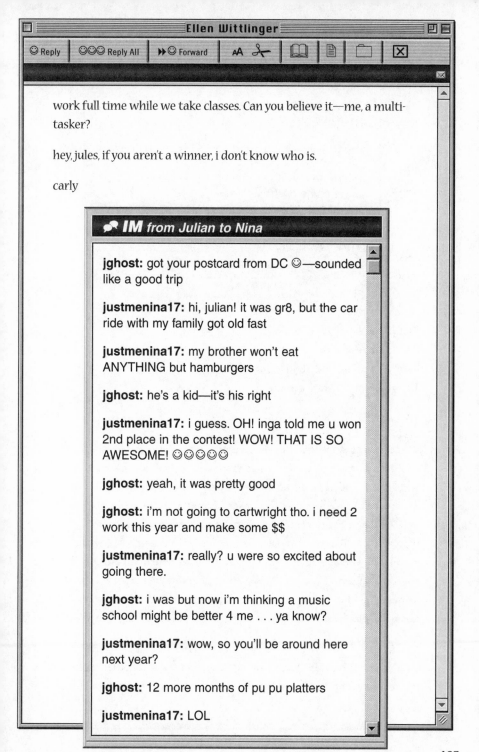

IM *from Julian to Nina*

jghost: got your postcard from DC ☺—sounded like a good trip

justmenina17: hi, julian! it was gr8, but the car ride with my family got old fast

justmenina17: my brother won't eat ANYTHING but hamburgers

jghost: he's a kid—it's his right

justmenina17: i guess. OH! inga told me u won 2nd place in the contest! WOW! THAT IS SO AWESOME! ☺☺☺☺☺

jghost: yeah, it was pretty good

jghost: i'm not going to cartwright tho. i need 2 work this year and make some $$

justmenina17: really? u were so excited about going there.

jghost: i was but now i'm thinking a music school might be better 4 me . . . ya know?

justmenina17: wow, so you'll be around here next year?

jghost: 12 more months of pu pu platters

justmenina17: LOL

justmenina17: maybe we could hang out sometime

jghost: sure—what are u doing this afternoon?

justmenina17: now? ummm . . . nothing—wanna come over?

B / u A A ▼ ▲ ☺

jghost: yeah, i really do

send   close

Subj: Power of Two
Date: 8/26/02, 10:56 P.M.
From: smallboyonherbike@boscore.com
To: ggillespie@Emmett.edu

Veev—

What a great weekend! I have to admit I was a *little bit* nervous about staying with you and Alice (and Jay). I don't know exactly why, maybe because I'd be in the minority as the lone heterosexual, but more, I think, because I've never been around you before when you were in a relationship with somebody. I think I thought you wouldn't act like the same old Genevieve. Or you and Alice would act like newlyweds or something and it would be embarrassing. Of course, that didn't happen. Well, you did kiss her goodnight in front of me once, but by then it seemed natural and I didn't even think about it until later.

I *really* like Alice, Veev. She's so much fun and so smart—I hope you stay with her forever! Just watching the two of you together made me feel so dumb for that whole fantasy thing I had going with Julian.

A relationship needs to be based on the day-to-day stuff, not just a couple days of locking lips. Looking back, I feel sort of bad about all the expectations I put on him. In my mind I'd turned him into a cross between Matthew Broderick and the young Fox Mulder. Sweet but mysterious, with a great voice. He *was* sort of shy and quiet when I met him at Cartwright, but my imagination turned him into a confident, big-hearted guy who'd stride off the plane and bowl me over. It's not his fault that's not who he is.

It was those damn roses. Not only did they screw up my relationship with Eli (which when I think about it was, day to day, pretty good), but they gave me the impression Julian was a romantic, someone who'd take a chance, leap at love! Not somebody who'd pout for three days because he was only the second best 18-year-old tenor in the country.

I know, you're right, he really needed the scholarship and I have no idea what that's like. You're right, you're right, you're always right. And, BTW, you were *fantastic* in the play. Have I told you that a hundred times yet? I laughed the minute you came on stage. And I loved taking the ferry to Ellis Island, and going to the Guggenheim Museum, and having dinner at that Turkish restaurant, and spending an afternoon at the Strand bookstore and meeting the almost-famous people at the theater, and seeing Mia Farrow in Central Park, and reading the *Times* on Sunday morning, and every single minute of the whole weekend! You fit in New York so well, I can hardly imagine you going back to Emmett now. Or maybe I just mean I want to come visit you in NYC again!

We leave Saturday morning for Cartwright. I'm taking my car and Mom and Dad are driving down in the minivan to bring the heavy stuff. I can't believe the summer is over and I'm really going! Suddenly I'm nervous. Did you feel like that before you started at Emmett?

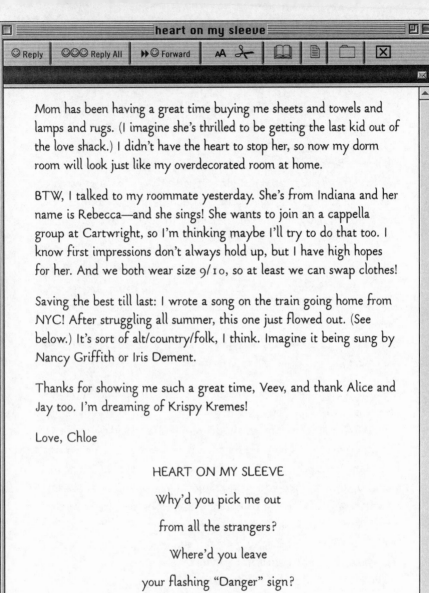

Mom has been having a great time buying me sheets and towels and lamps and rugs. (I imagine she's thrilled to be getting the last kid out of the love shack.) I didn't have the heart to stop her, so now my dorm room will look just like my overdecorated room at home.

BTW, I talked to my roommate yesterday. She's from Indiana and her name is Rebecca—and she sings! She wants to join an a cappella group at Cartwright, so I'm thinking maybe I'll try to do that too. I know first impressions don't always hold up, but I have high hopes for her. And we both wear size 9/10, so at least we can swap clothes!

Saving the best till last: I wrote a song on the train going home from NYC! After struggling all summer, this one just flowed out. (See below.) It's sort of alt/country/folk, I think. Imagine it being sung by Nancy Griffith or Iris Dement.

Thanks for showing me such a great time, Veev, and thank Alice and Jay too. I'm dreaming of Krispy Kremes!

Love, Chloe

HEART ON MY SLEEVE

Why'd you pick me out

from all the strangers?

Where'd you leave

your flashing "Danger" sign?

Who put the words

in your mouth I believed?

Who tattooed

your heart on my sleeve?

Reply   Reply All   Forward   AA

Sleeve, sleeve,

roll it down,

cover up,

all gone,

all alone,

throw a stone,

break a cup—

now I'm all grown up.

How'd you go

from Nobody to First Prize?

Who'd a guessed

that we could harmonize?

Why'd I think

you would never leave me?

Who tattooed

your heart on my sleeve?

Sleeve, sleeve,

roll it down,

cover up,

all gone,

all alone,

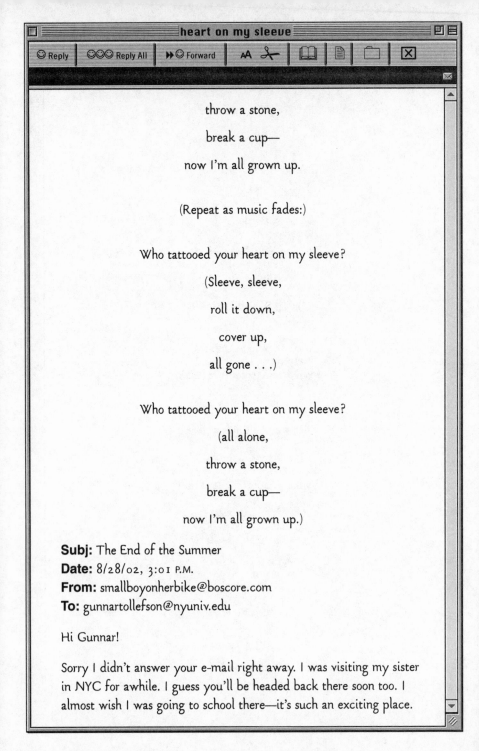

throw a stone,

break a cup—

now I'm all grown up.

(Repeat as music fades:)

Who tattooed your heart on my sleeve?

(Sleeve, sleeve,

roll it down,

cover up,

all gone . . .)

Who tattooed your heart on my sleeve?

(all alone,

throw a stone,

break a cup—

now I'm all grown up.)

Subj: The End of the Summer
Date: 8/28/02, 3:01 P.M.
From: smallboyonherbike@boscore.com
To: gunnartollefson@nyuniv.edu

Hi Gunnar!

Sorry I didn't answer your e-mail right away. I was visiting my sister in NYC for awhile. I guess you'll be headed back there soon too. I almost wish I was going to school there—it's such an exciting place.

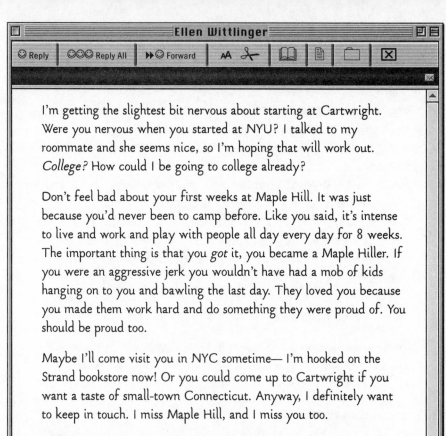

I'm getting the slightest bit nervous about starting at Cartwright. Were you nervous when you started at NYU? I talked to my roommate and she seems nice, so I'm hoping that will work out. *College?* How could I be going to college already?

Don't feel bad about your first weeks at Maple Hill. It was just because you'd never been to camp before. Like you said, it's intense to live and work and play with people all day every day for 8 weeks. The important thing is that you *got* it, you became a Maple Hiller. If you were an aggressive jerk you wouldn't have had a mob of kids hanging on to you and bawling the last day. They loved you because you made them work hard and do something they were proud of. You should be proud too.

Maybe I'll come visit you in NYC sometime— I'm hooked on the Strand bookstore now! Or you could come up to Cartwright if you want a taste of small-town Connecticut. Anyway, I definitely want to keep in touch. I miss Maple Hill, and I miss you too.

Chloe, soon to be known as chloegillespie@Cartwright.edu.

Subj: Life goes on . . .
Date: 8/30/02, 12:32 A.M.
From: jghost@flowire.com
To: CCinWonderland@hotmail.com

Hey, CC,

So, in between shifts at The Ginger Tree I've been filling out forms: some to defer my acceptance to Cartwright, just in case I decide to go there after all, some to defer my Menninger Foundation scholarships until next year, and some to apply to the Boston Conservatory, the New England Conservatory, Oberlin, and Juilliard. Hey, what the hell—I might as well try. Mom is actually okay with it—she knows I'll go somewhere next year, and I think she's sort of glad not to be alone just yet.

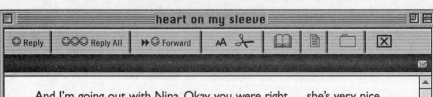

And I'm going out with Nina. Okay, you were right ... she's very nice and she likes me. (You will now kindly refrain from referring to her *knockers.*) It's not too hard to take having Nina like me after the cold reception I got from Chloe in Boston. When I think back on it though, I should never have tried to combine the contest with seeing her. I was so strung out about both things, I couldn't really do justice to either of them. Not that I'm blaming her for not winning the contest. I never thought I *would* win, until I got there, and then suddenly I just wanted it so badly I thought I *had* to win. And the contest definitely got in the way of being with Chloe. I somehow got it in my mind that *her* whole goal for the week was for me to win too! Stupid, huh? She probably would rather have spent the week swimming in that frigid ocean up there.

Anyway, I guess I learned something from the experience. Don't assume you know somebody *you don't know*! A second lesson might be: Listen to your sister when she tells you about girls. Nah!

Hey, it's great about you and Wes taking classes at the university. What are you taking? Who'd have thought YOU'D be starting college this year and not me? Hope it agrees with you.

Jules

Ellen Wittlinger

Reply | Reply All | Forward | AA | ✂ | 📖 | 📄 | 📁 | ✕

Subj: So, tell me
Date: 9/1/02, 11:31 A.M.
From: ggillespie@Emmett.edu
To: chloegillespie@Cartwright.edu

—How's it feel to be a college student? Are you all moved in? How many males do you have to share a bathroom with? (Very important question.) How's Rebecca the roomie? Are your sheets color-coordinated with hers? How fast did Martha and Tom peel out of the parking lot once they'd dumped your baggage on the curb? Tell all!

—Mostly writing to say your new song is kickass! I think this one steps into new territory. I CANNOT wait to hear you sing it. Really—WOW!

—Starting to pack here too, which is hard. Such a great summer! Alice and I are living together in an apartment off-campus this year, so at least we don't have to separate our stuff—just throw it all in together. I'll really miss Jay though. We're thinking maybe next summer we can do it all again. The Durang play finishes tonight and we'll be celebrating late I'm sure. Then tomorrow is the big push so we can leave here on Tuesday to make registration the next day. Ugh. I'm not in the mood for the realities of school.

—Lots to do today, but e-mail me before I leave. I'm dying to hear about Cartwright. Julian didn't show up, did he? Who are you meeting? Isn't it nice to be on your own? I hope your freshman roommate is better than mine was—remember her?—with the boyfriend who came to visit every weekend? If you think living with Martha and Tom is bad . . .

—Love, Veev

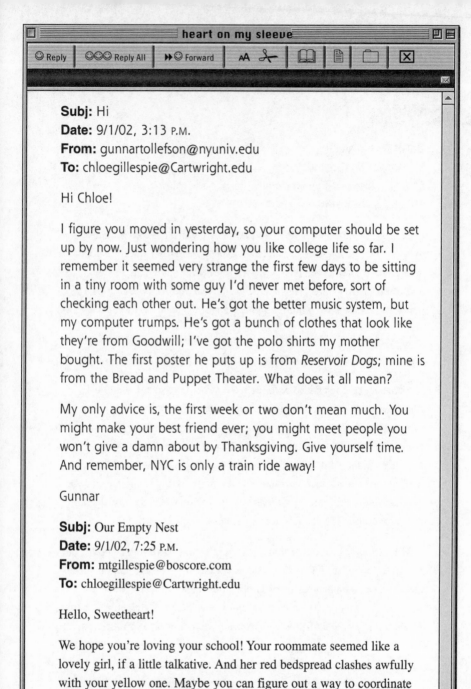

⊙ Reply ⊙⊙⊙ Reply All ▶▶⊙ Forward ᴀA ✂ 📖 📄 📁 ☒

Subj: Hi
Date: 9/1/02, 3:13 P.M.
From: gunnartollefson@nyuniv.edu
To: chloegillespie@Cartwright.edu

Hi Chloe!

I figure you moved in yesterday, so your computer should be set up by now. Just wondering how you like college life so far. I remember it seemed very strange the first few days to be sitting in a tiny room with some guy I'd never met before, sort of checking each other out. He's got the better music system, but my computer trumps. He's got a bunch of clothes that look like they're from Goodwill; I've got the polo shirts my mother bought. The first poster he puts up is from *Reservoir Dogs*; mine is from the Bread and Puppet Theater. What does it all mean?

My only advice is, the first week or two don't mean much. You might make your best friend ever; you might meet people you won't give a damn about by Thanksgiving. Give yourself time. And remember, NYC is only a train ride away!

Gunnar

Subj: Our Empty Nest
Date: 9/1/02, 7:25 P.M.
From: mtgillespie@boscore.com
To: chloegillespie@Cartwright.edu

Hello, Sweetheart!

We hope you're loving your school! Your roommate seemed like a lovely girl, if a little talkative. And her red bedspread clashes awfully with your yellow one. Maybe you can figure out a way to coordinate yourselves better as time goes on.

The house seems strangely quiet with both you girls gone. Daddy and I found ourselves wandering the hallways this morning, a little lost. I suppose we'll get used to it in time. We're going out with the Nevelsons tonight to brighten up our dreary lives!

Hope you're having a wonderful time at Cartwright. Write us with all your news!

Love, Mom and Daddy

Subj: When Fall Comes to New England
Date: 9/2/02, 11:51 A.M.
From: chloegillespie@Cartwright.edu
To: ggillespie@Emmett.edu

I don't know where to start! I've only been here two days, but it's been so FULL. First of all, Rebecca is cool—I think we'll get along fine. As soon as all the parental units had blubbered (hers) and air-kissed (Me&T) and staggered on down the stairs, Rebecca looked from her bedspread (screaming red roses) to mine (demure yellow daisys) and asked, a bit warily, "Did your mother buy yours?" I started laughing, and she said, "Me too. Let's stuff them in the back of the closets!" This afternoon we walked into town and found a store that sold Indian bedspreads, so we no longer look like we're sleeping in side-by-side cemetery plots.

I don't think Julian is here, although, of course, I haven't seen everybody on campus. I just have the feeling he isn't. There have been all sorts of freshman orientation activities—tonight there's a swing dance—if he's not there, I'm going to declare an all-clear. We don't register for classes until Wednesday, so these first few days are just for getting settled in, which is great. Rebecca and I have met a lot of other kids in our hall and we like most of them. There is one strange guy who only looks at your forehead when he speaks to you, but I think he's just very nervous. This guy,

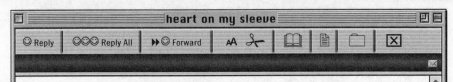

Baker, and his roommate, Pete, are the only guys who share our bathroom—two other girls, Ginny and Anne, also use it. We've worked out a system for knowing when it's in use, but it's weird not to have my own bathroom like at home. SPOILED BRAT? Yes, I am, but I'll adjust.

By the way, Rebecca doesn't have a boyfriend. She broke up with him before she left Indiana so she wouldn't be doing the long-distance thing. Yeah! So, no boyfriend sleepovers, at least for awhile.

I love it here! Just being on a campus is so cool. I really only know a handful of people, but I love bumping into them on the lawn or in the student union. It seems like I'll make friends quickly. Please don't tell me this is just the honeymoon phase, cynical sister. *I want to love it here!*

BTW, Martha says the house is too quiet now—they wander around the hallways, lost. Some people are never satisfied.

More news as it happens!

Love, Chloe

Subj: I Saw a Stranger with Your Hair
Date: 9/3/02, 10:32 A.M.
From: chloegillespie@Cartwright.edu
To: katewaverly@uver.edu

Hi Kate!

We did it! We're in college! What's it like at UVM? Do you like your roommate? How's your room? I love it here so much!

However, note my subject heading. I saw this girl here yesterday who looked SO much like you I almost spoke to her. I mean, I KNEW it couldn't be you because you're in Vermont, but she could have been

your twin or something. Or maybe I was just wishing I could see you. As much as I love it here, it's strange to always be with people you don't know very well. After I saw the girl who looked like you, I had this sort of homesickness thing for about an hour. I wished I could see you and Eli, if only for a few minutes. When you don't know anybody, it's almost like you don't exist. Or, your past doesn't exist, anyway. You're only who you are today, not who you've always been. Does that make any sense?

I think I might e-mail Eli too. Just a note. I miss him a lot. I've never started school without Eli right there next to me, you know? How could he be in MICHIGAN? I don't even know where Ann Arbor *is*.

Anyway, I like my roommate. We're both going to try out for an a cappella group tonight, and afterward we're going to a movie with some other kids from our hall. At least everybody else is a little bit lonely too.

Love you and miss you!

Chloe

Subj: Calling the Moon
Date: 9/3/02, 10:56 A.M.
From: chloegillespie@Cartwright.edu
To: elimather@unimich.edu

Hi Eli,

I got your e-mail address online—hope you don't mind. I just wanted to see (hear) how you're doing. Michigan seems so far away. I keep thinking of that Paul Simon song, *America*—you know it? About hitchhiking from Saginaw and being on the bus with Kathy. I always loved that song. So, what's it like there? I know it's a huge campus.

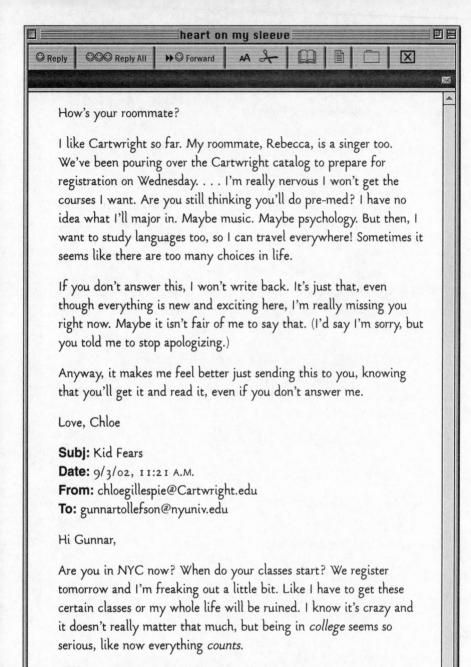

How's your roommate?

I like Cartwright so far. My roommate, Rebecca, is a singer too. We've been pouring over the Cartwright catalog to prepare for registration on Wednesday. . . . I'm really nervous I won't get the courses I want. Are you still thinking you'll do pre-med? I have no idea what I'll major in. Maybe music. Maybe psychology. But then, I want to study languages too, so I can travel everywhere! Sometimes it seems like there are too many choices in life.

If you don't answer this, I won't write back. It's just that, even though everything is new and exciting here, I'm really missing you right now. Maybe it isn't fair of me to say that. (I'd say I'm sorry, but you told me to stop apologizing.)

Anyway, it makes me feel better just sending this to you, knowing that you'll get it and read it, even if you don't answer me.

Love, Chloe

Subj: Kid Fears
Date: 9/3/02, 11:21 A.M.
From: chloegillespie@Cartwright.edu
To: gunnartollefson@nyuniv.edu

Hi Gunnar,

Are you in NYC now? When do your classes start? We register tomorrow and I'm freaking out a little bit. Like I have to get these certain classes or my whole life will be ruined. I know it's crazy and it doesn't really matter that much, but being in *college* seems so serious, like now everything *counts*.

I liked your story about your freshman roommate with the *Reservoir Dogs* poster. Did you get to be friends with him or not? I think my roommate and I will be friends—so far, so good. I sort of wish it was Thanksgiving already so I knew who my *real* friends were going to be. It does help to know that everybody who goes to college goes through the same thing.

Maple Hill seems like it happened ages ago! When I'm all nervous and feeling weird, I lie on my bed and think of walking in the woods past Blueberry Hollow and down to the lake. Just knowing that path is still there helps.

Thanks for writing, Gunnar. I really want to see you again. Let's get together soon, here or there.

Chloe

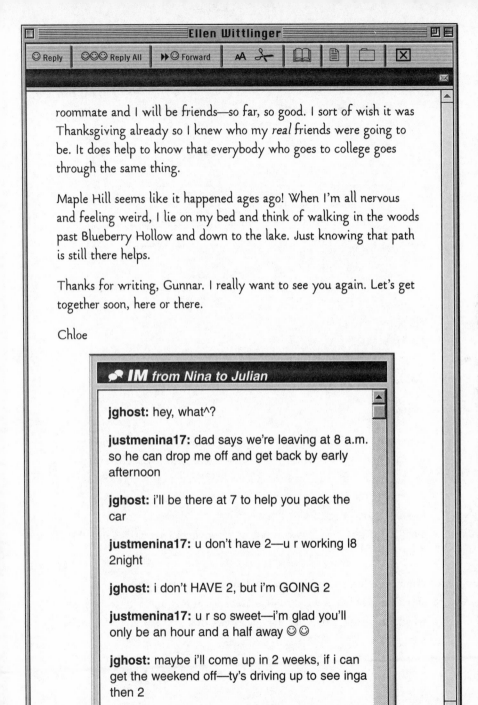

💬 IM *from Nina to Julian*

jghost: hey, what^?

justmenina17: dad says we're leaving at 8 a.m. so he can drop me off and get back by early afternoon

jghost: i'll be there at 7 to help you pack the car

justmenina17: u don't have 2—u r working l8 2night

jghost: i don't HAVE 2, but i'm GOING 2

justmenina17: u r so sweet—i'm glad you'll only be an hour and a half away ☺☺

jghost: maybe i'll come up in 2 weeks, if i can get the weekend off—ty's driving up to see inga then 2

justmenina17: i was HOPING you'd say that! YES, YES, YES!!!!!!! ☺☺☺☺

jghost: i'll just tell harvey i can't work. he won't mind—he thinks you're cute ☺

justmenina17: i don't care wot HARVEY thinks—wot do u think?

B *I* U A A ▼ ▲ ☺

jghost: tell u 2moro morning, soon as your dad is out of sight

send   close

Subj: Big bad blues
Date: 9/4/02, 9:12 A.M.
From: jghost@flowire.com
To: CCinWonderland@hotmail.com

Hey Carly,

I'm incredibly bored and lonely. Nina just left for school—I helped her pack up her car and then felt like some old broken toy she left behind. Ty is gone already too. Everybody's gone. I think I'm the only 18-to-22 year old left in Douglas, Florida. Suddenly this working thing doesn't seem like such a good idea, not that I have any choice. I already made plans to go see Nina in two weeks, but two weeks seems like months from now.

Mom was thrilled to hear you and Wes were taking classes. You should e-mail her once in awhile. You should e-mail ME once in a while. You never answered my question: What courses are you taking?

Okay, I'm in way too crappy a mood to write anybody a letter.

Jules

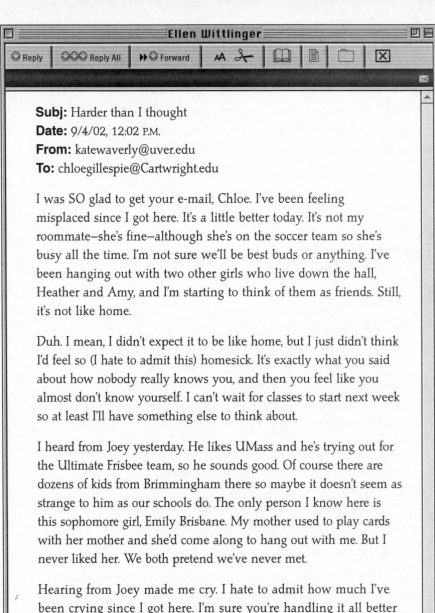

Subj: Harder than I thought
Date: 9/4/02, 12:02 P.M.
From: katewaverly@uver.edu
To: chloegillespie@Cartwright.edu

I was SO glad to get your e-mail, Chloe. I've been feeling misplaced since I got here. It's a little better today. It's not my roommate–she's fine–although she's on the soccer team so she's busy all the time. I'm not sure we'll be best buds or anything. I've been hanging out with two other girls who live down the hall, Heather and Amy, and I'm starting to think of them as friends. Still, it's not like home.

Duh. I mean, I didn't expect it to be like home, but I just didn't think I'd feel so (I hate to admit this) homesick. It's exactly what you said about how nobody really knows you, and then you feel like you almost don't know yourself. I can't wait for classes to start next week so at least I'll have something else to think about.

I heard from Joey yesterday. He likes UMass and he's trying out for the Ultimate Frisbee team, so he sounds good. Of course there are dozens of kids from Brimmingham there so maybe it doesn't seem as strange to him as our schools do. The only person I know here is this sophomore girl, Emily Brisbane. My mother used to play cards with her mother and she'd come along to hang out with me. But I never liked her. We both pretend we've never met.

Hearing from Joey made me cry. I hate to admit how much I've been crying since I got here. I'm sure you're handling it all better than I am. I don't hate it here or anything–it's just lonely. Sometimes I just can't believe Joey and I are broken up. I still love him so much, and I can't even imagine being with anybody else.

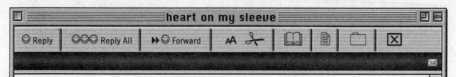

Oops! Just as I was sinking into despair Amy and Heather came to the door. They want me to go to lunch with them. So I guess I'm not as forgotten as I thought! Keep writing to me!

Love, Kate

Subj: new beginnings
Date: 9/5/02, 10:19 A.M.
From: elimather@unimich.edu
To: chloegillespie@Cartwright.edu

Hey Chloe,

I'm glad you wrote to me. It's kind of weird to be so far away from home and in such a different environment. I don't really know what Michigan is like—all I've seen of it so far is the University, and this place is so huge it seems like I'll never meet anybody except my roommates. I live in a quad, so I have 3 roommates—pretty good guys. I especially like Ted, who's a guitar player. (I guess I missed having one of those around.)

Yeah, I'm still thinking about pre-med, although it's kind of daunting how many years of school that takes. I don't know what else I'd do though—my language skills stink! You, however, could probably do anything you set your mind to. I KNOW you'll get into an a cappella group—how could they not take somebody with a voice like yours?

Okay, I really miss you too, Chloe, but I don't want to pretend that the last few months didn't happen. We broke up, and that was probably the right thing to do. So I feel mixed. I want to keep in touch with you, but I also want to get over you. You know what I mean? I actually went on sort of a date last night with this girl here who's a friend of Ted's. No big deal, but I need to do stuff like that. And you probably do too.

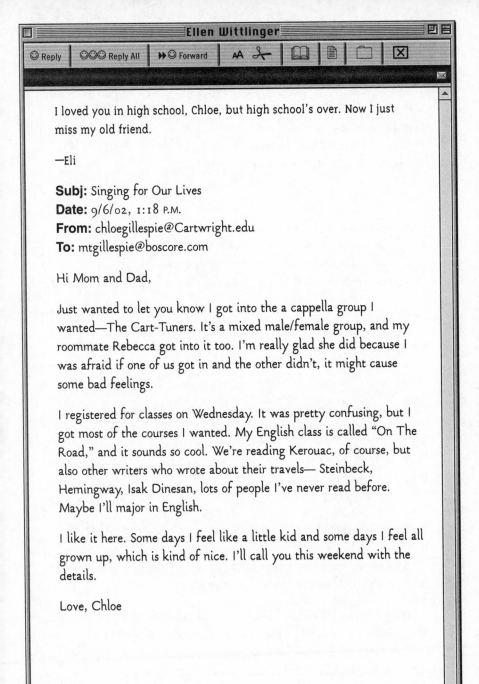

I loved you in high school, Chloe, but high school's over. Now I just miss my old friend.

—Eli

Subj: Singing for Our Lives
Date: 9/6/02, 1:18 P.M.
From: chloegillespie@Cartwright.edu
To: mtgillespie@boscore.com

Hi Mom and Dad,

Just wanted to let you know I got into the a cappella group I wanted—The Cart-Tuners. It's a mixed male/female group, and my roommate Rebecca got into it too. I'm really glad she did because I was afraid if one of us got in and the other didn't, it might cause some bad feelings.

I registered for classes on Wednesday. It was pretty confusing, but I got most of the courses I wanted. My English class is called "On The Road," and it sounds so cool. We're reading Kerouac, of course, but also other writers who wrote about their travels— Steinbeck, Hemingway, Isak Dinesan, lots of people I've never read before. Maybe I'll major in English.

I like it here. Some days I feel like a little kid and some days I feel all grown up, which is kind of nice. I'll call you this weekend with the details.

Love, Chloe

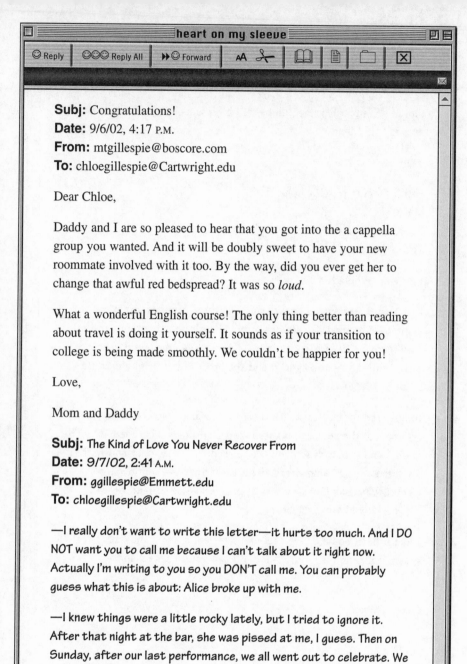

⊙ Reply   ⊙⊙⊙ Reply All   ▶⊙ Forward   AA ✂   📖   📄   📁   ⊠

Subj: Congratulations!
Date: 9/6/02, 4:17 P.M.
From: mtgillespie@boscore.com
To: chloegillespie@Cartwright.edu

Dear Chloe,

Daddy and I are so pleased to hear that you got into the a cappella group you wanted. And it will be doubly sweet to have your new roommate involved with it too. By the way, did you ever get her to change that awful red bedspread? It was so *loud*.

What a wonderful English course! The only thing better than reading about travel is doing it yourself. It sounds as if your transition to college is being made smoothly. We couldn't be happier for you!

Love,

Mom and Daddy

Subj: The Kind of Love You Never Recover From
Date: 9/7/02, 2:41 A.M.
From: ggillespie@Emmett.edu
To: chloegillespie@Cartwright.edu

—I really don't want to write this letter—it hurts too much. And I DO NOT want you to call me because I can't talk about it right now. Actually I'm writing to you so you DON'T call me. You can probably guess what this is about: Alice broke up with me.

—I knew things were a little rocky lately, but I tried to ignore it. After that night at the bar, she was pissed at me, I guess. Then on Sunday, after our last performance, we all went out to celebrate. We were just at a regular club, not a gay bar or anything, but Alice started to dance with this actress from the company. I guess she's a

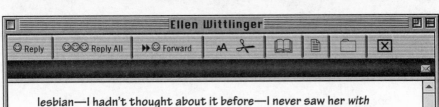

lesbian—I hadn't thought about it before—I never saw her *with* anybody. So the two of them are really heating up the floor, and I'm downing the margaritas and getting more and more upset. Long story short: After we got home we had a HUGE blowup. Alice said she couldn't stand me wanting to *own* her; she was young and wanted to have fun—she didn't want a *wife*. I couldn't believe she was saying that *now*, after this great summer, when we were headed back to school to live together.

—So then she dropped the big bomb. She's not coming back to Emmett this year. Apparently she's been thinking about this for several weeks, but hadn't said a thing to me. She talked to Ben Bernstein, our director, and he agreed to let her work with the company during the winter so she could stay on in NY. She even talked to *Jay* about it because she wanted to keep on living in the apartment, but he didn't want to say anything to me until Alice brought it up. And I guess she kept chickening out until finally she had to do something because we were packing to leave!

—You can imagine—the whole scene was a horror. I was even screaming at Jay, who obviously felt terrible keeping this a secret from me. He was put into an awful situation—I don't know how Alice could do that. Well, obviously I don't really understand her at all, do I? She must have been planning all this *when you were here!* Did you catch anything? I certainly didn't. I thought, sure, we'd had a little rough patch, but basically everything was peachy. What a little idiot I am.

—The worst part is that I can't really hate her. I want to, but, God, Chloe, she was my first love! She was the first person I ever fell for. I opened my heart to her. I feel like I'll never get over this, like I'm 16 years old again. I guess I thought that a woman wouldn't do this to another woman, as if we're a higher order of species. I must be the dumbest person on earth.

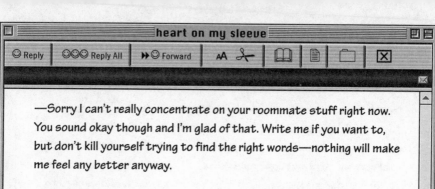

—Sorry I can't really concentrate on your roommate stuff right now.
You sound okay though and I'm glad of that. Write me if you want to,
but don't kill yourself trying to find the right words—nothing will make
me feel any better anyway.

—Genevieve

Subj: Tanglewood Tree
Date: 9/7/02, 11:50 A.M.
From: chloegillespie@Cartwright.edu
To: ggillespie@Emmett.edu

Oh, Veev, I'm SO, SO sorry this happened! I can't believe it either—
everything seemed so great between you when I was there two weeks
ago. I mean, it WAS great. Maybe this is just a temporary thing—
maybe Alice just wanted to stay in NYC for awhile. Obviously, the
reason she found it so hard to tell you was because she *does* have
feelings for you. I'm positive she does—I *saw* them!

Shit! How does it EVER happen that two people feel exactly the same
way about each other at exactly the same time? It seems almost
impossible when you think about it. One person always wants more.
You think you know what the other person is feeling, but you can't
really know, and somebody is bound to get hurt. I shouldn't be so
negative when you're already upset, but here I was thinking that you
and Alice had figured out how to do this being-in-love thing. I
thought if you could do it, maybe I could too someday.

What a lousy pep talk this is. Talk about finding the wrong words. But
I think you're right that there aren't any right ones. I just want you to
feel better, but I know I can't wave a wand and make it happen.

Of course you're not the dumbest person on earth. Maybe Alice is.
Or maybe I am. It turns out that Eli doesn't hate me, so maybe you
don't have to hate Alice either. But I guess you probably do have to

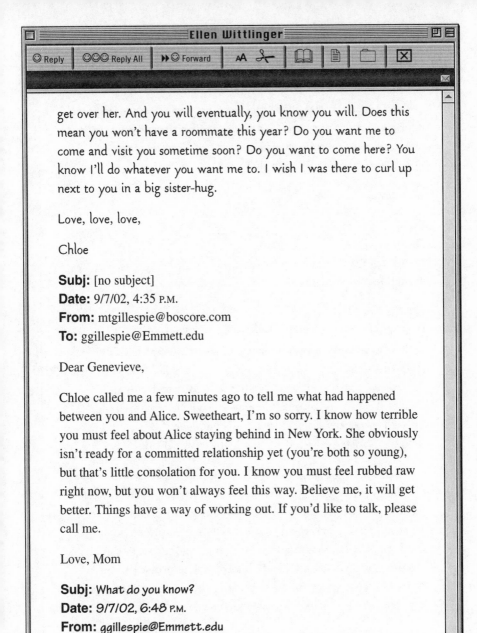

get over her. And you will eventually, you know you will. Does this mean you won't have a roommate this year? Do you want me to come and visit you sometime soon? Do you want to come here? You know I'll do whatever you want me to. I wish I was there to curl up next to you in a big sister-hug.

Love, love, love,

Chloe

Subj: [no subject]
Date: 9/7/02, 4:35 P.M.
From: mtgillespie@boscore.com
To: ggillespie@Emmett.edu

Dear Genevieve,

Chloe called me a few minutes ago to tell me what had happened between you and Alice. Sweetheart, I'm so sorry. I know how terrible you must feel about Alice staying behind in New York. She obviously isn't ready for a committed relationship yet (you're both so young), but that's little consolation for you. I know you must feel rubbed raw right now, but you won't always feel this way. Believe me, it will get better. Things have a way of working out. If you'd like to talk, please call me.

Love, Mom

Subj: What do you know?
Date: 9/7/02, 6:48 P.M.
From: ggillespie@Emmett.edu
To: mtgillespie@boscore.com

—*Things have a way of working out?* What is that, homespun platitude #465? I don't mean to sound ungrateful, Mother, but how can you

keep saying you *know* what I'm feeling? You don't! You and Dad got married right out of college—he was the only boyfriend you ever had—and you've been ridiculously in love ever since. Thanks for the sympathy, but don't expect a phone call. You *don't* know!

—Genevieve

Subj: school rules
Date: 9/8/02, 8:12 A.M.
From: CCinWonderland@hotmail.com
To: jghost@flowire.com

hey, kid, sorry you're lonely without your honeybunch. at least you HAVE a honeybunch now. be thankful for small miracles (and wise sisters). speaking of miracles, did you know that mom called me last night to say she wants to pay for my courses this year? actually, she *insisted.* two courses don't cost all that much, so i said sure, and i promised her i'd save as much money as i could this year so i can pay my own way next year when you need her dough. it was nice of her though—is menopause making her loopy or something?

wes is taking biology and geology courses. i guess science was always his thing—who knew? i'm starting out with english—i always liked that anyway and i figure i can use it wherever we transfer—and the other course is spanish. living out here it would be nice to be able to speak spanish—i already had 4 years of it in high school, so this is sort of a refresher course, and then i can take higher-level stuff. my first class is in—yikes—45 minutes so i have to get going. wish me luck. next semester i'm taking that history course!

Carly

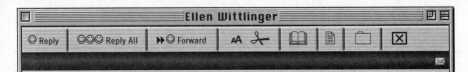

Subj: I know a lot more than you think
Date: 9/8/02, 9:30 A.M.
From: mtgillespie@boscore.com
To: ggillespie@Emmett.edu

Genevieve,

I was going to write you a letter instead of sending another e-mail—
you know how I feel about this public form of conversation. But then I
thought, no, if I'm coming clean, I might as well do it right out in
front of everybody.

I know that my relationship with your father looks problem-free to
you, but it was not always that way. Twenty years ago I would never
have imagined we would find a way to love each other again. The
story is one I never wanted to tell you girls—I always wanted you to
think Daddy and I had a perfect love so you would strive for that
too—but now I wonder if that was the best idea. You need to
understand what created our lives as they are today.

Yes, we married young, feeling confident that ours was a strong and
lasting love. Everyone feels that way at first. But a few years later we
were leading almost separate lives, together only because we lived
under the same roof. Dad had gotten his Ph.D., we were both busy
with jobs we liked, and we made very little time for each other. At
some point, I realized this was not good, so I proposed we begin a
family. Your father was surprised, but he agreed.

No sooner had I become pregnant—with you, darling—than I received a
phone call from a very distraught young girl. She was one of your
father's students from the college. Between her sobs she told me they had
been having an affair for six months which he now wanted to break off
because of my pregnancy. I guess it sounds ridiculous, but I actually felt
sorry for her, so young, weeping over the loss of my wayward husband.

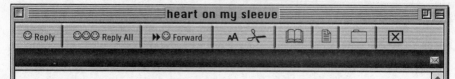

By the time your father returned home that afternoon, I had worked myself into a fury over his betrayal of both of us, or maybe I should say, all three of us: me, you, and the college girl. Knowing it would hurt your father terribly, I had already made an appointment to have an abortion. (This is why I never wanted to tell you this story, but really, the truth is the whole truth. When I think now that I might have gone through with it and not had my beautiful firstborn daughter, it makes me weep. Actually, just telling you is making me cry. I hope you can forgive me, Genevieve.)

Your father called the agency as soon as I told him and canceled my appointment. He was furious that I would consider giving up our child. (I did not call back to reschedule, so I think it was not really what I wanted either, yet I can't deny that first call.) We raged for days, blaming each other for every conceivable act of betrayal we could think of. We said terrible things designed to hurt each other deeply. I thought there was no possible way to ever bandage the wounds. Thank God, your father decided not to give up on us. I give him full credit for that. He found a wonderful marriage counselor and dragged me in to talk with her. Even in her office, we screamed at each other until the poor woman must have been ready to rip out her hair.

Finally she said to us—I remember because I think of her words often—"Yelling at each other is accomplishing nothing. As I see it, there are three things you can do, and it's time we discuss which it will be. You can separate right now, divorce, and share custody of your baby. Or, you can stay together, tamp down your anger for the sake of the child, and divorce when she leaves for college. Or, you can decide that those are lousy options. You can decide that people make mistakes, but it's possible to forgive each other for them. Then you can work to make this the very best marriage it can be. It's your choice."

Maybe that advice wouldn't have worked for every couple, but for us it cleared away the fog. It reminded us that we had once been very much in love and had both wandered off that path somehow. We forgave each other, and we have done so again and again over the years. When you understand that the choice really is yours, that you don't have to conform to societal notions of how you *should* act in one situation or another, it's so liberating! Most people (especially in those days) felt that if your spouse slept with someone else, the marriage was over. But why did we have to behave that way if we didn't want to? Suddenly we felt free to love each other *in spite* of our shortcomings—and maybe even *because* of them. I don't want you to think it was easy, especially in the beginning. We worked at it, and we still do, but we love our work, and it's made our marriage very rewarding. And no, your father never had another affair. Why would he want to?

I understand why my simple platitude was annoying to you. Of course, relationships don't always work out. I guess all I really wanted to say was: Don't give up on love. It's hard, but it's worth it.

Love, Mom

Subj: Meditation
Date: 9/9/02, 2:46 P.M.
From: gunnartollefson@nyuniv.edu
To: chloegillespie@Cartwright.edu

You are lying in a hammock between Redwood House and the big maple tree with the tire swing. You can hear kids softly singing "The Water is Wide," which you taught them last night at campfire. A guitarist practices too, and a piano is being quietly played. In the distance you can hear the potter's wheel spinning in the Arts Barn, and the low laughter of the theater group rehearsing their lines. Now imagine you rise from the

hammock and walk down the path, past Blueberry Hollow where a group is picking berries for dinner, past Dandelion House where the sound of a flute floats out the door, and on to the lakefront. The swimming area is empty, but a row of canoes slap lightly against each other as the wind curls the water into shore. You stretch your arms over your head and breathe in the smell of pines.

Repeat the above exercise until you relax, or until you hear the dinner bell, whichever comes first.

G.

Subj: Blown away
Date: 9/9/02, 8:51 P.M.
From: ggillespie@Emmett.edu
To: mtgillespie@boscore.com

Dear Mom,

—Thank you for that letter. I'm still reeling from it, but I'm so glad you told me all that stuff. At some point you should tell Chloe too, but probably not yet. I think your timing with me was perfect: You need to have been there to get it. I NEVER would have suspected you and dad went through anything like this. I thought you'd been in this crazy love since you were kids, which, now that I think of it, is pretty unlikely. I'm so impressed that you pulled out of such a terrible situation and found a way to love each other again.

—And I see now that you *have* overcome societal notions of how to act. Which, I admit, has sometimes embarrassed me over the years. But why *is* it taboo to kiss your husband in public? It's as if polite society frowns on acting loving. It's okay at the engagement party and the wedding, but after that: **stop**. Of course, people

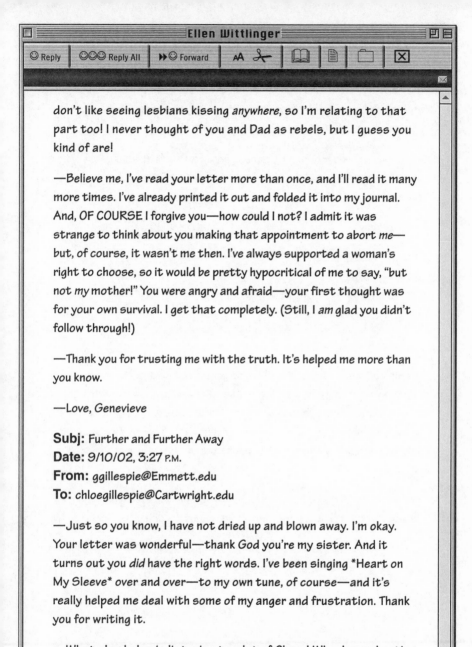

don't like seeing lesbians kissing *anywhere*, so I'm relating to that part too! I never thought of you and Dad as rebels, but I guess you kind of are!

—Believe me, I've read your letter more than once, and I'll read it many more times. I've already printed it out and folded it into my journal. And, OF COURSE I forgive you—how could I not? I admit it was strange to think about you making that appointment to abort *me*— but, of course, it wasn't me then. I've always supported a woman's right to choose, so it would be pretty hypocritical of me to say, "but not *my* mother!" You were angry and afraid—your first thought was for your own survival. I get that completely. (Still, I *am* glad you didn't follow through!)

—Thank you for trusting me with the truth. It's helped me more than you know.

—Love, Genevieve

Subj: Further and Further Away
Date: 9/10/02, 3:27 P.M.
From: ggillespie@Emmett.edu
To: chloegillespie@Cartwright.edu

—Just so you know, I have not dried up and blown away. I'm okay. Your letter was wonderful—thank God you're my sister. And it turns out you *did* have the right words. I've been singing *Heart on My Sleeve* over and over—to my own tune, of course—and it's really helped me deal with some of my anger and frustration. Thank you for writing it.

—What also helps is listening to a lot of Cheryl Wheeler and eating chocolate. Also, joining Lezzies Light, which is a comedy troupe on campus for ladies such as I. Laughter, as we know, is better

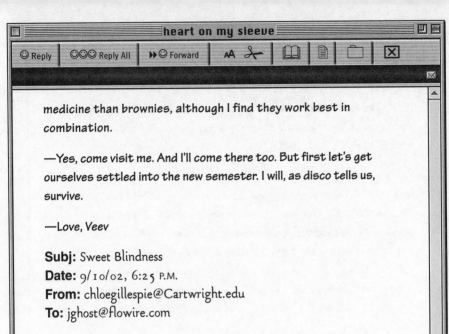

medicine than brownies, although I find they work best in combination.

—Yes, come visit me. And I'll come there too. But first let's get ourselves settled into the new semester. I will, as disco tells us, survive.

—Love, Veev

Subj: Sweet Blindness
Date: 9/10/02, 6:25 P.M.
From: chloegillespie@Cartwright.edu
To: jghost@flowire.com

Hi Julian,

It seemed like maybe I should write you a note. Not a thank you note and not exactly an apology either. I really don't know what to say. It seems like neither of us knew who we spent the summer writing letters to, and then we were disappointed when we found out. It was a crazy thing that happened, and, actually, I am sorry about it.

You aren't at Cartwright. I'm wondering where you are, what you decided to do. I like it here, but maybe you wouldn't have.

Anyway, I wanted to say something to you. Maybe just a nicer good-bye than I said at the airport.

Chloe

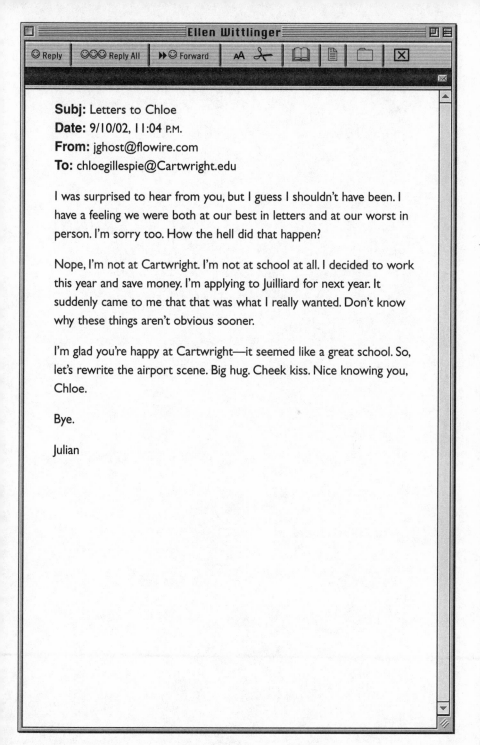

Subj: Letters to Chloe
Date: 9/10/02, 11:04 P.M.
From: jghost@flowire.com
To: chloegillespie@Cartwright.edu

I was surprised to hear from you, but I guess I shouldn't have been. I have a feeling we were both at our best in letters and at our worst in person. I'm sorry too. How the hell did that happen?

Nope, I'm not at Cartwright. I'm not at school at all. I decided to work this year and save money. I'm applying to Juilliard for next year. It suddenly came to me that that was what I really wanted. Don't know why these things aren't obvious sooner.

I'm glad you're happy at Cartwright—it seemed like a great school. So, let's rewrite the airport scene. Big hug. Cheek kiss. Nice knowing you, Chloe.

Bye.

Julian

Playlist

Are You Out There?	Dar Williams
The Great Unknown	Dar Williams
Here in the going going gone	Greg Brown
A Ha Me A Riddle I Day	Laura Love
When I Was a Boy	Dar Williams
As Cool As I Am	Dar Williams
Summer Wages	written by Ian Tyson, sung by Nanci Griffith
Frequently Wrong but Never in Doubt	Cheryl Wheeler
What Do You Hear in These Sounds?	Dar Williams
The Pointless, Yet Poignant Crisis of a Co-ed	Dar Williams
The Poet Game	Greg Brown
Eli's Comin'	Laura Nyro
Upstairs by a Chinese Lamp	Laura Nyro
Sensitive New Age Guys	Christine Lavin
Another Mystery	Dar Williams
In Love but Not at Peace	Dar Williams
Hard Times Come Again No More	written by Stephen Foster, sung by Nanci Griffith
Best Black Dress	The Nields
Might As Well Dance	Patty Larkin
Prom Night in Pigtown	John Gorka
If I Wrote You	Dar Williams
Closer to Fine	Indigo Girls
Punk Junkies from New York	Jim's Big Ego
Quit Hollerin' at Me	John Prine
Good Thing (Angels Running)	Patty Larkin
Little Lies	The Resophonics
Speed of the Sound of Loneliness	John Prine
Born to Run	Bruce Springsteen

Ellen Wittlinger

There's a Light Beyond These Woods (Mary Margaret)	Nanci Griffith
The Circle Game	Joni Mitchell
Wasn't That a Mighty Storm	traditional, sung by Tom Rush
Ain't Hurtin' Nobody	John Prine
Killing the Blues	John Prine
Butthead	Jim's Big Ego
The Babysitter's Here	Dar Williams
Car Wheels on a Gravel Road	Lucinda Williams
Cowards	The Nields
Allelvia, the Great Storm Is Over	Bob Franke
Leaving on a Jet Plane	Peter, Paul and Mary
Mr. Right Now	The Nields
This Happens Again and Again	The Nields
Love the One You're With	Stephen Stills
The Bottom of a River	Alastair Moock
Romeo	Jess Klein
Crazy	Patsy Cline
Power of Two	Indigo Girls
End of the Summer	Dar Williams
When Fall Comes to New England	Cheryl Wheeler
I Saw a Stranger with Your Hair	John Gorka
Calling the Moon	Dar Williams
America	Paul Simon
Kid Fears	Indigo Girls
Singing for Our Lives	Holly Near
The Kind of Love You Never Recover From	Christine Lavin
Tanglewood Tree	Dave Carter & Tracy Grammer
Further and Further Away	Cheryl Wheeler
Sweet Blindness	Laura Nyro